Love
Unfinished

Darian Wilk

The characters and events in this book are fictitious. Any similarity to real persons, living or dead, places, or events is coincidental and not intended by the author.

If you purchase this book without a cover you should be aware that this book may have been stolen property and reported as "unsold and destroyed" to the publisher. In such case the author has not received any payment for this "stripped book."

Email: Darian.Wilk@gmail.com
Website: www.DarianWilk.weebly.com
Print addition:
ISBN-13: 978-0-615-48405-1
ISBN-10: 0615484050
Library of Congress Control Number: 2011908193

Printed in the United States of America

*This book is dedicated to my husband, for his
endless support, encouragement, and understanding. To
my Mom, although she is no longer with me to see my
dream in print, without her this book would never have
been started. And to my friends Teri and Matt, for their
patience and help throughout this whole process.*

One

~CAROL~

May 23rd, 1946

The stunned congregation watched the explosion of red condiment, but Ted saw only the beautiful young lady with her face and paisley green sundress splattered with ketchup.

Her ocean-colored eyes were wet with embarrassment. She turned away from the gawkers and tried to discreetly lick her thumb and rub the splotches off.

Ted strolled up beside her, cleared his throat, and coyly offered a handkerchief. She raised a hand to shield her eyes from the beaming sun and gazed at the tall, thin dark-haired boy holding out his hand to her. Seeing him there so eager and handsome she felt something change inside her, although she didn't understand what it was.

She tried to offer a smile. "Thank you."

"It's very pretty," he said with an awkward nod at her stained dress.

"Thanks. It was anyway. Stupid Tommy and his tantrums. He always ruins everything," she said with a sideways sneer to her little brother pouting behind the tree. "My Mama's gonna be so mad when she sees this."

"Try this," he said, dipping the embroidered cloth into a pitcher of water. "My Mom always uses a wet cloth." His hand trembled as he rubbed a smear on her shoulder. "I, uh, maybe you should do it?" he said with a nervous chuckle and handed her the handkerchief.

She dabbed the dress with the wet hankie and glanced back up at him with a grin. "I think it's working."

"It should come out—"

"I'm Carol," she interrupted as she extended her hand.

"T-Ted," he said, and clasped his hand around hers. "I, um, you wanna go over there?" he said, nodding toward the swing set.

"Sure." She jumped up from the picnic table and started to walk past her infuriated parents scolding her brother. "Mama," she whispered from over her shoulder and pointed toward the swings.

June 16th, 1954

"Gosh, Mama…it's beautiful," Carol whispered as she fluffed out her skirt.

"I can hardly believe I managed to finish it on time." Mama clasped her hands at her waist as she took in the satin wedding dress. "You look amazing," she said, raising a hankie to her eyes.

"Oh, Mama, don't start. If you start crying then I'll start crying," Carol teased as she fanned her watery eyes with a hand.

"Mama grinned, dabbing her eyes with a hankie as she composed herself. "Goodness this heat. I hope my hair holds up." Mama pressed a hand to her up-do as she stepped closer to Carol. "Just look at you. I'm so happy for you, the both of you."

"It's finally going to happen, Mama! I can't believe it," Carol said, taking an anxious breath and gave Mama's hand an excited tug.

"There's just one last thing," Mama said, riffling through her purse and pulled out a hand stitched hankie. "It's from Aunt Sally. She wanted you to have it when the time was right." She unfolded the bunched up cloth and uncovered a brilliant gold brooch.

"Oh, Mama, I couldn't possibly—"

"Hush now, it's what she wanted. And I've just the spot for it anyhow," she said through a smile and carefully pinned the brooch in the V of Carol's neckline. "Perfect…"

Carol ran a finger along the small delicate swirls and the emerald jewel. "I don't deserve this much," her soft voice cracked.

"You deserve nothing less, baby," Mama said as she patted Carol's hand. "There, now you're the perfect bride."

The entire town was there to celebrate the marriage of the kids they all knew would marry someday. The preacher and deacons attempted to seat the guests crammed in the pews by setting up dusty folding chairs from the cellar. Women huffed in frustration, fanned themselves, and pressed worried hands to their delicate up-dos in the humid stagnant air.

Carol stepped onto the crisp white aisle runner, and her soft features were luminous in the golden sunset pouring through the faded stained-glass windows. With her loving eyes fixated on Ted waiting at the altar, the church hushed in romantic awe as the heat was forgotten.

Ted's legs trembled at the sight of this captivating woman as she walked toward, with her smile so bright it made the stars jealous. He took her hands into his and the instant her attention shifted from adjusting her train to his eyes, everything around them morphed to a gray blur. Verses the preacher read became a muffled slow motion speech, the whipping sounds of the makeshift paper fans faded to tiny flutters, and the anxious pounding of her heart slowed to a steady beat as she stood hand in hand with her best friend.

Carol looked radiant in the handmade dress. The long, lacy train was draped behind her as she gazed into her new husbands eyes. Carol cocked her shoulders back, standing tall and confident in the gown Mama so carefully made. Not a hint of doubt or worry flickered in her stare. *Everyone should be so lucky to marry their soul mate,* she thought, marveling the tender man gazing back at her. She heard the preachers cue, and then gently slid the simple wedding band on Ted's long finger as she recited her vows by heart.

"I now pronounce you husband and wife," the preacher announced with a wrinkled grin.

The crowd erupted into joyous clapping as the couple turned to face them. Her body exhaled in relief, grateful to start the path in life she was meant to be on. She tried to blink them back, but tears trickled down her blushed cheeks as they rushed down the aisle with their hands clasped together.

"You two need to be getting on to the reception. Folks are waiting for you," Carol's Daddy said as he closed the car door for her. "I'm getting your Mama, and then we'll be on behind you."

"All right Daddy. We'll see you at the hall," Carol said, waving as the car pulled away.

Carol loved the way the satin shimmered in the faint evening light. The embroidered lace trim glided between her fingertips; she could hardly imagine the abuse Mama's hands must have suffered sewing the pearls and crystals on the gown.

Ted smiled in awe at the young bride beside him, and raised an arm gesturing for her to scoot closer.

"I'm Mrs. Ted Parkman," she said as she scooted across the bucket seat, stretching her arm to admire the gold band on her left hand. "I can't believe we're finally married."

"Just think, this time tomorrow we'll be on our honeymoon! What do you want to do first, love? Do some site seeing? Maybe find something for the house?"

"I want to lie on the beach all day, just like a spoiled movie star!" she said through a chuckle. "Wouldn't that be lovely, Ted? And how you deserve the break with the hours you've worked lately."

Carol closed her eyes and pictured huge blue waves rolling onto the smooth sandy shore. "Oh it's going to be beautiful, Ted. I just know it," she said, opening her eyes from the childlike daydream.

"Sure turned out to be a nice night, huh? With those clouds earlier, I thought we'd be eating in the rain," he said, rolling down the window.

Huge elm trees hung over the small road like a canopy, shielding it from the clear evening sky. Ted sat up a little straighter, rubbing his tired eyes to focus better on the curvy stretch of pavement.

Carol leaned against him as she gazed at the stars peeking through the leaves. It almost felt like a carnival ride to her on the big hills, with dips and turns along the windy road. As they came down a large hill that felt like it might lift her right out of the seat, the car started into a sharp turn and pushed her into Ted as they drove.

As the car came around the bend they saw a tanker jackknifed in the middle of the two-lane route.

"Ted, look out!" she screamed as she instinctively braced against the dashboard for the impending crash.

Ted tried to swerve and slammed his foot on the brake. The tires screeched, the car clipped the side of the truck and whipped it into a spin. Carol's horrified shriek filled the quiet night as the car started to roll. Time seemed to stop. Before she could even think the car had skidded down the shoulder and slammed into the guard rail. Her limp, battered body hung helplessly half out of the windshield.

"Carol! Where are you?" Ted screamed with desperation. "Please...please...Carol..." he mumbled. His exhausted arm frantically reached in the air and caught part of her weathered dress.

"Carol!" He tugged on a tattered strip of her gown. He could only make out a hint of her white form. He grasped and fumbled in the darkness in search of her hand. He struggled to bring her slender hand to his lips, kissing her limp fingers and caressed them on his cheek.

Carol's head lay in a pool of blood on the mangled hood. Her beautiful wedding dress was a shredded mess with beads and crystals scattered everywhere. The delicate satin was smeared with bloody swirls and grime from the road. Her mind was filled with fog and confusion, muffling the vague whispers and strange noises around her.

A sudden gasp filled her lungs. She screamed in horror as piercing pain coursed through her body.

"Carol?"

"Ted...is that you?" she managed.

"Are you all right? I...I can't see," he mumbled. His exhausted body fell against the steering wheel.

"I, I think," Carol tried to take a breath. "I'm on the hood. It hurts." Bloody ran from her nose as she murmured. She tried to lift herself up, but her muscles had nothing left in them for movement.

"Can you feel me?" he stammered. His wearied eyes fought to stay open as a strange tingling numbness crept up to his fingers clutching hers.

"I, I can't feel you Ted," she cried in fear. "Ted, please help me!"

"I hear...someone's coming. Hold on, Carol," he mumbled. Dizziness swirled in his head. "I...I love you..." he said through a wheeze.

Her weeping slowed to faint whimpers; her eyes only catching quick flashes of light as sounds faded in and out around her. "Ted...I'm so tired," she said. Her slender hand went limp and fell to the dashboard.

"You hold on, do you hear me?" he said through a desperate cry. He started bawling and tried to squeeze life back into her hand. "Carol please!"

"Ted..." she whispered. "I, I lov..." She struggled to breathe but choked on the blood pooled in her throat. She lay with eyes wide and panicked, gasping before she collapsed like a rag doll.

"Carol?" he whispered. "Talk to me," he cried as he shook her arm to revive her. "Please, baby..." Tears streamed down his bloodstained face. Faint panicked yelling came toward the car and his foggy, exhausted eyes forced themselves shut.

"Please, God, I need my baby..." he muttered. His eyes flickered one last time, and then his body buckled beside hers.

Two

Dark stillness clung to her. No sight or sound filled her senses. At first a faint muffled noise trickled in, growing louder as her thoughts sparked and lit her soul alive. It was calming and rhythmic. A soft whisper of the gentle swishing of the ocean, with big foamy waves rolling onto the shore and back out again. A terrible weight pulled on her eyelids and her body with a paralyzing numbness. Carol strained to wiggled her fingertips and felt the rough crystals of sand between her fingers. The morning sun dotted beads of sweat onto her face, but was calmed by a cool breeze that drifted onto the shore and brought with it the salty scent of the sea.

Was it all a dream, she wondered as she dug her hand in the hot sand. *Am I on my honeymoon?* She grimaced trying to urge her muscles to lift her body up. As she gained focus, a flurry of visions of metal, sparks, and blood flew through her hazy mind. She gasped for air and instinctively shot up.

She squinted and covered her brow with a hand to see through the green blobs dotting her vision. As the fuzziness cleared, a breathless awe consumed her. The beautiful crystal-clear water and white shoreline stretched as far as her eyes could see. She took a hushed breath, pressed a hand to her cheek, and turned to share the moment with Ted. But he wasn't there.

Carol stumbled clumsily trying to stand and glanced down at her feet to see what they were tangled on. She was still in her wedding dress. A rush of panic engulfed her as she scanned the beach for Ted.

"Ted!" she called out. "Ted!" her hysteric voice screamed again. "Where am I?" she whispered. Frightened and her lip quivering, she spun around in dread glancing for signs of life on the empty island.

For countless hours she walked the length of the desolate shore. Her feet dragged through the sand, her muscles ached from clutching the weight of the gown, and caused her arms to give way and dangle like stretched rubber.

Exhausted, she collapsed onto the ground. The salty sting of sweat burned her eyes as it rolled from her forehead. She wiped her brows and tried to calm the furious pounding of her heaving chest.

"Where is he?" she asked no one as she twisted the wedding band around her finger. She stared down the shore, and a tear began to roll down her sand covered cheek when she saw the tiny hint of figure waving at her in the distance.

"Ted!" She jumped to her feet, bunched the dress up in her arms and started jogging down the beach. "Ted! Ted, I'm here!" she yelled, waving her arm in the air as she ran. The dark figure stood motionless as it waited. She smiled. "Ted I'm coming!"

Her sprint slowed to an apprehensive walk as her look contorted from delight to sudden bewilderment. Cautious, Carol stood at an angle as she approached the familiar face.

"Grandma?" She leaned in a little, "Is that you?" she whispered, eyeing the soft wrinkled features.

"Hello, Pumpkin," Grandma said with a warm smile.

"I, but…Grandma, you're, you're de—"

"Yes, Carol, I am no longer a part of Earth," she interrupted, cocking her head to the side. A tender gaze of patience poured through her hazel eyes. Her complexion glowed in the daylight, looking flawless and healthy. Her soft porcelain skin was warmed by her blushed round cheeks.

"Where's Ted?" Carol asked through a trembling whisper. "What's going on? Where am I?"

"He has been sent to his own waiting place, Pumpkin. His guide is with him now, I am sure," she assured Carol with a sweet grin and reached to press her hand to Carol's cheek.

Carol almost jerked away, still not believing this woman could be her Grandma. "Waiting place? I, I don't understand."

"It can take time to set in, Pumpkin. Be patient and I can explain."

"For *what* to set in?" Carol's brows pinched in worry as she shook her head in disbelief. "Where's Ted, Grandma!" she demanded.

Grandma let out a patient breath. "Hush now, Pumpkin," she whispered as she returned her hands to her lap.

"Why won't you tell me what's going on?" Carol collapsed to the ground, unable to restrain the surge of frenzied tears, and buried her face in her hands.

Grandma knelt on the sand, pulled Carol into a gentle embrace, and cradled her distraught grandbaby on the shore that Carol chose. Carol sobbed as she breathed in Grandma's comforting scent of baby powder with every panicked inhale.

Carol murmured into Grandma's shoulder as her mind ran wild with horrifying fragmented images and sounds. She saw herself from the side of the road as the car flipped, heard the crunch of metal and saw her body smash through the windshield. "Oh my God…" she breathed in terror and pushed Grandma away. "Am I, did I die?" She clasped her hands over her mouth in horror.

"Yes, Pumpkin, you did," Grandma said and reached to comfort her.

Carol slapped Grandmas hand away as she shook her head. "No, no, that's not right. I, I couldn't be dea—"

"Shh, Pumpkin, breathe—"

"Is, is this heaven? Did Ted— is he here too?" Carol cried as her black eyeliner drizzled from her tears.

"This is your waiting place Carol. Ted is in his own."

"Waiting place? Waiting for heaven?"

"No, Honey. Waiting to complete your soul's fulfillment, your destiny."

"Destiny? I don't understand…" Her feverish breathing grew to labored pants, sucking in more air than her lungs could handle.

"I know it's hard to understand, Honey. But you haven't finished your life's fate. So, you wait here, until it's time for you to go back."

"Go back? I don't understand. Why can't I be with Ted now? Please let me see him," Carol begged.

"You must find him again, Pumpkin, to finish what time wouldn't allow—"

"Please, Grandma, you don't make any sense."

"You must finish your lives together, by finding each other again."

"But I already had him…" Carol muttered. "Why won't you take me to him?"

Grandma caressed Carol's cheek. "I wish I could, Pumpkin. But you'll get a chance to love him in a new life, to find your Ted again." She bent her lips to a soft smile and ran her fingers through Carol's hair to comfort her.

"A new life! But, I, I don't want to—" Carol shook her head. "I want to be with Ted now. How can we find each other if we're strangers!" she cried as her tears flowed freely down her face. "Why can't I be with Ted?" she said through a sob.

"You must trust in the strength of your love. That is what will pull you together again."

"But if he doesn't remember me? How will—"

"His heart will remember. Love will remind him. If only the faintest feeling of familiarity, you'll know that you're meant to love each other."

"I, I don't want to, Grandma," she muttered with a shaky voice. "I want to see him now."

The breeze grew stiff and cool, covering her pale arms in goose bumps as a shiver crept down her spine. The clear horizon dimmed to perfect shades of gold, crimson and purple as her time there dwindled. Carol had never seen anything so beautiful before. The rolling waves slowed to mere ripples in the water. The sand felt cold and soothing against her tired, blistered feet, and she felt a twinge of comfort ending her first day there wrapped in Grandma's arms.

Grandma knew the change churning in the distance. "Ah yes, your time comes soon," she said as she turned back to Carol. "It's time for me to leave now, Pumpkin." The fullness of her love beamed in her tender smile. "You looked stunning." Her eyes welled up as she looked down at her grown granddaughter, turned, and walked away.

Carol jumped up and began chasing after Grandma. "Wait!" she screamed as she sprinted across the shore. "Don't leave me. I don't want you to go! Please, take me to him," she yelled as she tripped and fell.

She scrunched into a tight ball, holding herself as she bawled on the cold sand and watched grandma fade into a billowing mist. She started to rock herself, sobbing and muttering as she swayed in the darkness. "I want to be with Ted…Please, I want to be with Ted," she whispered over and over until the sky grew black. And then darkness took her again. The cool breeze vanished. She heard no soft swishing of the waves. She lay on the cold ground, holding herself in the darkest of black. Waiting.

Three

~EMMA~

June 20th, 1992

Emma cracked the window to let in the cool evening air, hoping it would distract her from his annoying drumming on the armrest. The barrier between them seemed to soak up the air around her, stealing her breath before her lungs could fill. Her gaze drifted to the figure beside her. He was handsome with firm muscles filling the sleeves of his Oxford shirt, calm and lost in his own thoughts.

"I think we need counseling," Emma said, not hearing the words come out of her mouth.

"What?" he said, cocking his head toward her.

"I think we need counseling, Craig. I think we need—"

"Counseling? Like, marriage counseling?"

"Well, don't you agree?" she said, shifting on the cold leather seat.

He ran his fingers from his forehead to the nape of his neck, took a deep breath, and rubbed the knot in his shoulder.

"It wouldn't suit our image well. You know how people around here like to talk," he said as he straightened his tie.

"The superficial smiles, the mindless chatter at these stupid events. Is that really all that's left of us?"

"The election has been hard on both of us," he said as he put a cool hand on her knee. "But doing something like that would be detrimental."

"Detrimental to what, your election or our marriage?" she said, crossing her legs and watched his loveless hand fall from her knee. She tightened the shawl around her bare shoulders and raised her eyes to his.

He fidgeted with a cufflink and straightened his sleeve. "Once the election is over, things will be better. Just ride it out, Emma."

"Ride it out? I don't want to just *ride out* our marriage—"

"What do you expect, Emma? We've been married for eight years. Young love can't last forever."

Resentment tore through her well-trained patience. She crossed her arms and let a fierce stare rest on his unfaltering gaze.

"Of course I don't expect that, Craig. I'm not—"

"You really want to be pawing all over each other like teenagers? I think we both realized a long time ago the motives behind our marriage."

Emma froze staring at his polished onyx eyes.

He took a peaceful breath, raised his cheeks to the charming smile people loved, and took her hand in his. "We may not have the perfect marriage, darling, but our needs keep us together. It makes our marriage work."

"Marriage shouldn't feel like an arrangement, Craig. That's not what I want for us."

He gently kissed the diamond ring on her left hand as his eyes rose to hers. "Now, darling, you know where you would be without me," he said with a smile. "And I cannot fulfill my dreams without you. We're a team, you and I."

As he caressed her hand on his smooth cheek, she was desperate to feel a flicker of love between them in his touch.

"So, you see, we're perfect for each other. Don't let being tired spoil a perfect understanding."

"I don't want an *understanding*, Craig. I want love, what happened to—"

"Oh, Emma," he laughed, shaking his head as he let go of her hand. "That childish imagination of yours. Let's not discuss this anymore."

"We need counseling Craig. We need something. I can't keep going on like this, being married to a stranger," Emma said as she faced him square.

Craig reached into his briefcase and started flipping through the week's agenda. "Ah, remember that you have to attend that auction tomorrow. We need to have a presence established among the people."

"Doesn't it bother you that we're like—like business partners?"

"Marriage *is* a partnership, is it not?" he said with a sideways glance.

"What about passion? What happened to that?"

"It's really important for us that you be there tomorrow. Hopefully more collected then you are now," he said as he closed the planner. Craig tipped his head back against the headrest, closed his eyes, and interlaced his fingers on his lap.

"Craig?" she said, leaning forward and saw his relaxed, closed eyes. "Craig?"

"I'm tired, Emma," he said without opening his eyes, shifted on the seat, and turned his back to her.

"But…Craig?" she said softly. His eyes clenched tighter, and she knew no response would come from his lips.

The limo seemed to split in half from the quake of their crumbling marriage. She took a solemn, empty breath watching the husband she lost to greed. Her watery stare shifted to the window as the city lights faded to specks as the car coiled up the hill. She scooted closer to the door, enforcing the chill between them.

"I can't do this," she whispered to no one.

****

Hints of morning sun crept through the taut curtains, dotting flecks of light in the dark, loveless bedroom. Emma whimpered in her sleep as she rolled over and dug her head deeper into the feather pillow. Sweat beaded on her face as muffled screams, sparks, and suffocation twisted her dreams into a familiar fright.

"Find me," a voice whispered as her eyes shot open to wake. Her fingers trembled as she placed a hand on her heaving chest. She forced deep breaths to soothe her frantic heart as she took in the elegance of the posh Victorian room.

"It was just a dream," she assured herself and took in another breath. "Just a bad dream," she whispered. She rubbed her shoulders as if to wipe off the surreal nightmare and slid out of bed.

The swift clacking of the butler's approaching steps echoed off the marble floor in the hallway. The air hinted of musk and laundry detergent as he popped his head in the doorway. "Ah, you're up. Wonderful. Good morning, Mrs. Beckett."

"Of course I'm up, Edward. Why wouldn't I be?" she said, splashing cool water on her face as visions of the nightmare still flashed through her mind.

"Are you feeling all right, ma'am?" he asked and almost touched her shoulder.

"Do you have today's schedule?" she said, patting her face with a towel.

"You're to leave for the auction at eight, ma'am."

"Have you heard from Olivia? She was due back in town last week, but I haven't heard from her."

"Well, Ms. Child does seem to have loose restraints on schedules."

"Perhaps she'll call for lunch, being Monday and all," Emma said, scooting by his thin body in the bathroom doorway.

"I'm afraid that wouldn't work. Mr. Beckett called earlier. He requests you meet him for lunch," Edward said, making himself comfortable on her vanity chair and crossed his legs.

"Did he say why?"

"It's of no importance, I'm sure," he said with a flick of his manicured nails.

"Of course he didn't," she said to herself and leaned into the mirror to inspect the puffy circles engulfing her washed out gaze.

"You're to head straight to his office after the auction. I have already instructed the driver of this."

Dreading the unexpected lunch, her stomach coiled into knots. "Yes, of course."

"Well, then, I'll leave you to ready yourself," Edward said with an abrupt twist of his feet and left the room.

"God forbid I don't stay on schedule," she said to herself, leaning close to the mirror and pressed a fingertip into the squishing circles. She let out a groan as she turned and eyed the walk-in closet. "Another day in the life of a trophy wife." Craig's fascination with being envied slid its slimy fingers into every crevasse of their lives, and her apparel was no exception. Her well-trained eye was mindful of his wishes.

With her feet planted to the ground, Emma's stance wilted in the full-length mirror examining the modern-day Jackie O. that looked back at her. People saw only a beautiful, prominent woman in society, but she loathed the pathetic woman in her reflection. She tugged on the chiffon blouse, neatening the tuck in the waistband as she twisted her feet, second-guessing the ankle wrap shoes. With one last scrutinizing turn, *they might pass inspection*, she thought.

"You look lovely."

Startled, Emma spun around toward the voice behind her.

"God, Prudence," Emma said holding a hand to her chest. "Thank you. Is it too casual?"

Prudence was in her early twenties, Emma would guess, with shoulder length mousy brown hair, stunning hazel eyes, and a curvy youthful body.

"I've never been to an auction," Prudence said with a half shrug. "But the top is very cute." Prudence smiled and untwisted the strap on Emma's blouse.

"I'm like a damn puppet," Emma muttered, wiping a smudge of eyeliner from her eye.

"Excuse me?" Prudence said.

"I'm sorry. I must sound like a whiny, spoiled rich girl to you," Emma said as she turned to face Prudence. "Well, what do you think?"

"Very nice, ma'am. Pretty as always."

"Just the way he likes it," Emma said, scowling at her reflection before turning to the door.

******

Emma thought only of last night's conversation with Craig while she rode to the auction house.

"I can't let him destroy me," she whispered to herself, nibbling on a fingernail as the car approached the parking lot. "What is life without love?"

"Pardon?" the driver said.

"Oh, nothing, just talking to myself," Emma said as the car stopped.

Scattered throughout the parking lot were groups of spoiled socialites engaged in superficial conversations shrouded with plastic smiles. *I am not like them*, she thought as she walked toward the mass of people being herded into the auction house like sheep. Once inside she immediately felt the twinge of regret and looked for a way to avoid the woman meandering down the first aisle. Andrea Norton couldn't be a day older than Prudence, Emma guessed, as she stared at the thin beauty admiring a hideous zebra print chair. But Joe didn't marry her for her personality. Everyone knew that. Andrea is a former Playboy Bunny - Miss July in fact.

"Oh my God! Emma, I'm so happy to see you!" Andrea squealed when she spotted Emma.

"Andrea, what a pleasure," Emma said as they exchanged a hug.

"I have been trying to get a hold of you, you naughty thing!" Andrea smiled and smacked Emma on the arm. "I was just saying to Joe today how I just can't get you on the phone."

Masterfully hiding her disgust for the black-haired Bunny, Emma smiled and said, "Well, with Craig running for—"

"I tell you, if Joe was only half as sweet as him, I'd never let him out of my sight!" Andrea said with a wink. "I don't know how you can pull yourself away from that man."

Suddenly sickened by the admiration for Craig, Emma hoped to change the conversation. "So, what brings you to the auction today?"

"We've just bought a house in the hills. It has this terrible country motif," Andrea said with a curled lip. "I told Joe, I can't possibly vacation there until it's *completely* remodeled."

"Oh, yes, how terrible." Emma's tone dripped with sarcasm.

"Come on, let's see what goodies we can find," Andrea said, wrapping her arm around Emma's.

Andrea giggled and squealed as she poked fun at the others in attendance. "God, what a mess. Look at her dress," Andrea chuckled, nodding to a woman by a few paintings. "Deserves a closer look, don't you think?" she said as she pulled Emma with her.

As Andrea heckled and teased, Emma drowned out her squirrel-like giggles and bent over for a closer look at the paintings.

"It's quite nice, don't you think?" Emma said, stretching to admire the pastel scene behind the velvet ropes.

"Ugh, old and *ugly*," Andrea said.

"You think so? I think it's quite nice."

"I thought you had better taste than that," Andrea snickered. "Oh, hold that thought," she said, held her index finger up to Emma, then bounced away to greet a handsome man across the room.

"It's the Victorian era I believe," said an attendant to Emma's interest in the collection.

"Who's the artist? I can't make out the signature."

"The owner says it's a Shivley painting?" The attendant nodded toward a man in the back chatting with the manager.

"Shivley you say? Hmm."

"Just a moment, I'll get him to clarify," he said as he scurried toward the owner of the painting. He gestured at Emma as they spoke, then the small group walked toward her.

"It's a very old piece. Lovely palette for its time," the manager said, extending his hand to Emma. "I'm Charles Hubert, auction house manager."

"It's interesting yes." As Emma shook the manager's hand, her heart sped to an eager thud as she stole a look at the quite man standing just behind them. He was much taller than Craig, *must be at least six and a half feet*, she thought.

"The artist is relatively unknown. Only a handful of his paintings can be found today. Probably because of his color choices at the time," the man said with a smile and reached to shake her hand.

His slender face had a cute notch in the chin she wanted to press her finger into. He had a handsome, boy next door kind of sweetness about him.

As they held their stare, he realized he still held her hand. His eyes flickered embarrassment as he jerked his hand back and tucked it in a pocket.

She fidgeted with a piece of her skirt pinched between her fingers and wiggled on her feet on the heels of her shoes like an awkward, self-conscious teenager.

The two seemed to forget the manager still stood there. "If you have any further questions, feel free to ask the staff," he said before excusing himself.

"How you did?" Emma pressed a hand on her forehead. *I sound like an idiot.* "How did you, ugh," she smiled, glanced at the floor and tried to catch her breath. "Where did you find the painting?" she managed.

He blushed being caught in her gaze and fidgeted with his already straight tie. His stubble covered cheeks bent to a faint smile. "I'm sorry, what?"

Emma's flushed cheeks raised to a smile. "I said where did you find it?"

"A farmhouse in Arkansas, if you can believe it." He rubbed the back of his neck and cleared his throat. "I'm sorry, I don't usually go to these things, my partner does. He's better with people than me." Two faint dimples appeared as a boyish grin lit up his face. "I, uh…" his voice cracked through a nervous chuckle.

"You, um." Emma smiled and tried to look away, but couldn't pry her gaze from his. "We must have met before," she said.

He grinned. "I think I would remember that," he said.

"Are you sure? It feels like—" she blushed, realizing she was staring again.

"I know, but I don't think—"

"Perhaps at another auction?" she said.

"No, I don't usually—"

"Go to these things, your partner does," she interrupted with a nervous laugh.

Emma found herself stepping closer to him and wanted to wrap her arm around his.

He stood motionless, taking in every feature of the woman before him. "Stunning," he hushed.

"Pardon?"

"Nothing. I'm sorry," he said, a rosy hue covering his cheeks. "I can't help but—"

"Come on, let's get good seats. I want to watch that one," Andrea said as she stepped between the two, nodding to a woman by the zebra print chair. "She's eyeing my stuff," she said, not acknowledging Emma's conversation and pulled her away.

"It was nice chatting with you," Emma said, smiling over her shoulder as Andrea continued pulling her.

Four

Emma peeked over her shoulder throughout the auction searching for the strange man, but saw only excited, spoiled faces celebrating their win. Now back in the seclusion of the car she resisted smiling as she thought of him. The rush of his presence was something she hadn't known before, yet felt guilty letting it overrun her thoughts. She glanced down the street through the window. Her excitement of the forbidden flirtation was quickly subdued by the sight of Craig's building.

The town car pulled up to the white stucco building's side entrance where an attendant helped her out of the car. As she walked through the grand halls busy interns and secretaries scurried about around her clutching stacks of files wearing flustered looks and hurried steps.

As Emma approached Craig's office, his secretary sat filing a snagged nail with her head cocked, and resting a phone on her shoulder.

"Yes, I understand the dilemma. But Mr. Beckett has several meetings today and simply cannot move the appointment," Shelia said into the phone.

Emma cleared her throat to gain Shelia's attention.

Shelia glanced at Emma with a hint of annoyance and spun her chair to turn her back to Emma.

"Well, flip through your little calendar to see what you can move then, Carrie," Shelia said.

"Excuse me, Shelia," Emma whispered.

Shelia raised a hand over her shoulder to hush Emma without looking at her.

Emma waited for a moment. "I'm sorry, Sheila, but—"

Shelia whipped her chair around, snickered at Emma and pointed to the phone resting on her shoulder.

Emma hoped she wouldn't intrude into a meeting, and quietly opened the door.

Craig was perched on the edge of his desk with one leg casually propped on a side chair. His face flushed a warm peachy color as he spotted Emma in the room. He seemed to glide in slow motion; his dark eyes sparkled like polished onyx looking at her and still made her heart pound a little faster. The man was handsome; even she had to admit that. His tender grin almost made him tempting, until she felt the coldness of his lips pressed against hers.

"Hello, my love. I'm so glad you could make it," he said, then cupped his hand on the small of her back and leaned in for a hug. "Don't screw this up for me," he whispered into her ear.

"Emma, gorgeous as always," said a raspy voice beside her. Craig stepped to the side, and there sat Richard Daminski, sipping coffee in the corner chair. He was in his late sixties, short, and balding terribly with an oil slicked comb-over. Richard was filthy rich, eerily creepy with his crooked smile, and one of Craig's biggest supporters.

"Oh, Richard, I didn't see you hiding there!"

The fat old man grunted trying to push himself out of the chair. He panted shuffling to Emma and kissed her on the cheek. "Such a beauty you are—"

"Don't go getting any ideas there, Rich. There's plenty of interns for that." Craig chuckled and pulled Emma closer to him.

Emma chimed in with a pleasant smile. "Now, you two behave."

"Well, shall we?" Craig suggested and gestured to the door.

During lunch Emma learned grotesque eating habits would be a vast improvement for Richard. He chomped on his lobster as if it were his last meal, letting little bits of meat flick off his tongue and land on the tablecloth. Richard broke into obnoxious laughter. "Woops, looks like that one got away from me!" he said as he picked up the hunk of food and tossed it in his mouth.

After the main course and two deserts Richard seemed to have his fill. He leaned back in his chair and not so nonchalantly loosened his belt. "Now, for the business at hand," he said, picking at his teeth with a fingernail.

Craig squeezed Emma's knee underneath the table; his cue that she was to turn on the charm.

"Seems that *preservation fund* we thought might be sending some funds our way could be on the chopping block," he said, picked a piece of food off his teeth and flicked it at the floor. "Damn auditors, always got their noses in other people's business."

"Would that affect the—"

"Might have an impact on contributions. If ya' catch my drift," Richard interrupted.

"Would it be helpful if I called in a few favors?" Craig asked.

"Unless your friends are Regan himself, probably ain't going to do a damn bit of good!"

Craig dug his fingernails into Emma's kneecap.

"Oh, Richard, don't be so dramatic," she said with her gentle, well-trained tone.

"Ain't drama, sweetheart. It's politics."

"I'm sure someone as intelligent as you can figure out a workaround," she said, flashing a charming grin at the round-faced businessman.

"Honey, I love your enthusiasm, but I know when not to put my dick in a noose."

"Richard!" she teased and swatted his hand. "Now, Richard, if we let Rumbart win that will be the end of us all. You know how those types are."

"Look, I hate that brown-nosed Democrat as much as the next guy but—"

She knelt back in the plush chair, crossed her arms, and shook her head with solemn disappointment. "If he manages to pull ahead of Craig and wins the spot, you know the first place he'll start looking when he gets elected Richard."

"I'll have time to tidy the books up before he—"

"Look what he's done to Wakefield. Ruined him already," she said. "He sees no place for businessmen like yours - and Craig's - *type*, in politics."

Richard started gnawing on a toothpick and fixated his stare on the drab beige tablecloth. She could see his crooked wheels turning, envisioning legislature rejections, tax increases, and millions falling out of his pockets.

Craig tapped her leg, a small gesture of approval she supposed. Emma had softness about her, a gentle likeability that swayed people in the direction she wanted them to go. She was a priceless commodity for Craig's endeavors.

They shared a few minutes of lighthearted chatting back at the office before Richard politely excused himself to another meeting, leaving her and Craig alone. The dark stain of the massive wood accent furnishings made the room feel cramped and suffocating. The sleek chocolate brown chairs echoed his forceful masculinity. Emma stood in the center feeling minuscule and worthless in the refined office.

She hesitated before sitting in the stiff leather chair as her timid mouth opened, "Well, that ended well, didn't it?"

"That fat old bastard, trying to back out on me like that!" Craig said and threw his jacket at the sofa.

She flinched as the balled up fabric whooshed by her head.

"Stupid old prick better grab ahold of his balls."

She took a deep, quiet breath. "He won't pull out. He has as much riding on this election as you. Well, more actually," she said, almost wincing in reluctance.

He grunted, whipped his chair around, and faced the sage green wall covered with his prized awards.

The faint ticking of the gold clock seemed to mock her as she sat in silent agony. *Am I supposed to leave*, she wondered, watching his chair turned away from her. She almost yelped as his chair spun around but caught her poise moments before he eyed her.

"I suppose you might be right. This time. If he doesn't find some other way to filter it, it'll hurt him more than me. I can find another source, but few lawyers will do for him what I have," he said with a cocky tone of assurance.

"Yes, of course. There are plenty of avenues."

He bent over his desk and started to thumb through a file. "That's it, you can go," he said, nodding at the door. "Oh, wait—"

Pausing for a half a second, she almost expected him to say thank-you.

"We're going to a fundraiser this weekend that's not on your schedule. There are several people attending and it would help us if your smiling face is there with me. Particularly Sharon McCormick - I have a meeting with her husband and it would do us well if she came home with happy tales to tell," Craig said, not looking up at her.

"Craig, I don't mind doing some of these things to help you, but you know how I feel about lying like—"

"I won't hear it, Emma. I need his backing, so it needs to be done and that's it."

"Craig," she said, softening her tone as she took a step forward to catch his look. "I know you had good intentions with this election business—"

"*Business?*" he repeated with a raised a brow.

"But, I think that…perhaps your plans have veered off a bit. Don't you think?" her voice cracked with hesitancy.

"How the hell do you figure that? We're right on track."

"It just seems, well, your drive as a lawyer was to give us a comfortable life. And it has," she said, taking his stiff hand inside hers. "It just seems that this election and all, it goes above wanting a good life, seems a bit… a bit greedy, perhaps."

He shook her hand off. "You think I'm greedy?"

"I'm concerned this avenue you're exploring, with Richard and the people like him. Maybe it's clouding your judgment a bit."

"Perhaps you're just too weak willed for the challenge."

"Craig, I have only good intentions here—"

"I thought I rid you of that southern trash honesty. I see now that I haven't," he said, scooting his chair back and eyed Emma.

"I am not southern trash, Craig. Damn it, why do you—"

"Look at you, one unkind word and you're all flushed and cursing like a hillbilly," he said with a smirk.

"It's dirty money, Craig," she said through clenched teeth.

He shot up from his seat, arching his back like a lion ready to pounce on its prey as he pressed his face against hers.

Her breath stuttered as she resisted the urge to slap him.

"You go with me. You smile. Be charming. Win people over like I taught you," he whispered in her ear. "Or I'll have no more use for you." He stood back, adjusted his tie, and tucked a pile of files under his arm as he began walking to the door. "We'll go to the fundraiser, happy and smiling, okay?" he said and reached for the doorknob.

"I won't be your puppet, Craig," she said, spinning to face him.

"I've done all of this for you, because I love you. Now I need you to do something for me. Or you'll force me to come to other...measures, we'll say," he said, his smirk stretching to a full smile as he left the room.

****

This is the last time I'm doing this, no more, Emma thought as the huge front door creaked open. The swift clatter of sudden footsteps filled the mansion as employees scattered with pretend busyness.

Edward appeared from the study with his hands clasped behind his back and an unsettling grin stretched across his face. "I trust you enjoyed lunch?"

"Yes, of course," Emma replied, quickening her pace toward the stairs.

"Would you care for a beverage ma'am?" he hollered after her.

"Wine, have it sent to the office please."

A throbbing headache squeezed her head as she rummaged through file cabinets in Craig's office.

"If he refuses to change, well, then that will have to be it," she said to herself, riffling through papers. "There has to be something in here," she said, tossing a file to the side and pulled out another one. "God where does he keep it all?" She took a deep breath as she clutched a pile of papers against her chest. "I can't believe my name isn't on any of it. Not a single account?" She rubbed her temples. "How can I get out?"

Emma continued scouring bank statements and investment summaries, hoping to find any way to hide money for herself. As she moved to another filing cabinet, a black blob of uniform sprinting across the yard caught her eye outside the window. A winded maid whispered something to Prudence who was embraced with a young man under a tree. Prudence turned to run inside. The young man tried to reach for Prudence, but she spun her head back and said something over her shoulder as she continued to run.

Minutes later the hurried swishing of Prudence's skirt came jogging down the hall. She barged into the room, sweating and almost panting.

"Good afternoon, Mrs. Beckett. Which wine would you like?" She appeared almost panicked, and her fearful hazel eyes avoided Emma's look.

Emma bent her head to the side. "Who was that boy?" Emma asked, surprised by her bluntness.

Prudence's guilt filled eyes shifted to the floor as she tucked her nervous hands in the apron pockets. "One of the landscaping crew, ma'am."

"Emma, please, call me Emma," she said with a warm smile. "Are you two close? Dating?"

"I, well, I know it's against policy." Her fearful voice cracked like a boy in puberty. "We, I mean he and I, well, we—"

"That's a yes then?"

"Yes, ma'am, err, Emma."

Emma turned back to the young man still waiting by the tree.

Prudence's look grew painful and cautious. "Am I going to lose my job now?"

Emma pondered the question, and then nodded her head with a faint smile. "My usual wine, only a small glass please."

"Oh, ma'am, I mean, Emma, thank you so—" Prudence's body lit up with gratefulness, making her smile stretch like someone had pulled her cheeks back with hooks. She bent her head in repeated nods of thanks as she backed out of the room.

It had been so long since Emma was sincere in her motives; she had forgotten what it felt like. She sat on the corner of the desk, kicked her shoes off and relished the moment of doing something she alone wanted to do.

The wine almost sloshed out of the filled glass as Prudence rushed back into the room.

"Come, sit with me while I look for some papers." Emma smiled and motioned to the chairs across from the desk.

The young maid was reluctant to sit down, but obliged her employers wishes.

"Now, tell me about that cute man out there. He looks lost without you." Emma pointed to the gardener who still waited, kicking dirt at the tree.

"Well, I guess it started last summer…"

****

Uncertain if Craig would join her for supper, Emma instructed the chefs to start serving without him. She felt ridiculous sitting at the enormous birch table with thirteen empty chairs around her. Three grand chandeliers lit the luxurious room with a subtle, romantic glow, and cast a soothing stream of light on the Helen Allingham oil paintings lining the longest wall.

She drummed her fingers on the table, looked around the big empty room, and tugged on her earlobe. Even after this many years it still seemed strange calling for someone to collect her dishes. So she waited, twirling the cloth napkin in a circle, and listening to the soft sizzle of wax melt off the candles.

A quiet chuckle snuck out as she remembered the man from the auction, his sweet grin, so nervous and fidgety around her. *I can't remember the last time a man smiled at me like that*, she thought. As she held back a grin a loud thud resonated through the silent halls. Emma jumped suddenly hearing Craig's voice. "God, he's in another mood," she said and shifted in her chair.

Craig threw the doors open and swiftly walked to the head of the table. He glanced at her distastefully. She felt small and worthless again, as if the room grew around her trying to swallow her whole.

"You don't even seem happy to see me," he said.

"I, uh, I'm just surprised to see you dear," she said. "With the Daminski meeting today I thought—"

"Don't get me started on that fat slob," his sharp tongue snapped. He waved an impatient hand in Prudence's face while she set a bowl of soup on the table.

Anxious, Emma twisted the napkin around her finger until it was plump and purple. She could feel his rage brewing across the table and she scrambled for a response. "No, of course. I'm sorry." She glanced at Prudence from the corner of her eye and motioned in warning to exit quickly.

"I called a few people. They're going to help *persuade* Richard into riding it out," his jagged voice spouted as he bent to slurp his soup.

"I'm sure you're pleased by—"

29

"This is ice cold! Do they actually expect me to eat this shit?" he said and dropped the spoon in the bowl.

His anger frazzled her, causing her thoughts to fumble over each other and squeeze her heart into pounding panic. *I should let him rant. No, I should distract him, change the subject.*

She sat straight with phony confidence. "Craig, I, I was thinking about our reservation tomorrow."

"Oh for the love of God, Emma," he said and slammed back against the chair. "You're really going to bother me with babble right now?"

Her jaw clenched and she looked down at her empty bowl on the table.

"Well?" He crossed his arms and locked an impatient glare on her.

"Please don't take that tone with me, Craig. I'm not one of your employees."

"I've had a terribly long day, you didn't even greet me, and I can't even stay home because I have to meet someone for drinks," he said, taking a deep breath in self-pity. "So excuse me if I'm a little short. I'm running myself ragged for you."

"You're not doing this for me anymore, Craig. Quit putting that burden on me."

"Why on earth would I go through all this for myself? I want to do great things for people, why do you hate that so much?"

"Why can't you just be great for me?"

"Damn it, Emma. I'm too tired for this tonight."

"Then stop talking to me in that tone!"

"Fine. What was it you wanted to say?" he said, leaning back in exaggerated attention.

"I, I was just going to see if you needed to cancel."

"Cancel what?"

"Never mind. It's not important," she said, throwing her napkin on the table and crossed her arms. "You're clearly not in the mood. So forget it."

He threw his hands up. "First you snap because you want to talk, now you don't want to talk. What *do* you want Emma?"

She tightened her arms, raised her brows and stared back at him. "We'll discuss it later, when you're not so…edgy."

As dinner dragged on, she listened to his furious ranting about Richards's stupidity and lack of gumption. He collected his wits and bid her goodnight before vanishing to another late meeting. As the front door slammed shut, she could sense the entire house exhale in relief.

She inhaled deeply trying to let go of tension from his whirlwind appearance. A light sound ruffled behind her, she looked back as Prudence peeked out from behind the kitchen door.

"He's gone," Emma said.

"I wasn't sure." Prudence wheeled out a cart to collect the dishes from the table.

Emma sank in the chair as the flickering flames on the candles pulled her deeper into an almost catatonic state.

"Are you all right, Emma?"

"How could anyone be all right like this?" Emma said.

"Is there something I can help you with, ma'am?"

Emma's somber empty eyes met Prudence's puzzled stare. "If you'll excuse me," Emma said as she stood and left for her bedroom.

Emma paused in the bedroom doorway, surveying the medieval cell.

"How did we get like this?" she said to the darkness, walked to the bed and crawled in without even bothering to undress.

Five

Time refused to pass that night. Emma's closed eyes only flashed pictures of Craig's scrunched, hateful face staring at her from across the dinner table. She was used to his rough edges, his callous manner, and over the years she could adjust without a passing thought. But lately he had become something darker than she thought even he was capable of being.

Curled up on the window seat, she watched the world outside carry on in morning routines. This glamorous life became her death sentence. There was nothing for her anymore, no one to reach out and help save her from the beautiful prison.

"I can't live like this." The full weight of her fate felt heavy on her chest, crushing her will to carry on. She twisted the massive wedding ring and squeezed it between her fingertips. "Does he really not love me anymore? Did he ever love me…" She traced a circle around the diamond as she tried to convince herself all was not lost.

Edward rapped on the door as he opened it. "Good morning, Mrs. Beckett. I trust you slept well?" he asked, eyeing the untouched bed.

"It's a little early, isn't it?" she said as she covered herself with a robe.

"Perhaps a little," he said, and glided a fingertip along a stack of books atop the dresser. "Miss Child called for you last night." He ignored the barrier between employer and employee, continuing to snoop through items on her desk. "She would like to meet you for lunch...at your usual place?" he added with suspicion, glancing up from a stack of photos.

"Oh wonderful, she's finally back in town!"

"Should I ready the driver?"

"No, I'll drive myself, I think," she said with a cringe, knowing how Craig thought not utilizing their driver reduced her to common folk.

"Hmm. As you wish ma'am."

Fed by the excitement of seeing her only friend, Emma trotted to the bathroom and not thinking that she left Edward unattended with her belongings. Olivia was the one spark in her life not even Craig could control. No one controlled Olivia Child.

****

Olivia Child was anything but an ordinary Winfield socialite. But her wealth and stature allowed her the unchallenged freedom to be so peculiar. She made no hesitation to flaunt her A-list status, was categorized by most as a blend of classy and tacky, yet was confident enough not to care which side of the fence she sat on.

The Childs always provided services with questionable methods, and it paid off. It seemed secrecy came with a high price tag. Olivia was born with a silver spoon in her mouth and expanded the family business in ways people were afraid to imagine. And Olivia loved it.

She waited at a bistro table on the patio, spinning the stem of the wineglass between her fingers and eyeing the men around her for anyone of interest. "Emma, darling!" she hollered, leaped from her seat and trotted to hug Emma.

Olivia was dressed somewhat sensibly, for her, and wore an orange spaghetti strap dress with a gold belt. It was the monstrous platinum necklace and four-inch heels on unsteady feet that caused a second look.

Emma wrapped her arms around Olivia. "Why do you insist upon leaving me?" she whispered.

Olivia squeezed tight and frowned at the miserable thing in her arms. She gave a gentle, playful shake to Emma's shoulders. "It was a terrible divorce, darling," she teased. "I only made away with seventy-five percent of what he was worth! Of course I needed time to recover from that," she said as she laughed. "Come, come, sit!" she said and escorted Emma to the table.

"God how I've missed you, Olivia. I can't stand when you're gone for so long," Emma said as they settled in their chairs.

"I know, darling, but you know what you need to do—"

"I haven't a clue how to deal with him anymore," Emma interrupted, then sipped her wine. "It's unbearable. He thinks he can save the world, but crushes anyone in his path to get there. How did he get so...cold?"

Olivia motioned to the waiter and waved her glass in the air. "Lots more," she slurred, unconcerned with the disapproving looks from her intoxicated hollering.

"He's been so distant with me. Works so many hours, then makes me feel guilty like *I'm* the one making him work so much," Emma said as she rubbed her temples.

"You look tired, darling," Olivia said, raising Emma's head and touched a finger to the circles around her eyes.

"Between Craig and not sleeping well, well I must look a terrible mess," Emma said somewhat embarrassed.

"Not sleeping? I should introduce you to the lovely Prince Valium. I can't sleep a wink without it."

"It's silly, but I keep seeing this man—"

"Now that's my kind of dream!" Olivia laughed.

"No, not like that." Emma smiled. "I think he's supposed to be my husband? But I don't recognize him. He's injured somehow, and I want to save him but..." Emma took a breath and hoped she didn't sound crazy. "I'm covered in blood, and I can't find him. Then I wake up screaming," Emma said as she shrugged.

"It's probably that bastard husband of yours bleeding poison into your dreams even," Olivia said before finishing her drink.

"He's not a *bastard*. The money's just gone to his head."

"Just like the rest of this damn town. It's no wonder he fits in so well. You'll never learn will—"

"I don't need to be mothered, thank you."

The waiter filled their glasses. "Just leave the bottle," Olivia said without thanks, grabbing it from his hands and poured wine to the rim. "You know what your problem is? You're going about this all the wrong way."

"Do I get advice from the great goddess of relationships now?" Emma chuckled as she raised her glass.

"Men are to be used like tissues." Olivia paused and tipped her head to let out a puff of smoke. "Used only a few times then tossed to the side."

"Oh God, Olivia—"

"I'm serious! That's all they're good for. You can't rely on them. Especially the types like Craig."

"He's not a *type*."

"Of course he is! And no matter how much you try to hide it, you're just like me—"

"I am not. God, you're terrible!" Emma laughed.

"It's true!" Olivia insisted. "You crave passion, attention, *love* and affection. That's no different than me," she snickered with a silly grin. "The only difference is I actually have the balls to go out and get just that."

"I'm married, Olivia. I took vows. No one said marriage would be easy," Emma said with a defensive glare and turned away with a huff.

"God, you're so stubborn," Olivia said and halfheartedly pushed Emma's shoulder. "He only sees you as a tool to be used now. You're a tool to him, a pawn, just like every other trophy wife. You make him look good."

"I am not his tool," Emma said, scrunching her face into pinched anger. "I may have let love get in the way of better judgment, but I am not some pawn."

"Then what are you? If not there for him to shove around, what are you?"

"Every marriage has troubles, Olivia. They have bumps and hard times."

"You're not being so brash to say that this is normal are you?"

"It's just, you wouldn't understand it," Emma said and looked over her shoulder in fake distraction.

"He'll never leave you. He won't look like the bad guy like that. You must leave him. It's the only option to rid yourself of that wretched man."

"I can't leave him, what do I have to my name?" Emma said, raising her brows as she waited for the answer that didn't need to be said. "Exactly," she said to Olivia's silence. "I don't have a dime of my own, and there's nowhere I can go that he won't find me." Emma once thought it sweet that Craig wanted to handle the finances, to take care of her. But now there was no hiding his true motives for it, to trap her.

"You're just a trophy wife like the rest of them, you know I'm right," Olivia urged, nodding to a table of perfectly poised women having lunch.

Emma hunched over the table trying to be discrete. "I can't leave him, you know that," she whispered. "He tracks every purchase, every move I make. He'd find me."

"Well, I hate to compare myself to him. But people like Craig and I are very well connected. It's rather unfortunate that he could hunt you down, just like that," Olivia said with a snap of her fingers. She tapped a finger to her lips as she thought. "What about fake ID's, new birth certificate? I may know someone who handles that sort of thing."

"Would that stop *you* from finding someone, a simple name change?" Emma raised an eyebrow.

"I have my ways of finding things, I suppose," Olivia said with a smirk. "Well poo, then he could do it just as easily."

"I spent an entire day searching through everything. Everything. I just don't see how it's possible." Emma took a breath and shook her shoulders. "I don't want to talk about that anymore, not today anyway. It doesn't seem right."

Thoughts of the evening ahead flooded Emma's mind. Her stomach rolled with uneasy nerves for discussing divorce on such a day. She finished off the wine and held her glass for Olivia to refill it.

"So, what are you going to do about tonight then?" Olivia asked.

"We're having dinner at Del Mar."

"Oo la la, tres chic, I met my fourth husband there," she teased.

"To our anniversary..." Emma said with wide nervous eyes and gulped her wine.

Olivia raised her glass in a halfhearted toast. "Well, did you buy yourself something nice at least?"

"I was hoping he did," Emma said, rolling her eyes at the naiveté.

"Uh huh...I can bet how that goes," Olivia said. "It's pointless you know, right?"

Emma's focus wandered to the street, watching tall blonde and dark-haired beauties peer into shop windows.

"He's killing you," Olivia said with pity for her friend.

Emma's attention snapped back. "It could change, go back."

"Go back to what? The way he always ignored you, beat you down?" she yelled. "God, Emma, when are you going to get your head out of your ass and stop the incessant justifying!" she hollered and threw her lighter on the table.

"Shh!" Emma glared at her and glanced around in embarrassment. "It's not as simple as it seems. We do love each other, Olivia."

"Love. Ha! You really believe that crap?"

"I have to…"

Olivia tried for a supportive smile and grabbed Emma's hand. "This kills me, you know. You're the only real thing in this damn town I've got." She let go and brought a hand to her cheek. "I've got more power than I know what to do, yet here I am, helpless to my true friend."

"Your friendship is enough. Things might change—"

"Change? Don't be ridiculous, darling." Olivia leaned closer to Emma and lowered her voice to a whisper. "You know, he could have, well, an *accident?*"

"Don't you dare!" Emma demanded.

"I can't just sit by and watch him do this to you Emma. I just can't do it anymore," Olivia begged. "If we can't get you out, then let's be rid of him."

"Don't talk like that! I'll work on a plan, I will—"

"Why won't you just let me have my way with him?"

"After tonight, well, I'll start working on something. But absolutely not what you're inferring," Emma said, glancing around secretively.

"Wonderful, I know the sexiest pool boy for a rebound fling," Olivia smiled.

"God, Olivia, you're shameless!"

****

The valet attendant held out his hand, struck with awe by the striking woman climbing out of the limousine. Emma wore a long, shimmery black gown. A deep scooped back exposed her tempting, silken skin. Her golden soft curls had a glossy sheen as they draped over her shoulder. Oblivious of the admiring eyes upon her, she craned her neck and scanned the parking lot for Craig's limo. *Not here yet, I guess*, she thought. She flashed a pleasant smile, nodded hello to the doorman and was promptly met by the maitre d' in the lobby.

"Good evening, Mrs. Beckett. Do you have a reservation?" he asked with a French accent too thick to be authentic.

"Yes. Two under Craig, I'm sure."

"Ah, yes, of course. You look lovely tonight! Please, right this way," he said, then bowed and shuffled off to escort Emma to a table.

As she slid the organza shawl off her shoulders her bare skin almost glowed in the orange hue of the candlelight. Her striking aura consumed the men around her. They stopped and turned to gaze at the gorgeous woman at the corner table.

"Could you tell me if my husband has arrived yet? I didn't see his car. Perhaps he's at the bar?"

"Ah, oui madam, he has not arrived yet no," he answered and then walked away.

She ordered a bottle of his favorite wine, a bit too bitter and coarse for her taste, but she wanted to start the evening off right.

Ill at ease with Craig running late, her hope started to waver. *Things have not fallen apart*, she repeated to herself. She tried to shake off the nagging worry and take in the romantic air of the atmosphere. Surrounded by doting, loving couples, hope started to flutter inside her. *He'll show, of course he'll show. It's our anniversary, he'll be here. He's just running late…*

Their table sat in a corner cove, kitty-corner to the floor-to-ceiling slate fireplace. A pillar candles centerpiece wafted the sweet scent of vanilla and strawberries, and was surrounded by velvety rose petals scattered atop a smooth-edged mirror. *The perfect setting*, she thought, and leaned in with closed eyes to let the delicate scent soothe her.

Patrons came and left, but still, she waited. Her posture slumped as an hour past with no messages from her husband, and she became all too aware of the meddling eyes around her. Customers hunched close to the other, whispering, and gave secretive sideways nods toward her table.

"Emma, so wonderful to see you here," said Tiffany Mitchell, a woman only capable of only jealousy and vengeance. "Look at you, sitting all alone like this," she said with a mocking pout. "Has your husband up and deserted you again?" She smiled, picked up a rose petal, and crumpled it between her fingertips.

"Tiffany, of course you're here," Emma said, clenching her jaw shut and sighed. "Craig is running late. You know how busy he gets."

"Running late...mm hmm, sure he is," Tiffany said with a smirk. "I don't think I'd have the strength to be seen at a place like this, all by myself." Tiffany curled her lip at the rolled up rose petal between her fingers, flipped her hand over, and flicked it on the table. "But you country girls are a different sort of breed, aren't you?" Tiffany nodded and walked away before Emma could respond.

Emma craved to berate Tiffany and cause a scene, but all she could muster was a glare across the room. She was certain all eyes cast her way as Tiffany belittled her so swiftly. She didn't have the strength to look up and see how many sets of eyes watched her in amusement. She was disgraced and running out of excuses for her thoughtless husband.

"Would you care for another bottle, ma'am?" the waiter asked.

"No, thank you," she said and tried to form a polite smile. "Could you tell me, has my husband left a message for me yet?"

"I don't believe so. But I can check again if you'd like."

Her gaze drifted to Craig's empty chair. "Would you please bring the menu? I'd like to order while I wait."

Her stomach reeled into twisted knots as emotions bubbled to the surface. The last thing she wanted was to choke down a seven-course dinner. But if she didn't force herself through the meal looking pleasant and deliberate, word would get out that the beloved attorney had stood up his wife. *Why do I even care what these people think?* she wondered as she smiled and nodded to a gawking couple at the next table. *They already know he deserted me.*

Desperate to keep down every bite of her soufflé, she tried to ignore the pain of being forgotten. Yet the nagging thought kept whispering that Craig didn't even care that she sat alone. Whatever it was that he was doing, it would always be more important than her. *Maybe I did marry the wrong man after all,* she thought, choking down another bite. She couldn't look up from her plate; she felt the burn of eyes watching her from every direction. She slid her arm across the table, grabbing Craig's gift off his place setting and scooted it toward her hoping to hide it by her purse.

God, they're right aren't they? she thought. In front of the flashing cameras they were an adorable couple, perfectly at ease as they moved through events hand-in-hand. But at the end of the day there was nothing he liked more than to be rid of her. *My marriage is dead, isn't it,* she thought as she ran the satin bow on his gift between her fingers.

"How could I possibly afford a divorce?" she whispered to herself, daring to ponder the notion of freedom. *There is no way to withdraw money where he won't notice, where his damn accountant won't tell him.* She twisted the two-karat ring off her finger, tempting herself with a life without the heavy burden. The full force of her broken heart pushed her to the brink of the unknown.

"Strawberries for you tonight, madam?' the waiter asked

Startled, Emma gasped.

"I'm so sorry to have frightened you," he apologized, and almost reached out to her.

"Oh, no, no, that's fine. I was just lost in thought. No, not tonight, thank you. Just the check, please," she said with a tortured smile.

She signed the receipt and left the table with as graceful a stride as she could muster. In a quiet hush rumors and gossip began to fly around the room behind her as she walked passed obvious gawkers.

She peeked over her shoulder to take one last look at the empty table in the corner, with Craig's delicately wrapped gift beside his untouched place setting. The coat check helped her with her shawl, and then she left the restaurant.

"Please take me home, Phillip," she begged the driver as she sank in the limo. She had waited three hours to flee and only wanted to dive in the car and disappear underneath the cover of the night sky.

Looking at his spot beside her, her eyes welled up and years of neglect charged through her carefully built walls. "Bastard..." she whispered.

Six

The ride back to the mansion was insufferable. His lingering putrid cologne smothered the air and Emma crumpled with nausea. She wasted all her strength holding back the raging river of her broken heart. The car pulled up the driveway and her anxious stomach rolled like a typhoon as she peered out the window to look for his car.

The limo stopped by the magnificent fountain in the courtyard. Beautiful sculpted angels danced in the water pouring down on them. She paused as the driver helped her up and quietly stared at the commanding entry to their home. Massive two-story pillars ran the width of the stone castle; huge slate steps led up to the grand Cathedral doors where his family's crest hung proudly above them. Cobblestone paths veered away from the house to lush gardens dotted throughout the property. It was painfully perfect.

Yet to Emma the lavish refurbished castle only echoed with misery, despair, and entrapment. The dull, cold stone home seemed mysterious and dark, like a shadow loomed over it even if the sun shone high. A whimpering voice inside her begged for escape. To run the farthest her legs would carry her. To save her from the slow death this life was bound give her. *Leave, please leave*, the voice cried out. Ignoring the urgency bellowing inside, she took a woeful breath and made her way up the large steps.

"Did you find your evening pleasurable, ma'am?" Edward said, stepping out from the shadows in the foyer.

"Why are you here?" she snapped. "Shouldn't you be in your quarters by now, Edward? I have no patience for you tonight."

He stood bewildered by her challenging tone.

Emma froze, with eyes wide and equally shocked by the outburst. Submissiveness urged her to apologize, but forceful despondency pushed her over the edge. "Well? What could you possibly want?"

"I, well, I was expecting to see Mr. Beckett, ma'am—"

"And you feel that your business with him is more important than I, his wife!" Her hands trembled as she hollered, she begged herself to stop but something kept forcing the brash words out before she could stop them. "Well? Stop the damn stammering and get it out already."

"I, uh, it's not important, ma'am. My apologies for the intrusion," he said. He bowed and whisked himself into the darkness from where he came.

Her knees collapsed beneath her. She stumbled and braced herself on the bureau by the hallway. Her heart thumped so hard it hurt. She raised a shaky hand to her lips, and then hobbled to an armchair just inside the hallway. Her lungs burned like the wind had been knocked out of her. She giggled and cried, thrilled and petrified by the outburst.

After a few moments she fumbled through the darkened hallways to the seclusion of her room, where she locked herself in the bathroom. She sat dizzy and weak, unconcerned with how long she cowered there and longed for the comfort of hiding in a nights sleep.

She pulled herself up and walked to the side of her bed. She traced a finger along the amethyst satin sheets as she stared at the loveless bed.

"How long has it been since we slept together..." she said to herself. She reached for his pillow, squished it in her tingling arms, and took a deep breath. "How long has it been since he touched me, and meant it?"

She turned around and collapsed on the bed. "I don't think I care," she said through an exhale. A fire started to boil inside her belly, filling her with contempt. "No, I deserve an answer," she said as she bolted up from the bed, tossed his pillow to the floor and ran out of the room.

****

Incapable of controlling her emotions she restlessly shifted in a chair as she waited. She heard the clanking of the metal handle on the front door and froze. Her heart beat like a drum line in her ears, her breath quickened, and she glared at his large figure casually strolling into the house.

"Where were you?" Her raspy voice boomed through the darkness.

Startled, Craig looked around the foyer searching the shadows for where she hid.

"I said, where were you?"

"Emma? What are you doing up at this hour? Where are you? Come in the light so I can see you" he snapped as he flipped on a lamp.

Slow steps brought her to a small stream of moonlight drifting in from a window. She paused for him to catch sight of her. Her robe hung open and crooked, arms dangling like dead weight on her little frame, and with a face void of emotion. "Where. Were. You?" she said again.

"What business is it of yours?" he yelled, took off his coat and turned to scorn her.

"I'm your wife, that's what business it is!" she said. "I sat in that restaurant for three hours. Three hours!" Her voice echoed through the barren halls.

"It is not my concern how long you sat where—"

"How could you desert me tonight? Tonight!"

Furious, he stormed toward her in four huge steps and leaned into her face. "I don't know what the hell you're talking about you crazy bit—"

"Why would you do that to me?" she bellowed so loud her voice cracked mid-sentence.

He bumped his chest into her body, pushing as he walked and forced her against the wall. "You will ask me nothing. Nothing! Do you understand me?" he shouted. His eyes glowed glassy with rage as he huffed. Any woman in her right mind would be terrified.

She stared into the dark eyes she once melted in. "Why would you do that...don't you care? What's wrong with you?" she said with eyes welling up as she hollered.

"I am in no mood for this shit, Emma—"

"Don't you love me anymore? Do I mean nothing to you?" she begged through a scream.

"What the hell has gotten into you?"

"You have no idea what day it is, do you? How can you be so heartless?" she said softly.

"I suggest you get your ass upstairs or I swear to God I'm going to—"

"You think you can scare me?" she said.

"If you don't shut the hell up I'll do more than scare you."

"You're just like your father!" she screamed and shoved his body away. "Beat people down to think they're nothing—" She put all of her weight into pushing him again.

Craig stumbled from her force. "Don't you ever compare me to him—"

"I'm not going to take it anymore!" she yelled. "Don't you care about me, about us? Don't you care what day it is?"

"Why should I care about you, Emma?" he screamed and pushed her into the wall. "Tell me, why should I give a shit? Because you're my wife?" he said as he laughed.

"I can't believe I used to love you…used to be proud of you," she said, curling her lip as she eyed him from head to toe. "Look at you, look what you've become. You're disgusting! You don't care about anyone but yourself!" she screamed. It was as if his image unraveled itself before her, revealing the inner layers she tried so hard to ignore. She cocked her head as she examined his face. His gorgeous features seemed distorted and ugly. She saw him for the first time as he really was, a monster. She reached to touch his foreign face but he jerked and smacked her hand away.

He glowered at her, utterly enraged yet thrown off by her demeanor.

"I don't know what the hell has gotten into you, but I won't stand for it!" he screamed.

Emma tilted her head. "I can't believe I wasted so much love on you," she whispered, took one last look at him, and then turned around in a foggy haze toward the stairs.

Seven

The night held no mercy for Emma. Her dreams shifted between an ugly, grotesque Craig, and her nightmare of the man she had somehow lost. As the night wore on, the dream changed. A woman cried, begging her to find him as the man called out to her from the distance. His blurry form twisted and morphed into the man she met at the auction. Her soul ached to find him, to heal the pain of the crying woman. She reached to touch him and saw that her hand was covered in blood. She woke to the sound of her crying, "I will find you!" She closed her eyes as she panted, and a pang shot from somewhere deep within. "It's just a dream," she repeated as she tried to catch her breath. As she opened her eyes a speck of white caught her attention from the corner of her eye. A shudder slid down her back from the huge, gorgeous bouquet of lilies placed on her nightstand. She slid across the bed and grabbed the small white card tucked inside it.

'Sorry to have missed our anniversary dinner. I have arranged a surprise to make it up to you. Be ready by ten. Love, Craig'

Emma slipped her hands around the thick stems, bent down and inhaled deeply. "Oh Craig..." she whispered. *I knew he still loved* me, she thought as her bouncy step carried her to the bathroom, *he's just busy, distracted with work. How selfish of me to forget that.*

The car pulled up to Magnolias Spa and Retreat and Emma's heart filled with delight. She strolled into the mint colored lobby with a confident strut, sure that Craig would be waiting for her in a private room.

A young receptionist sat perched in front of a large tranquil waterfall. "Morning Miss, may I help you?"

"I believe I have a reservation, Mrs. Beckett?" Emma said.

"Oh, Mrs. Beckett, welcome! We have a wonderful day planned for you! Please," she nodded to an attendant clutching a terrycloth robe with his arm held out to the hallway beside him.

"Will my husband be meeting me?" Emma asked from over her shoulder.

"Ma'am?" Her brows scrunched in confusion. She began shaking her head as she flipped through her appointment book. "I only have a reservation for you, ma'am."

The fleshy pink color washed from Emma's face. The serene surroundings distorted into ugly shades of musty-gray, and instantly she felt a fool. Her feet refused to step forward, her knees locking themselves in place. *So whimsical and trusting,* she thought, watching the water dribble over the glassy rocks. *So stupid to think he'd be here...* She felt sick and instinctively clutched her stomach as her heartache rolled in her belly.

"Ma'am?" the concerned attendant stepped toward her and cupped a hand under her elbow. "Are you all right?" he glanced back at the receptionist who shrugged. "Ma'am?" he asked again. "I think you should sit down."

"Of course he isn't here..." Emma whispered.

"Pardon —"

"Do you have a phone I can use?" she muttered back at the receptionist.

"Yes, of course," she answered. "But I think it's best if you—"

"I don't care what you think is best. Call me a taxi, please," she said and snatched the phone from the girl's hand.

It was quite the contradictory sight. The businessmen and politicians watched the two women at the bar with aroused curiosity. One woman was flamboyant; dressed in a cleavage-oozing silk tank top with an outrageous floral pattern, skintight purple pants and huge diamond rings on nearly every finger. The odd, gorgeous woman was surrounded in a cloud of smoke. She had wild eyes and exaggerated gestures as she was in feverish chatter with her friend.

The other woman, equally slender and breathtaking in her simple manner, sat almost motionless as she talked. Her mauve strapless dress fluttered in the breeze, teasing the men as it crept up over her knee. She was oblivious of everyone around her but her friend. Her delicate touch cupped a glass as she stared off down the shore. The mysterious awkward duo was more than enticing on an otherwise mundane Friday morning.

"So he was just going to send you off for the day? Hoping that would appease you?" Olivia's eyes were crazed, engulfed by the conversation.

"I suppose that was the plan—"

"Thought that would shut you up, I bet."

"That would suit his normal tendencies, wouldn't it?" Emma shrugged. "He thinks I'm a sap for love. Perhaps he's right?"

Olivia nibbled on her straw and said, "The nerve of that—"

"And then I called you. It's the only logical thought to cross my mind in twelve hours."

"Good lord, darling." Olivia stamped out her cigarette in the ashtray, waved her glass for a refill, and turned her attention back to Emma. "So, now what will you do? I wouldn't dare bet the egotistical prick will give a shit that you skipped out on your *special* day," Olivia said as she mocked him.

"As long as I don't interfere with his day it makes no difference to him what I do. I just have to *behave*." Emma sighed and looked out on the stretch of white shoreline. The hot sand was covered with lounge chairs and young women enjoying a lazy summer day, smiling as they flirted with handsome strangers. It seemed ages ago life allowed such lackadaisical freedom.

"I remember who I used to be, you know. That girl you met…" Emma said dreamily, watching a young woman chat with a lifeguard.

Olivia's glower stretched to a nostalgic smile. "God, what a spirit," she whispered. "You were a feisty little thing back then," Olivia chuckled.

Emma smirked. "I was something then, wasn't I? Turning heads, ready to take on the world." She laughed as she shook her head. "If I only knew…" Her eyes locked on the condensation soaked napkin beneath her glass. "Seems like a stranger to me, that girl. I can hardly imagine I was ever like that. So trusting and free."

"She's still in there, darling," Olivia said and nudged Emma with her shoulder.

"I don't think I could be like that no matter how hard I might wish it. All that's left is what you see before you," Emma said, gesturing to herself. "A beaten down, hopeless romantic clinging to a dead marriage. Pretty pathetic, isn't it?"

Olivia frowned; the sweet country girl was only a memory now.

"There's nothing left of her anymore I don't think. God, how I wish there was though," Emma said. "She would tell him and storm right out without a thought!" Emma laughed remembering her spunky, former self.

"Don't lose hope, darling. Just, just become a new, redesigned version," Olivia said, offering a faint smile and laugh.

"Like an upgrade?" Emma laughed.

"Exactly! Like a revised version, just older and saucier. Like having plastic surgery, without the surgery."

"Revised," Emma said to herself. As she let the thought linger, urgency bellowed within her. Without a thought she turned back to Olivia and said, "You have your annual benefit tonight don't you?"

"Blasted thing has given me such a headache planning it. Too bad Craig has another function, bloody bastard hogging all your time like that."

Emma rolled her eyes. "You know, to hell with his function," she said and nodded. "Yeah, to hell with it!"

Olivia's eyes flickered with delight at defiance. "You know, if those ignorant pricks really knew who he was—" Olivia said as she waved her glass at the restaurant packed with businessmen. "that worthless prick wouldn't stand a chance in this town." Olivia glared through her sunglasses, despising the men in tailored Italian suits and smooth shaven faces.

Emma sat secretly tickled by the thrilling idea of revolt. Whatever it was that sparked the notion inside her grew fierce and determined.

Olivia darted back to Emma. "So it's settled then. I'll send my driver for you, we'll show that man—"

"I really should use the—"

"Shh, nonsense," Olivia waved her hand frivolously at Emma. "Be ready by six o'clock, darling," she said with a devious smile, shot up from her seat, and clutched her purse under her arm. "Now, I have much to do. I'll see you tonight, darling, beautiful as ever I'm sure." She kissed Emma's cheek and rushed for the exit before Emma could mutter a word in protest.

Olivia stormed toward her car parked crooked and halfway on the curb in front of the restaurant's entrance.

The valet attendant waved at her improperly parked Mercedes. "Uh, ma'am, it's in the red zone," he said, pointing to the bright-red line painted on the curb. "You can't leave it there, or we'll have it towed."

"Oh, hush. I'm leaving," she snapped and rolled her eyes. "You people just don't care about anything, do you?"

"Without people like *us*, you wouldn't even have a job. Jerk," she said, then waved her middle finger in the air and slammed the car door shut.

The car made a terrible scraping sound as it clunked down off the curb. The tires squawked when they hit the pavement and she peeled off without glancing for oncoming traffic. Olivia grabbed the car phone, weaving in and out of the lane while she dialed.

"Hi, it's me. I need a favor," she said dryly, digging through her purse as she drove. "I've got nothing solid to go on yet, but I need the dust blown up around someone. Can you boys handle that?"

"Depends on the dirt you're looking for," said the man. "You don't have anything to use as a starting point?"

"Just the whims of my imagination," Olivia said through a sly laugh.

"Then how do you know there's something to find? We're very cautious about these types of things."

"Oh, I'm sure there are oodles to be found. No one is that pretty."

"How quickly you need it?"

"I need something by tonight. Can you do that?"

His voice cracked with hysteric laughter. "We're not *that* good. We need more time—"

"Damn it, what am I supposed to do for tonight then? I've got to have something."

"The whims of your imagination baby!"

"Yeah yeah, laugh it up, Johnny. When can you get it to me?"

"I can start today sure, I won't even ask for a retainer. But I won't have anything solid for a couple of weeks. Assuming there's actually anything to find."

"There is, I assure you," she said with a disgusted groan. "All right, it will have to do I suppose. I'll just have to make something up for now then. Pick from the standard scandalous ideas. I haven't the time to wait for you people to get started."

"Hey, listen now—"

"Oh calm down, Johnny. You know I simply adore you boys."

"Sure you do," he said with a laugh.

"Of course I do! How would I ever bury someone without you!"

Eight

Olivia worked a crowd like no other, even putting Emma's skills to shame. She treated everyone as the favored guest, and they savored the attention. But tonight, she had more intentions than simply looking for a potential boy toy.

She chatted with the cliques she detested the most, politicians and bank rollers. She whispered sordid fictitious tales, putting her plan into action through the buzz of gossip.

Olivia stood with Mrs. Marchavie - old, dirty money.

"I can't say for sure, but I heard it from a very reliable source," Olivia whispered.

The short twitchy woman lived for gossip about high profilers. It made her eyes wide with hunger, devouring every white lie Olivia fed her. She gasped with shock, held a hand to her cheek, and almost smirked. "The Cayman Islands?" she hushed.

"That's what he said. It's tucked away there so they can't touch it. He hasn't paid taxes in over a decade," Olivia replied, then quickly excused herself. A slick smile tugged on her cheeks knowing Mrs. Marchavie would soon do the dirty work for her, of course distorting the tale as she spread it throughout the room.

"It's just too simple," she said to herself and sipped champagne. She scanned the massive crowd trying to spot her next target in the array of black suits filling the ballroom. "Ah, there he is!"

Olivia smiled and nodded to partygoers as she worked her way through the crowd toward Allen before he was out of sight.

"I have been looking for you everywhere, darling!" Olivia's voice oozed charm as she wiggled her shoulder against his arm.

"You can't possibly need a new husband already!" he teased.

"Wouldn't you like to know?" She winked and slid her hands around his bicep.

Olivia couldn't stand him, most people couldn't. Allen Talbert was neither attractive nor intriguing by any social standard. Unfortunately for Olivia, he was the one who controlled or influenced the dirty behind-the-scenes work of the California political system. He was the puppet master for those who dreamed of climbing to the top, Richard Daminski's right-hand man, and precisely the man she need to speak to most.

"Walk with me, darling. I've much to tell you of your favorite pet," she said, gesturing to a corner of the room not filled with people yet.

"Really now?" he said with amused suspicion.

He wrapped his arm around her waist when they stopped, just past a horde of eavesdropping ears.

"Now tell me, you seductive manipulator. What have you heard of my favorite toy?"

"I can't say for certain—"

"Can you ever?" he said as he laughed.

She raised a brow and pouted in playful disappointment. "I've heard it from a very reliable source."

"And who might that be?" he prodded.

Olivia nodded indirectly toward a group of people letting his imagination fill in the blank.

"Really now!" he said, brightening his face with intrigue.

She smirked, content that he had found a satisfying candidate for reliability in the nameless group. "Well, I have heard that he has quite the taste for the ladies."

Allen erupted in laughter, grabbing his stomach as he bellowed. "Who here doesn't? I don't think there's one faithful man in the lot of them."

She obliged him a moment of laughter, then widened her eyes expressing urgent juicy tales.

"No, no, darling. It's not of the *clean* type," she whispered. "Not our kind, you see?"

Allen grunted under his breath as his faced flushed a brilliant shade of hate. It's been rumored that his mother was a drug addicted prostitute that left little Allen alone for hours while she worked for money to get a fix. Olivia knew the quickest way to make Craig's money stream cease flowing was if Allen thought his puppet had taken a liking to shady ladies on street corners.

He tugged on his shaggy uneven goatee as he observed the crowd. "If you'll excuse me, Olivia, I have some business to take care of." He bent down and kissed her on the cheek.

"Of course, darling. Please, do enjoy the party."

"As always, you have a way of livening up even the dullest of situations," he said with a smile, and then disappeared into the sea of tuxedos.

A content sigh slipped past her lips as she strolled around the room again, smiling and exchanging kisses while she contemplated the next person to pull into her web of deceit. By night's end a flood of midnight calls to accounts would be made as Craig's free ride came to a crashing halt, leaving his name tainted and questionable. Hit him where it hurts the most, her mother always said, and that is where Olivia thrived.

****

Spotlights waved in the brilliant evening sky, boasting an amazing event was happening tonight. Limos lined up for blocks like the Oscars. Emma's jittery hand tapped on the armrest as she waited for the limo to pull up to the red carpet. She closed her eyes and took a few deep breaths before the driver came to open the door. Not only did she make the defiant choice to skip Craig's fundraiser, but the paparazzo was there to publicize that she wasn't by her husband's side. *There's no undoing this now*, she thought as the door started to open.

The photographers stretched over the velvet ropes, hanging on top of one another, with cameras feverishly clicking attempting to get the perfect shot of the select guest list.

"Julia, Julia! Miss Roberts, over here!" they hollered outside the car.

"Keep it together Emma..." she murmured as she swung her legs out of the car. The cameras flashed and flickered with frenzy. "Mrs. Beckett! Mrs. Beckett! Where's your husband? How does he feel about the latest ratings poll?" the journalists shouted. She posed for the zealous media, gracious as always and showcased her winning smile, gave a courteous wave then strolled inside the mansion as casually as possible.

Once past the horde of media her legs wanted to collapse. Sheer panic stabbed her lungs and she stumbled on her long gown. Her face flushed shock white as her ankle twisted. She wanted to disappear before she came crashing to the ground in an awkward fall. It was like tripping in slow motion, dragging out the embarrassment. The crystal chandeliers in the grand hallway slowly glided through her vision when her legs buckled and she tipped backward. Her arms swung out in halfhearted flailing, grasping at air to brace herself.

Someone grabbed her arm and braced her before she caused a scene. Her pale face was stunned, more surprised by the strange hand than the impending fall. She glanced up and saw only the side of his face. He had a well-defined jaw and soft brown hair.

"I, these shoes, I'm so—" she said with an embarrassed, shaky voice.

"Shh," he whispered as he continued pulling her forward. "Just keep walking and they'll probably never notice." His voice was raspy and smelled of wintergreen gum.

Without thinking she followed his gentle guiding grip out of the main hallway toward an alcove by the entrance to the ballroom.

They stopped by the steps and looked out at the gathering of the country's wealthiest individuals. His hand was warm, tender, and still cupped under her arm although her stance was steady. She smiled looking up at her strange savior and her cheeks flushed a bashful pink.

"Oh my, it's you—"

"From the auction, I remember," he said, rubbing the back of his neck as his bashful gaze met hers.

"I, uh, you saved me from quite the scene back there."

"They can be pretty ruthless, I guess. It's the least I can do," his gentle voice offered with lips bending to the familiar boyish grin.

Returning the smile came natural to her. "Yes they can." She blushed catching herself gazing in his eyes again and diverted her stare to the floor. Her pulse soared so fast she felt light headed. She needed to sit down but didn't want to leave his side.

"Well, I, I should be—" he stuttered, and then nodded toward the ballroom behind them.

"Oh, I'm sorry. Of course, please, go ahead," she said, glancing at the huge crowd and felt a twinge of disappointment.

He paused in mid-step halfway down the stairs and look back over his shoulder. The warmth of flirtation made it impossible to hide her smile. Emma hoped his hesitation meant he would come back and cup his hand under her arm again.

He continued down the steps while still watching her and almost fell face first onto the floor. He looked down at his clumsy feet, caught his balance, and turned back toward her again. They stole one last look, and then he made an awkward dash toward the sea of guests.

Within seconds his handsome face was lost amongst the masses of dark -haired heads. She tried to follow the glimmer of his body through the crowd but the room seemed to consume him, and she lost him again.

Emma mingled with collected groups scattered throughout the room being graceful, polite, and spouting witty responses to odd comments about her husband's absence.

The night wore on with continuous prodding about her husband and backhanded compliments about her attending the charity ball alone. She meandered from one clique to the next and was greeted by the same inquisition. *I still can't get away from him, and he's not even here*, she thought.

"Yes the lunch was lovely. I haven't seen Richard in ages." Emma smiled as she was cornered by Allen Talbert.

"He rather enjoys your company, but who doesn't?" Allen replied with a grin.

His tender tone and sympathetic eyeing made her uncomfortable, like someone had exposed a secret she didn't know she had.

"Craig, is he here with you tonight?" he asked, glancing around the room.

"He has another fundraiser tonight. I was hoping to—"

"Figures, never around when you need him."

If you only knew, she thought, but offered an apologetic smile. "My driver knows, perhaps I could ask—"

"I'm sorry. I'm being rude again. Everyone has to be good at something though I suppose, right?" he said through a chuckle.

"Is it about the meeting, any progress?" she said without concern.

"Seems there's a new development, I'm leaving to meet with Richard now. Or trying to anyway." His rough voice grumbled as he twisted his overgrown eyebrows. "Been trying for an hour to get to the damn door, but these bloodsucking bastards keep getting in my way," he said while checking his watch. "See, there I go again. I'll excuse myself now before I say anything else." He smiled as he extended his hand.

"Always a pleasure, Allen," she tipped her head as he kissed her cheek.

Desperate for a moment of solitude, Emma tucked herself into a secluded corner and unconsciously scanned the crowd for the man from the auction. Unable to spot him, she started watching guests through the champagne bubbles floating in her glass. The room was a stunning rainbow of glittered and sequined gowns, accented by black blobs of tuxedos dotted around them. Women flirted and gossiped while businessmen talked finances and politics. *I cannot be a part of this anymore, this is disgusting*, she thought, repulsed by the room filled with pretend interest and obligatory laughter.

As she contemplated sneaking toward an exit, a great force divided the crowd in front of her like parting waves. Here approached Olivia slowly working the guests, liquoring them up for extra zeros on their checks, no doubt. Olivia managed to spot Emma and excused herself from the doting crowd.

Olivia made her way toward Emma, cupped her hand around Emma's arm, and guided her toward the bar. "Ugh, the muck I have dredged through this evening," Olivia said.

Emma giggled. "It's horrible, isn't it? Did you see the Zimmermans? She looks like a parakeet with that hat on."

"Oh, darling, you don't even know the shit I've been through tonight!"

"You can't pout at your own party, you live for these things," Emma teased.

"God, darling, I think I'm giving up on parties. All I need is a man who can't speak a lick of English with a wonderful, perky ass. Let me say I've had no fun tonight."

"Remind me again why I agreed to this," Emma chuckled.

"Because you're reinventing yourself, darling," Olivia said with a smirk.

"Ah yes, that's right. Rebellion, being true to myself, blah blah. It's coming back to me now." Emma laughed.

"Perhaps we're both misguided about tonight." Olivia laughed, and then helped herself to the rest of Emma's champagne while they waited for the bartender.

"Let's sneak out, before anyone notices," Emma said and winked.

"And miss this glorious torture? Never!" Olivia laughed, wrapped an arm around Emma's, and they walked back toward the other partygoers.

As they mingled Emma felt secretive glances surrounding her. She cocked her head toward Olivia. "Why are people staring at me so strangely," she whispered.

Olivia hid a smirk. Her fictitious tales of Craig's corruption had swept through the entire event by now. "I don't have a clue," she replied.

****

Emma wiggled her jaw and shifted on her feet contemplating how to pass the time without the sanctuary of Olivia's company. She decided to meander toward the display tables of the silent auction.

"Lovely array isn't it?" said a kind looking woman beside Emma at a table of antiques.

"Yes, gorgeous," she said truthfully. She surveyed the assorted treasures and found herself drawn to a small gold brooch set back from the larger pricey pieces in front. The old accessory entranced her, filling her with the enthusiasm of finding a familiar belonging you lost long ago. *I know I've seen this before, but I can't recall where. Look how pretty the detail is, so dainty...*

"Beautiful isn't it?" said a raspy voice.

Surprised to see the strange savior standing behind the table, she smiled and said, "Well, hello again. Yes it certainly is. I swear I must have seen it before, but I can't recall. I wonder why no one has bid on it yet."

"It's probably not flashy enough," he replied, nodding toward women oozing glitz and not even glancing at his table. "I'm sorry, I shouldn't have said that."

"I think it's lovely," she said as her eyes met his bright green eyes like dew covered grass. "I, uh..." she said. Her face grew hot and started to flush. "Are you working this event too then?"

"My partner deserted me again, so here I am," he said and tried to laugh.

"Well, I'd be lying if I said I was sorry to hear that," she said, and blushed at hearing herself flirt. "So," she said, clearing her throat to compose herself. "You must own quite the shop then, with two auctions like this?"

"It's just a small store really. We're out by Crystal Lake."

She twisted on her heels as the moment of silence lingered. Flirting was harder than she remembered. She shifted her focus back to the brooch, leaned over the table, and traced its swirls with a fingertip. Being mere inches from him her heart thudded so hard she thought he might hear it. Emma inhaled deeply, stealing a hint of his scent so close to her.

The soft sound of Etta James started to fill the ballroom. Couples wandered to the dance floor as her sultry voice poured through the speakers. "At last, my love has come along..."

Without thinking he stepped around the table and held out a hand. "Dance with me?"

She looked down at his open hand, knowing she should trust the moment, and clasped her hand in his. He escorted her to the dance floor, wrapped an arm around her waist, and pulled her so close she could feel the thumping of his heart on her chest. Her hands threatened to tremble; she could scarcely find the breath to make it through the dance.

All the mindless chatter around them hushed to white noise as they slowly spun on the cramped dance floor.

"I haven't danced with someone in a long time. Wasn't very good then, either," he said.

Seeing his bashful smile made her temperature sore. She closed her fingers tighter around his. "Well, you already know how clumsy I am," she said.

Her awestruck stare took in each part of him. There was something familiar about him drawing her into him. She longed for his hands to pull her closer, to roam her body without the barrier of clothing between them. The thought of their bodies intertwined in passion was dizzying. Her face grew warm and flushed like she had been kissed by the sun.

"I really hate these things, parties and crowds like this," he said, then started rubbing his thumb on her hand. "I, well, I'm kind of glad now though. That Harvey couldn't make it that is," he said, quickly averting his look.

"I'm not supposed to be here tonight either," she said, cocking her head to catch his gaze. "Seems something wanted us here tonight though, doesn't it?"

They held each other's look as she wrapped her arm tighter around him, stepped in closer, and lay her head on his shoulder. An anxious stuttered breath escaped him. He placed a jittery hand on her bare back and was nearly overcome by the delicate skin underneath his fingers.

It took everything in her to resist tipping her head to taste the sweetness of his lips. The tingle of anticipation slid a shiver down her spine. His long fingers tightened their hold on her and she almost sighed in desire.

He raised their clasped hands to his face and gently pressed her hand to his cheek. He closed his eyes and took in the warmth of her slender hand pressed to his skin.

They twirled and spun for what felt like hours, but the song was finally over. The dance floor was suddenly over-run with twenty-something's grinding to the newest rap song. They stopped, still holding each other, and she lost herself in his gripping eyes.

"I'm afraid I still haven't caught your name," he said with an intrigued smile.

"It's Emma, Emma Beckett."

"Beckett?" he paused. "Like, Beckett, that lawyer, Beckett?"

The color slid from her face. "Yes..." her disappointment hushed.

The arms around her waist went limp and fell to his sides. He cast his eyes down to the black and white checkered floor as he tried to collect himself.

"I, well, I should be getting back to my table," he said, nodding over his shoulder. "Thank you for the dance, Emma," he added, struggling to offer a grin before turning to walk away.

"Wait," she said and reached for his arm. "We could, um," she said, pleading into his broken gaze. "Can we still talk, at least?"

He slid her hand off his jacket sleeve. "I'm supposed to be working."

"Please, wait," she said, taking a step closer. "I, I didn't even get your name."

"James, James Dover."

"James," she said, taking in his tender face one last time. "Thank you, James. This was the best time I've had in, well—"

"The pleasure was mine," he said with a casual smile, turned, and disappeared into the bouncing bodies around them.

On the dance floor alone, tipsy people swaying and grinding around her, she watched James walk away. She felt broken, as if her heart plummeted into the deepest shadows of her soul. Every step he took away from her took the air she breathed with him. She stretched to the tips of her toes, scanning the crowd for his face. He was gone. Her eyes filled with tears, she turned and ran to the balcony behind her.

The railing felt cool against her warm, trembling hands.

"Emma, where the hell have you been?" Olivia slurred, staggering away from a man she had been speaking to. She kicked off her shoes and sighed as her throbbing feet were released from the red stilettos. She leaned against the railing beside Emma. "What's the matter, darling? It looks as if you're having a worse time than me," Olivia said, resting a hand on Emma's shoulder.

"I'm not quite sure," Emma said through an upset giggle and wiped underneath her eyes.

"Look at you, you're a mess, darling."

"I met a man, James. We danced, and," Emma said, letting his name rest on her lips. "It was the most beautiful moment really. Sounds ridiculous, doesn't it?" she said, trying to chuckle as she wiped her eyes. "But it doesn't matter. It's completely ruined now."

"Darling, you must slow down, I've had a lot of drinks tonight. What ruined this Jim guy?" Olivia said.

"This damn thing on my finger," Emma's furious voice cracked as she yanked on her wedding ring to tug it off. "This stupid commitment I made. This, this damn promise to a man that doesn't even love me!" The ring slipped off and she held it precariously over the edge of the balcony.

"Honey—" Olivia said, still confused as she grabbed the arm holding the ring. "Slow down, darling. You're not making sense. What are you talking about?"

Emma spun around and plopped on the patio bench with her hand open and the ring in her palm. Regret filled her lungs as she let out a breath staring at the swarm of dancers twenty feet away. "It was one of those moments…"

Olivia sat beside her and cocked her head. "What moments? Darling my head's fuzzy, you must slow down."

"Like, like when something inside tells you to hold onto it, no matter the cost, you know?" Her watery eyes lifted to Olivia's. "One of those rare chances in life you're lucky to get. You hold it and run away with it…or before you know it, you've lost it."

Still unsure what was happening, Olivia hugged Emma as she said, "What are you talking about, honey?"

"James. James Dover." Emma smiled a sad, sweet smile. "You know that sappy, fairytale stuff you dream about when you're a girl? Meeting a man, everything blurs around you, and something inside you tells you it's his arms you're meant to be in?" she asked, looking up at Olivia.

"Of course, every girl dreams about that sort of thing. I've been chasing it for seven marriages now."

"I had that. I just know it," Emma whispered, stood and walked to the doorway of the ballroom. "And now he's gone. Because of this," she said, spun around and stretched her arm out with her wedding ring in her palm. "This has ruined everything. Ruined me." Her arms went limp, the ring fell to the ground and bounced across the cement to the edge of the balcony.

Olivia shot up and scooped up the ring before it rolled off the edge. She took Emma's hand in hers and placed the ring back in Emma's palm. "Soon, you'll be free."

Emma looked up at her, laughing a desperate, broken laugh. "Free? I'll never be free. Craig will never let me go."

"You need to keep this," Olivia said and closed Emma's fingers around the ring. "You'll understand, one day."

"I'll never have that again, will I?" Emma asked, nodding to the dance floor. "My faithfulness to a dead marriage has ruined something else, hasn't it?"

Olivia pursed her lips and just shook her head.

Emptier than she had ever felt, Emma called the driver to take her home. She laid her head back on the smooth headrest, closed her eyes, and brought James' brilliant smile alive in her mind. "My heart was wrapped up in clovers. The night I looked at you…" she sang to herself with tears trickling down her cheek. She wanted to live like that forever, twirling around on the dance floor in his embrace. But the chill of reality shuttered through her body as the car turned into her driveway.

As she brushed the curls out of her hair, she couldn't help wondering where he was, what he was doing, if he was thinking of her, too. She closed her eyes, felt his lips pressed on her hand, and then flicked off the light and climbed into bed.

"Why did I let him go?" She swallowed hard, trying to gulp down the pain of losing the man she somehow knew she was meant to love. "I shouldn't have let him go..." she said through a sob, rolled over and buried her face in the covers.

Nine

Emma envisioned Craig barging into the house like a typhoon, things crashing and falling behind him as he raged through the halls. But the night held no intrusions, no midnight arguments, and the morning brought with it a quiet haze.

Emma curled up in a plush whicker chair overlooking the rose garden. The gentle swaying of the delicate flowers pulled her deeper into the fog looming over her.

"Morning, Emma. Here's your tea," Prudence's cheery voice chirped as she placed the saucer on the end table.

"Thank you," Emma replied, still staring at the peach-colored petals.

Prudence turned to leave, but Emma couldn't tolerate another minute left alone with her thoughts. She grabbed Prudence's arm. "Please, will you stay with me?"

"Of course," Prudence said, somewhat alarmed by the frazzled look in Emma's eyes. "Is something wrong?"

"Yes, no," Emma stammered. "I'm fine," she said with a pathetic attempt to smile.

Prudence laughed. "Doesn't sound like fine. What's going on?"

"I had the most wonderful, yet terrible night," Emma whispered as she scooted closer to Prudence.

Prudence bent forward toward Emma, both glancing around to ensure secrecy.

"I met a man the other day," Emma said, biting her lip as she smiled. "Sweet and, I don't know, familiar kind of, you know?"

Prudence grinned, leaned closer, and propped her elbows on her knees.

"I thought I'd never see him again. He's not the type to be in Craig's circle," Emma said and curled her lip. "But there he was, at the party. And, God, I can't even describe it really," Emma said with a faint giggle and pressed a hand to her cheek. "We danced…" Emma collapsed back in the chair as she remembered the feel of his hand against her back. "I can't believe I danced with another man," Emma whispered and looked around, sat back up and leaned close to Prudence.

"It's just a dance, Emma. There's nothing wrong with dancing," Prudence said.

"It wasn't *just* a dance. It was magical, thrilling. It was so much more than that—"

"Oh, you didn't, well, you know, did you?" Prudence whispered.

"God, no," Emma said with a flicker of disappointment running through her. "It just, I can't even wrap my head around the whole thing."

"You must've been all kinds of sneaky to pull that off in front of Craig," Prudence said.

"I skipped his fundraiser," Emma said. "I don't even want to think about what he'll have to say about that," she said with a shiver.

"He never even came home, I heard." Prudence raised an eyebrow as she crossed her arms. "Maybe you shouldn't be feeling so guilty about just dancing, huh?" she said with a nod.

Emma's forehead scrunched. She turned to Prudence with a scrutinizing stare. "No…" she said, raising a hand to her lips. "He isn't having an…" Emma's nibbled on fingernail. "He wouldn't, would he?"

"I don't think he's ever talked to me before, other than 'Hey you, get me this, get me that.' Guys like him though, well…" Prudence shrugged.

"He may be a lot of things but I don't think he'd…" Emma took a breath and looked at Prudence.

Prudence cleared her throat. "So, are you going to see that guy again?" she said and winked.

"I don't think he wants anything to do with a married woman. Not a *Beckett* anyway. I don't think I've ever felt that way so quickly with a man. Not even Craig."

"Sounds like a keeper to me," Prudence said with a smirk.

"Already got a keeper," Emma frowned, lifted her left hand, and wiggled her ring finger.

Prudence nudged Emma's shoulder. "I have to go work but I'll check on you later, okay?"

Emma tucked her legs up under her skirt, slouched in the chair and turned back to the massive garden outside the floor to ceiling windows. The calm breeze whispered to her, a silent urgency begging her to find him again.

She chuckled remembering each clumsy stammer, his bashful gestures, and hesitant soft touch. It was the kind of thing she hoped to find in her husband.

Emma heard the front door whip open, followed by Edwards's speedy walk and muffled apologies. She glanced at the clock, realizing she had been sitting there for two hours dreaming of a man she wouldn't see again.

"Where the hell is she?" Craig said from the hallway.

Emma clasped her hands in front of her and took a deep breath. Craig charged through the doorway like a tornado ripped through a house. He burned a deep, hateful glare into her eyes.

"What the hell do you think you're doing?" he screamed.

"What are you talking about?" she said, crossing her arms on her chest.

"Do you have any idea what this could do to our image?" he said, tossing a tabloid magazine at her.

Emma scanned her picture on the cover, captioned by fictitious tales of their divorce.

"You can't just up and skip my fundraisers without even telling me," he said. "You made me look like a jackass," he said, waving his hand at her. "I kept telling people you were running late, but there you were," he screamed, ripped the magazine from her hand and pointed to her picture. "All prettied up someplace else!"

"Craig, just calm down," she said as she stepped toward him. "I'm sure everyone adored you—"

"I do not appreciate being made to look the fool," he said through clenched teeth.

"Stop overacting. So I missed one of the, what, hundreds of dinners I've been to?" she said, raising her eyebrows as she returned his glare.

"You think you can just do as you want huh, with no regard for me? Just willy-nilly whatever you want," he said, shifting his stare to the rows of neatly placed champagne bottles by the buffet table. He grabbed a bottle and squeezed it in his white knuckled grip over her head.

Emma took a step back. "Craig," she said, holding her hands up in front of her. "Don't do that. Put that down."

"You're right," he said and lowered his hands.

Emma felt herself breathe.

"That would leave a scar. You're too pretty for scars," he said, and suddenly charged forward.

Emma stumbled around the chair as she rushed backwards. "This, this is how you're going to treat me?" she said, swatting his hand away as she tripped over an ottoman. "Don't do this, Craig."

"This is what you deserve!"

"No one deserves this!" she screamed, staggering as she tried to stand and fell back against the wall. "You're just like your father." Her eyes locked with his. "You're a monster!"

Craig cocked his hand back and slapped her so hard his own hand tingled and burned. "I am nothing like my father!" he screamed. "You will never mention him again—"

"You are your father, evil, brutal—" she said, cupping her hand over her swollen cheek.

"I am a better man than he could ever dream of being!"

"You're nothing!" she screamed, gained her footing, and glared in his eyes. "You're a loser, just like he said you were. Just like he is!"

"I'll show you what my father was like," he said, charging for her and wrapped a hand around her neck. "Is this what you want?" he said, slamming her against the wall. "You want me to show you what Daddy's like?" he asked as he tightened his grip on her airways.

Her eyes grew huge; she grabbed at his hands to pull them off and shook her head.

"What's that?" he chuckled, leaning in toward her face. "No, you don't want to know what Dad's really like?" he said with a grin.

She shook her head again, he withdrew his hand, and she fell to the ground. Emma held a hand to her neck, "You're going to pay for that," she said through a cough.

"You'll do as I say, when I say, or I swear to God I'll ki—" he said, shaking a fist in her face.

As she looked at the hate seeping from his eyes, she knew she would never be free of him. He would find her, and kill her. "It won't happen again..." her mournful voiced hushed.

"Damn right it won't. You're nothing without me. *Nothing*," he said, and then stormed out of the room just as quickly as he came.

Seconds after the door slammed shut Prudence poked her head into the room and saw Emma crumpled on the floor.

"Oh, God, Emma, what happened?" she said in a horrified whisper as she ran across the room. She tipped Emma's head up, examining the swollen eye.

Emma took a shaky breath. "He hit me."

"Prick," Prudence whispered. "How could he do that to you?"

"I can't do this anymore," Emma said, taking Prudence's hand off her check and raised her eyes to Prudence's. "I have to get out," she whispered.

"I'll grab you some suitcases," Prudence said, jumping to her feet.

Emma grabbed Prudence's skirt. "No, wait."

"You said you want to—"

"I can't just leave, you wouldn't understand. I need a plan," Emma said, staggering to her feet. "I have to figure out a way—"

"You get in your car and go, that's how," Prudence said, handing Emma a towel.

Emma shook her head as she placed the towel over a cut on her cheek. "He'll find me that way, he will." Emma looked at the splotch of blood on the towel, then back up to Prudence. "He'll find me. I can't just leave." Emma inched closer to Prudence and locked her eyes with Prudence's. "I have to, to *disappear*. No trace of me, anywhere."

"He'll do it again," Prudence said, nodding to Emma's swollen face.

"I know," Emma said. "He'll kill me someday too, if I'm useless to him."

"I don't get it, I'm sorry," Prudence said, throwing her hands up as she sat down.

"I don't want to live like this, die by his hand," Emma said, watching the doorway he stormed out of. "But I can't simply leave. He knows people, they'll track me down and...I have to set up a plan. I need help though, will you help me? Please?"" Emma said, stepping closer to Prudence. "I won't be able to do it alone," she said with petrified eyes locked on Prudence.

Prudence bit her lip as she looked at Emma's swollen eye. "Of course, whatever it takes."

"Thank you," Emma whispered as her eyes welled up. "I, I thought I married a good man..."

Prudence opened her mouth to speak but hesitated. "I'll, I'll get some bandages. Go up to your room and we'll get you cleaned up."

Ten

Olivia basked in the afternoon sun with bored housewives by the pool at the country club. She looked unusually simple with no outrageous accessories and hair pulled up into a messy ponytail.

"He took money from his own charity? Doesn't he have that thing for the kids? You know, those poor ones somewhere?" Andrea asked.

"Africa's Angels, that's the one, darling," Olivia answered.

Misty Willard gasped in unison with Andrea. "I mean people do, well, certain things, to get ahead. But to take money from poor kids—"

"People have standards!" Andrea chimed in, bending forward to nod at Misty on the other side of Olivia. "Does Emma know about it? I mean she used to be a do-gooder type, didn't she? A nurse or something?"

"She was a social worker, a long time ago. I mentioned something the other day and she didn't have a clue what I was talking about. She was just as shocked as me. She's too sweet to stoop that low," Olivia said.

"Oh absolutely!" Misty said, agreeably tapping Olivia on the arm. "My word, that poor thing is going to go down in flames if this gets out."

The three beauties sat in silence, shaking their heads at Craig's impending demise. Misty leaned close to Olivia. "Does she have a stash? You know, in case things get, bumpy?" she whispered.

"She's too honest to even think of such a thing," Olivia said as she laughed.

"You always need a stash," Andrea said.

"Poor girl is going to need it," Misty said.

Andrea primped her hair as she said, "God, I just can't believe it. I always thought he was so nice."

"We all did," Olivia said and tried not to roll her eyes.

"Wait until Joe hears about this—"

"And Charlie too. He's going to be pissed," Misty replied.

"It's a damn shame, dragging her down like that. You gotta stay clean you know? Don't take money from kids," Andrea said, adjusted the strap on her bikini then leaned back in her chair.

"I think her only chance is that her name's not on anything," Olivia said.

"Oh, well that's good for her then, you know, should word get out somehow," Andrea said.

"They can't bring her up on charges or anything then, I don't think. Should it come to that and all," Misty added.

"I can tell you this, my Joe isn't giving him another cent. Not if that's the kind of man he really is—"

"Taking money from kids, it's disgusting!" Misty interrupted.

"Poor girl is in for a bumpy ride. We'll take care of her though…" Andrea added, pushing her sunglasses back up the bridge of her nose.

It was no accident Olivia chose these two misinformed women for this particular spin of Craig's questionable methods. They were both heavy donators to children's charities. They held it close to their diamond crusted hearts and practically threw money at whoever came begging for it. It wouldn't be long before they ran home to tell their husbands the horrid story and demand they sever ties with Craig.

Olivia let her head fall back on the lounger, closed her eyes, and almost smiled. She thought it due time for him to lose what mattered most to him. It would be an injustice, really, to not bring his fraudulent acts to the attention of the public. She let out a relaxed sigh imagining the evening news stories that would be running and the morning articles exposing his corruptions. She couldn't help smirking with joy at the thought of his misery. *Serves him right.*

****

Craig rubbed his forehead. "What do you mean you're pulling out? You can't pull out now," he said. "No I—" he groaned and pinched the bridge of his nose while the man ranted in his ear over the phone. "No, I don't know what you're talking about." He shot forward, hunched over his desk, and lowered his voice to almost a whisper. "Look, you have far more to lose on this than me. If I go down, there's a whole lot that can take you down too." He heard a click. "Hello? Hello? Damn it!" he yelled and slammed the phone on the base.

"Sheila! Sheila, get your ass in here!" he said with his finger pressed on the intercom.

"Craig, what is it? I've been so worried out there," she said look of pity and ran her fingers through his hair.

"Not now," he said, cocking his head away from her. "Get me Talbert on the phone. I'm not going to let this election go to hell, not like this."

"Of course, right away, Craig," she said and rushed back to her desk.

He paced the length of the room while he waited for Sheila to connect the call. "What the hell is going on?" He stopped, sat on the edge of the windowsill, and took in the distinguished office he worked so hard to hold. The hunter-green walls were filled with commemorative plaques, pictures of him cutting red ribbons, and his favorite articles broadcasting his great achievements as California's honorable attorney. The room was a self-made shrine, and he felt it all slipping away from him.

"I have Allen on line three," Sheila's voice called out from the intercom.

Craig rushed back to his desk, took a deep breath, and picked up the phone. "Allen, how are you buddy?" he said, trying to sound as casual as possible.

"Craig, glad you called. Saves me the trouble of trying to get ahold of you."

"What's on your mind, Allen?"

"Seems we need to hold back on contributions for a while, Craig."

Craig held his breath a moment. His biggest donators withdrawing contributions was dizzying. He fell into his seat. "What, why, Allen? Has something come up in the audit?"

"We won't be able to contribute for an undetermined amount of time, Craig. That's about all I can tell ya."

Craig could almost feel Allen's smirk through the phone. He stood no chance without Allen and Richard funding him.

"Hello, Craig, buddy you there?"

"Yes, yes, I'm here. There has to be another way around it. Pull it from your Korean source, or the company in New Zealand? There's a way around it, Allen. You just need to dig a little deeper."

"Sorry, Craig, we've searched all avenues. There's just no place to pull it from. But you're a charming fella, I'm sure you'll come up with another idea." Allen said, almost chuckling.

"Yes, of course," Craig added through a laugh.

"Best of luck to you, Craig," Allen said as he hung up the phone.

Craig hung up and slouched in his chair. He looked up at the ceiling and spun the chair in circles as he thought. Calls like Allen's had been coming in all week. Every deep pocket he weaseled his way into was dumping him out all at once, and he hadn't a clue why. Sure he made some promises he more than likely couldn't keep once he was elected, but that's just how it always went. People understood that.

"Sheila!" he hollered.

She sprinted through the door already frazzled, with a stack of files pouring out of her arms, and loose strands of hair sticking this way and that. "Yes, Craig?"

"Call my accountant. Tell him I needed him here two hours ago. And get me Richard on the line. Now," he said, and then paused with an odd look at her disheveled appearance. "And do something about your hair for Christ's sake, you look terrible."

She ducked her head in embarrassment as she smoothed out her hair. "Yes, of course. I'm sorry," she said with a pout.

"Don't be like that. I don't have the time for it now."

"You'd *better* have time for it later," she said, glaring before she went back to her desk.

"I've got to get to Richard before Allen does…" he whispered to himself as he paced while he waited.

"I have Richard for you," Sheila said from her desk, stood, and closed his office door.

He took a deep breath and straightened his tie. "Richard old boy, how are you today?"

"I've seen better days, Craig."

"I'm sorry to hear that, Rich. Allen just called me and gave me some disturbing news—"

"Yes, I figured he'd be calling you."

"So you know he wants to pull of our agreement then?"

"I've seen a lot in my time, and I know when to step away, Craig."

"I have to say, Richard, I'm not understanding why you guys are pulling out. We're so close, doesn't seem to make much sense to bail now," Craig said with persuasive ease.

"Well, Craig, some people might say Allen and me aren't the most upstanding of citizens, but even cockroaches have standards."

Craig shook his head, baffled as to why they would back out with only a few months left to go. "I'm sorry, Rich, I really just don't understand why. Perhaps you could shed some light on the subject?"

Richard grunted, probably unbuttoning his belt from eating too much, the fat old bastard.

"You see, Craig, little voices have been whispering all week about some very questionable acts on your part—"

"Questionable acts?" Craig snapped.

Richard continued, "Neither of us really wants any part of that. We make enough trouble for ourselves as it is, you understand."

"Who told you? What did they say?"

"Now you know I can't tell you that," Richard said as he laughed. "Now look, I'm sorry we won't be able to contribute anymore. But once all this blows over, should you turn around, don't be afraid to give me a call."

Craig listened to the dial tone and rubbed the brewing migraine between his eyes. "Who the hell is doing this?" he whispered. He closed his eyes and ran through faces and names, analyzing everything he could think of.

"Craig, Floyd is here," Sheila said, peeking in from behind the door. "And I've called Larry. He'll be filling in for you this afternoon at court, but says you owe him a round of golf for it."

"Thanks, Sheila, please send Floyd in."

The young accountant clutched a thick, expandable file holder under his arm. He wiggled his nose to inch his glasses back up his nose. "Afternoon, Craig, sorry I couldn't get here sooner—"

"No, no, Floyd, thanks for coming so quickly. Please, sit," he said as he shook Floyd's hand.

"We have to move some things around, fast," Craig said.

"Sure thing, Craig. What's the rush?" Floyd replied as one brow rose with curiosity.

"Seems my name has been thrown into the rumor mill. I need to tuck away as much as I can to weather this."

"That explains the calls I've been getting," Floyd said.

"Calls?"

"Notifications really, cancellations of monthly deposits."

"Perfect," Craig said as he massaged his temples. "What are we working with here then? What kind of numbers am I looking at?"

"Well, let's see." Floyd flipped through his file and pulled out a few sheets of paper. "Considerably less than you were set to have. So we should disburse what you have in odd increments to all of your offshore bank accounts." Floyd bent and thumbed through his briefcase beside him. "I just need you to sign these to get the ball rolling," he said as he handed Craig authorization forms.

"Can't we just dump it in the Cayman's? Seems that would be much faster."

"Transfers like that would draw a lot of attention," Floyd answered, peering up from the papers. "It's best if we can move things in smaller amounts. It's less likely to raise red flags."

"Can you make this work?"

"It'll take a few tricks to scoot by the IRS, but I'll do what I can."

"Thank you, Floyd, I'm sure you'll stretch it as much as you can. Will this be done by the end of today?"

Floyd's eyes widened with surprise. "Today?" he checked his watch and wiggled his jaw. "With time differences and wire delays…it'll be tight, but I can probably move a large portion of it. But I'll need a few days, at least, to have it all transferred."

"You're a lifesaver, Floyd," Craig said smiling, stood, and shook Floyd's hand.

"Don't thank me yet, Craig!"

With Floyd gone to start transferring his money, Craig sat down for a much deserved afternoon drink. "Hello, vodka, how are you today…" he said as he wafted the bottle under his nose. He sank onto the sofa, crossed his feet on the coffee table, and took a big swig.

He admired the prestigious awards decorating his walls as he chugged the vodka and let out a mournful groan. "How the hell am I going to fix this?" he said, pausing before he took another drink.

Eleven

Even though Craig had all but disappeared, Emma spent over a week cooped up in the house, too afraid to be seen with brown and purple splotches on her face. She would hear Craig come and go at odd hours, but never did he sit in the same room with her or talk to her. It wasn't guilt about his actions that kept him away, but she relished his absence regardless.

After another dinner in solitude she strolled out to the pool, pulled up her dress, and dipped her feet into the cool water. In the pitch black yard, the in-water lights made the curvy pool look as if it were glowing. She twirled her feet around, making a small whirlpool with her pointed toes. She lost herself in the swishing water and didn't hear him come up from behind.

He sank into the patio chair behind her and stared off in the darkness beyond the pool. Emma caught a faint whiff of his musk cologne in the crisp breeze, turned and glanced behind her shoulder.

"Someone's sabotaging me," he said, not breaking from his trance.

Her stare drifted around for a moment as she contemplated a reply, but she returned her gaze to the crystal-clear water and wiggled her feet.

"I don't know who, yet. They're trying to rip it all apart at the seams." He kicked off his shoes, rolled up his pant legs, and walked to the pool.

Emma's heart half-fluttered for a second, almost anticipating him to push her in and hold her head under the water. But Craig sat down beside her, plunked his bulky feet in and whooshed his legs around. They sat for a few minutes, twirling their legs this way and that as they sat in silence.

He took a deep breath. "I can't figure out who, or why. Every avenue I've tried, to no avail, everyone seems to be turning on me." Without looking at her, he slid his hand across her leg and cupped her hand in his. "You won't turn on me, will you, love?"

Emma kept her focus on the waves and her red toenails wiggling in the ripples. So long she had clung to a futile hope that he would show her affection, embrace her, and need her again. But his touch made her feel dirty, like her hand had just been dipped in sewer sludge. *You know he doesn't mean it*, she thought to herself.

He raised his head up to her, waiting for some type of loving response. She cocked her head toward his, almost looking through him as she took in his solemn face.

"You shouldn't ask me that," she said, and then looked back down at the water. "Where else could I go?" she said in a whisper. She knew she should have covered her statement with some quick believable lie, but she didn't care to. And he didn't seem to care to retort. He sat quietly holding her hand in the glowing light of the pool and twirled his legs in the water like a child.

"I can always count on you, can't I?" he whispered, giving her hand a gentle squeeze in strange appreciation.

Emma wanted to feel disgust for putting up with his mood swings, deceit, plotting, and scheming. Except the water entranced her, coaxed her into an odd accepting calm.

They sat together for an hour in silence, and then finally she stood to leave for her bedroom for the night. He stood and followed behind her. She changed in the darkness to avoid seeing his black eyes watching her, but she felt them, staring at her, thinking something about her in the heavy darkness. She tried to pretend it were any other ordinary night, pulled back the covers, laid down, and wiggled into her pillow.

The bed bounced as he climbed in. He nuzzled up beside her, wrapped an arm around her waist and pulled her close. Her body tensed; sickened that there was so little sentiment between them that his mere touch repulsed her. She felt his breath on the back of her head as he inhaled her scent like a long forgotten soothing aroma and relaxed into her.

He ran his hand along the outside of her thigh, lifting her nightgown as his hand slid higher. So long she hoped for a night like this, Craig showing her love again, and the night finally came.

"I need you, Emma," he whispered in her ear as he rubbed her thigh.

"Do you love me?" she asked, her body stiffening as his hands roamed.

"I need you," he said again, pressing his lips on her neck.

"But do you love me?" she said, and rolled over to face him. "I need to know you love me."

"Why must you ruin such a moment?" he said as he plopped his head back onto his pillow.

"Why do you think that's such a ridiculous question for a wife to ask her husband?"

"You and this sappy, 'Tell me you love me' stuff. Can't you just go with the moment?"

"Why can't you say it? If it's true it shouldn't be this hard."

"*Want* has nothing to do with love," he said, flipped her over and climbed on top of her. He pulled up her gown and sat for a moment examining her body.

"Shouldn't you be doing this with someone else?" she said, pulled down her nightgown and hoped to catch a glimmer of his reaction in the darkness.

He stared at her for a moment before bending toward her ear. "She's busy tonight," he whispered, and then scooted her nightgown back up. "Let me have you," he whispered. "Don't you love me?"

She could feel him smiling. "I won't do this with someone who doesn't love me," she said, rolling over to turn her back to him.

"Fine, I love you. Better now?"

She turned to face him in disbelief. "I can't believe I ever saw love in you. What happened to you?"

"You're so beautiful. Let me have you," he said, almost ignoring her as he slid his hand down her bare arm. "Come on, we can pretend we're young. I just got out of college, you're all dirty getting out of the factory. Play along, won't you?"

There was no love in his touch, no tender thankfulness for her years of devotion. He needed to feel powerful; she felt it in every second of him not caring about her.

"You can have me when you love me," she said, yanking the covers back over her.

"Why do I even bother with you," he said, rolled over and pulled the covers to his side of the bed.

"I was just thinking the same thing about you," she said as she scooted away from him.

After an hour she finally heard him snoring, and she started sliding out of the bed. She tried to take slow, silent strides on the tips of her toes to the seclusion of the bathroom.

With the door locked, Emma waited a minute to be sure he was still asleep before she turned the shower on. She stepped into the shower and let the warm water rain onto her trembling body. She closed her eyes, slid down the cold tile wall, pulled her legs into her chest and sat on the floor as she held herself tight and let the water pour down to wash away his smut.

Craig had never made her feel so dirty before. She scrubbed her skin until it was bright-red and raw, but she could still feel his grimy touch on her flesh. She saw his face above her, felt his hands slide down her legs and she wanted to scream.

Twelve

Craig's transition from dominator to fake loving husband was almost overnight. But it was desperation that made him cling to he;, she wasn't a fool. Like an addict hocking family treasures to get a fix, he craved praise and would go to any lengths to feel the warmth of applause. Using Emma was his only option to revive his hero-like status. She was the one thing that could hush the lies and calm the fears of his bankrollers before the winds of rumor blew down to the voters. Over a month had passed trying to regain her trust through superficial affection, and he received nothing but contempt from her.

"I wish I could stay with you all day like this," he whispered, as he nuzzled against her cheek.

"It's almost quarter to seven. You should go or you'll hit traffic," she said, brushing his arm off as she reached for her robe.

"Why do you keep resisting me like this?"

"I'm not resisting you. I'm resisting this, this fakeness you're oozing," she said.

"Isn't this what you want?" he said, flashing a charming smile.

"You don't love me anymore, Craig, let's not pretend—"

"I tried to show you love, affection, all that crap you like. I tried last—"

"All that *crap*? That's exactly it, you don't know real love at all," she said and laughed.

He charged across the room, grabbed her by the arm, and spun her to face him. "Have I not given you everything? Look at this house, these clothes—" he said, yanking on the silk robe draped over her shoulders. "You'd have none of this without me."

"You still don't get it, do you?" she chuckled through a cold glare. "I didn't want this, I only wanted you. I could have cared less about all this crap."

"Don't get high and mighty, Emma. We made this together. You were there every step of the way."

"I wanted to see you happy, because I loved you, because I thought we would do great things together," she yelled, shaking his hand off.

"I don't recall seeing any frown on your face when you quit working at the factory, or when you hung diamonds from your ears, or filled a room with thousands of dollars worth of clothes—"

"You can keep it, I don't need that. I don't want that!"

"Don't be silly, now. We've built a great life together."

"No, *you've* built a prison," she said as she crossed her arms on her chest.

"Listen, if you don't keep up your end of the bargain—"

"My end of the bargain? What are we now, blood brothers? Do we have a secret handshake too?"

"Look." He groaned and stepped so close his chest brushed against hers. "I tried to give you what you wanted—"

"You did this for yourself," she said. "You did this because you want the world to praise you. And you can't do that unless I tell them how great you are—"

Craig pushed her shoulders, making her fall backward into a chair. He bent over with a pointed finger in her face. "If you do not do what I need you to do—"

"Have I not been beautiful for you?" she yelled. "Have I not been deceitful, tricked people into thinking you're a good man!"

"And if you don't continue to do that, I'll have no use for you."

"There's nothing you can say anymore that's going to scare me, Craig. You've already taken everything from me."

"No, no, my love. I won't divorce you," he said with an evil grin.

"I'm going to leave you, Craig. You'll wake up one day and I won't be here. You'll see," she said, clasping her robe shut.

"You know there's nowhere you can go where I won't find you. I know far too many people for you to be able to just slip away like that," he said, laughing as he straightened his tie in the mirror.

"I'm tired of being scared Craig. I'm tired of your idle threats. What you've turned into is worse than fear."

"Okay, country bumpkin, if you want to go back to that speck on the map, shithole place you called home, be my guest. Go ahead and try to leave me, see what happens," he said and threw a dress at her.

She stood, clutching the dress against her chest, inching toward the door.

"Like I said, I won't divorce you. I won't even bother to make you come back home," he said, and then grabbed her wrist and pulled her close. "I'll just dispose of you…" he whispered, glaring for a moment then let her arm drop.

"You don't scare me," she said, emphasizing the pause between each word as she leaned close his face.

"I have ways, you can count on it," he said, kissed her forehead, then turned and left.

****

Prudence dipped a rag into a bucket and as she wrung out the water she spotted a fresh, deep purple blotch on Emma's wrist. Emma tipped her head about to speak but caught Prudence staring. She looked down at her wrist and twirled her finger around the purple circle.

"Pretty isn't it? It almost matches my top," Emma said with a sarcastic roll of her eyes.

"I don't know how you can laugh at something like that," Prudence said, stretching to clean the top of the window.

"Abuse has a strange effect on people I think. It almost makes you numb, or paralyzed maybe," Emma said. "Listen…" Emma peeked around before she scooted closer to Prudence. "I've figured out a way," she whispered and waved for Prudence to come closer. "To get some money without him knowing, I think."

Prudence bent to wring out the rag again so she could listen and cocked her ear toward Emma.

"He's checking my charge cards, but I've got jewelry. I was thinking, if I can sneak it to you, can you take it to a pawn shop? Sell it for me?"

They heard the click of Edward's high shine shoes coming down the hall.

"Yes, ma'am, I've only a few more windows then I can tend to your dress," Prudence said somewhat loudly and watched Edward pass by from the corner of her eye.

"It's a terrible stain, I don't know what I did to it," Emma said, playing along as she peeked around the corner. She tiptoed back beside Prudence and sat down.

"I know a few places. What kind of stuff is it?" Prudence whispered.

"Nothing *too* fancy or expensive. He'll notice if the very nice pieces are gone," Emma said, then slid her hand into her pocket and pulled out part of a necklace to show Prudence. "Things like this."

"I don't know how much I can get for that," Prudence whispered. "But I'll do my best."

"Whatever you can get for it, I just need the money." Emma checked behind her, then tucked a handful of necklaces into Prudence's apron pocket. "Thank you."

Prudence patted Emma's hand and nodded. "Yes, ma'am, I'll tend to that right now," she said, picked up her bucket and left the sunroom.

"I'll be heading into town per Mr. Beckett's orders, would you care for me to take care of anything while I'm there?" Edward said as he strolled into the room.

Emma sighed, brought a hand to her cheek and tapped a finger while she thought.

Edwards look moved to the purple mark hugging her wrist like a bracelet. Bright in color, still tinged with small red splotches, it was fresher than the mark on her face she tried to hide weeks before.

"Are you all right, ma'am?" he asked, nodding to her wrist.

Emma had forgotten the bruise already and quickly tucked her hand underneath her thigh. "Yes, just clumsy these days I guess," she said and avoided eye contact. "I believe Craig has some dry cleaning that needs to be picked up."

"Are you sure, that you're all right I mean?"

"Yes, fine, thank you," she said, taken aback by the softness in his stare. "That should be all," she said, nodding to the door.

Edward walked to his room in a haze, shut the door behind him and slunk into a small writing chair. He sat for a moment, mind spinning, flashes of Emma's recent bruises whipping through his thoughts. A whirlwind of remorse stormed through him. He sat straight and nodded his head. He knew what needed to be done.

He dragged a chair to a large armoire, grunted as he climbed up and stretched his lanky arms to reach something off the top. He pulled the chair back, sat down and gently placed an old striped hat box on his desk. He grabbed a handful of items, flipped through a pile of papers and pictures, then stopped and ran his thumb along a Polaroid.

"I think its time to use this...." he said through a breath. "Although not how I intended." He flicked the photo in the box and slammed the lid back on.

****

Craig strolled with a cockiness extreme even for him. He tucked his hand loosely in his pocket as he glided through the hall toward his office, confident he was putting the pieces back in place. With new funding rolling in, his ladies reminded of their places, he impressed even himself.

"Afternoon, Craig," Sheila said as she spun around in her chair. Her young, tanned legs uncrossed as she stood, and her black skirt rode dangerously high up her thighs.

"Did you hear from that Mitchell somebody yet?" he asked from over his shoulder, glancing down at her delicious legs.

"Yes, he's on his way now. I was just about to call you actually," she answered, fighting a cringe. Craig hated surprises. She tried to catch him before he shut the door. "Craig!" she said and quickened her pace behind him. "That's not why I was trying to call you."

"Well, what is it?"

"This was delivered for you, not by any type of courier." She handed him a large red envelope devoid of writing.

He looked at it curiously. "Who delivered it?"

"I don't know. A middle-aged man in a cheapish, navy suit. Squirrely eyes, creepy almost."

"Did he say anything?"

"He handed it to me and said 'Make sure Craig gets this.' I didn't recognize him, that's why I was going to call you." She ran his smooth tan lapel between her fingers and flashed a small, supportive smile.

Craig slapped her hand off as he glanced around, tucked the envelope under his arm, and closed the door. He tossed the strange envelope on the desk, slid his jacket off and sat down. The fist page had a handwritten note.

'Men who misbehave never go unpunished. You should have been more careful with the people you hurt.'

His face scrunched in uncertainty. He looked around his empty office, heart fluttering with worry and tore open the package it came with.

Shelia hadn't heard a peep in over an hour; she bit her lip and pressed the button on the intercom.

"Is everything all right, Craig?"

"If I need you I'll call for you," he snapped.

"Well, you have to be in court in an hour don't forget. I'll let you know when your driver has arrived."

Papers covered the top of the desk like a rainbow of deceit. He ruffled his hair as he leaned over the mysterious package. He thumbed through photographs of him with mistresses at hotels, receipts for dinner dates and secret weekend getaways. The copies of checks that never made their way to his accounting books, and copies of tax deductions for charities that didn't exist alone could ruin him.

He took a deep, strained breath and wondered why there was no list of outrageous demands or warnings. *Would there be more packages? Who else might have gotten copies?* His mind ran wild with questions with nowhere to look for answers.

"Craig?" Shelia's voice cracked through the intercom.

He jumped as his heart shot to his throat "What?"

"Mr. Mitchell is here sir," she said, sounding as pleasant as possible.

"Yes of course! Just a moment," he said.

He scooped up the papers and crammed them in a drawer. He had no idea how he was going to make it through a surprise meeting with a client.

Thirteen

The heat of the day warmed her solemn face, bits of her pain seeming to slip away with the wasted afternoon. Emma dipped her head into the water, raised a hand and rubbed the tiny scar on her forehead. She let her long legs float out before her in the pool.

Prudence carried a tray with iced tea, set it down and began pouring Emma a glass.

"I've taken care of those things you asked me to," she said, not looking at Emma as she poured.

Emma glanced to see who was around. The landscaping crew was too far off to hear them.

"How much did you get?"

"Only a couple hundred. I tried for more, but the guy said there wasn't anything too special about them. Just gold and diamonds," Prudence said, walked over and handed Emma a glass. "Can I?" she asked, nodding to the water.

"Of course. He's not here, so don't worry," Emma said, then held Prudence's glass while she slipped her shoes off and stuck her legs in the water. "Was it a lot of trouble for you?"

"It's on my way to my Aunt's house. I go there on my Saturdays off usually." Prudence wiggled her toes in the refreshing pool. "I stuffed the money inside a pair of socks in your drawer, the tan pair on the bottom."

"Thank you, so much. I have some more things set aside that he won't notice missing."

"Want me to try another place, to see if I can get more?"

"All pawn shops are like that, don't worry about it. At this point I just need the money. Disappearing is expensive." Emma tipped her head back, letting the sun warm her skin. "The pawn shop back home was the worst. Guy would give you a quarter of what something was worth, then sell it for twice that right in front of you," Emma said, rolling her eyes.

"I never figured you to know about pawn shops," Prudence teased, nudging Emma on her shoulder.

"I was a vastly different person once. Things weren't all flashy and glamorous back there, believe me. Grew up by corn stalks, factories, and *real* cowboys. Even had me a cowboy hat," Emma said as she with an exaggerated twang.

"A real country girl, huh?" Prudence laughed. "Walking around feeding chickens and stuff?" she said as she giggled.

"Helped a cow have a baby too." Emma nodded with a grin.

"Well, you sure don't look like a country girl now," Prudence said, nodding to Emma's Gucci sunglasses. "No twang in your talk either, never would have guessed it, really."

"Craig had me take speech classes, said my twang made me sound stupid."

"Figures—"

"After my parents died is when things got bad. I didn't make enough to cover the mortgage, lost the house. I worked at the factory, but even double shifts didn't make you much."

"Then how did you meet Craig? Him I'd never guess a country boy!"

"He was something different then too, let me tell you. He was a city slicker passin' through town," Emma said, exaggerating the southern drawl again.

"Nice, huh? Must've been, I guess," Prudence said while swirling her feet in the pool.

"Sexy too, sweet, so caring…and, God, those eyes! Turn you into a pile of melted butter, I swear."

"You miss it?" Prudence asked.

"Sometimes. Not the factory, but my parents, the farmhouse they had. Life was so much simpler then." Emma climbed out of the pool and started squeezing the water out of her hair. "I was working a second job at a diner when I met Craig. I worked for free food, really," she said, sat at the patio table and leaned back. "He was like this hero, come to save me. All he needed was a white horse and suit of armor," she said. "I couldn't believe a guy like him would fall for a girl like me. I thought I was *so* lucky," she said as she shook her head.

"Love makes us a little blind sometime, I guess," Prudence said, standing to dry her legs off.

"I don't think he ever loved me, not really," Emma said, handing Prudence a dry towel. "I guess he just saw me as *trainable?*" Emma took a deep breath and stared at her wedding ring. "Wasted love," she whispered to herself, then slid her sundress over her shoulders.

Emma stretched her leg onto Prudence's armrest, comfortable in the quiet afternoon. Prudence leaned back, untied her apron, tugged on her scratchy cotton uniform, shifted her weight and settled in.

Edward burst through the French doors onto the patio. His forehead was covered in sweat and face beet-red. "Ms. Child is here," he said through a pant. "In quite the hurry today it seems," he said, wiping his brow.

"Olivia? Wonderful!" Emma said and leaped from her seat.

Prudence excused herself as Emma trotted to the foyer with Edward right behind her.

"Olivia!" Emma said as she came around a corner to the foyer.

"Emma, darling!" Olivia said, holding her arms out to embrace Emma.

They hugged for a moment as Edward stood to the side behind Emma, eyeing Olivia.

Olivia caught his glare. "Tsk, tsk, darling, servants don't sneer. Servants fetch drinks." Olivia clapped her hands like calling a dog. "Come, come now, be a good boy and fetch us something. I'm so very parched!" she said with a snide grin.

Emma chuckled halfheartedly. "Come, I have iced tea on the patio." Emma took Olivia's arm and guided her through the maze of hallways.

"*Just* tea, oh that will never do. It's nearly evening and I'm not the least bit intoxicated!" Olivia cringed, everywhere she looked was cold rock or huge wooden beams. Emma lived in the most beautiful prison she had seen.

They settled on the patio. "Oh, Emma, Emma, I feel likes it's been ages since I've seen you!" Olivia said, slipping her sunglasses down from the top of her head.

"It has been a while, over a month now maybe?" Emma said.

"Has it really? God, where has the time gone?"

"Down the bottle I think," Emma said, nodding to the miniature bottle of vodka Olivia poured in her tea.

"Hmm, perhaps," Olivia said, licking a dribble of vodka from her thumb. "But it makes life so much easier to deal with."

"I really wish you would cut back Olivia. It scares me to see you drink so much," Emma said, scowling at the empty liquor bottle on the table.

"I have to say, darling, I'm sorely disappointed," Olivia said. "I was hoping to come here, only to find out you've taken off some weeks ago, just disappeared into the night," she said, sipped her drink and licked her lips. "I thought we agreed you work on a plan, embrace that rebelliousness inside you just itching to get out?"

"I have been working on something," Emma said, deciding perhaps Olivia had the right idea and took a miniature bottle from Olivia's purse and poured it in her tea.

"Has that bastard you call a husband tricked you again, with some ooey-gooey nonsense?"

"You do have the strangest way of showing concern," Emma said with a smile.

"Well I can't start crying about it, darling, that would ruin my mascara. I can't go around town looking like a raccoon, now can I?"

"Just so you know," Emma said, bumping Olivia with her knee. "I have been working on something. It's going to take a bit more time I think. I'm really not getting enough money as quickly as I'd hope," Emma said, pursing her lips and stared at her wiggling toes.

"Why didn't you say so!" Olivia said, riffling through her purse and pulled out a checkbook. "So, how much, ten thousand, fifteen?" she said, wiggling her pen in her hand.

"I already told you I won't take your money."

"God, you're ridiculous, only person in this damn town who doesn't have their hand out," Olivia said. "Don't be so stubborn," she said, stuffing a wad of bills into Emma's bikini top.

"Olivia, I said—"

"Stop it, what's this to me? I wipe my ass with more than this."

"Thank you," Emma said, realizing there was no resisting Olivia. "This will help. I may need the number of a few of your, *contacts*, too."

"So how long till you're rid of this dreadful place? I mean really, it's so very ugly for being so pretty...just reeks of him everywhere, bastard."

"A few months I think. I have to be untraceable, you know," Emma said.

"Months! Good God, darling. That's far too long to be stuck with this shit," Olivia said, nodding to the scar on Emma's temple.

"He's hardly here anymore anyway. I think he's finally given up on me...or me on him? I'm not entirely sure where it fell apart."

"Oh, now isn't he tasty," Olivia said, nodding to a gardener in the distance. "Sweat dripping down those biceps like that, yummy!"

Emma looked over her shoulder, squinting into the sun.

"Reminds me, whatever happened to that Jimmy, or was it Jon, Joe? Oh, you know that man," Olivia said, waving her hand in the air. "The one from the party, had you in hysterics. How are things with the two of you? You know I love a good scandal. Is he what spurred on your courage?" Olivia said, winking.

"James, you mean," Emma said, feeling the warmth of a flush creeping up her skin. "No, he and I, well, there isn't a he and I really."

"Oh, pity, he had you so worked up like that I thought—well who knows what I thought."

"I think he was put off by my being married," Emma said, remembering the hurt in his eyes.

"Imagine that, a man with morals. Who knew?"

"Don't tease, he's a wonderful man," Emma said, smacking Olivia's hand.

"I'm sure Jimmy is wonderful, can't recall the last time I saw you in such a frenzy like that."

"James, his name is James."

"James, Jim, it's all the same. Shame things didn't work out between you two."

"Probably best. If Craig found out, God, I can't imagine what he would do."

"He's a prick of a man," Olivia said, curling her lip. "Look what he's done to you," she said, running a fingertip along Emma's scar. "Bastard deserves a taste of his own medicine."

"Don't go sending one of your goons to do something," Emma said, raising a brow with a stare of insistence.

"How is the jerks election going these days anyway?" Olivia asked with a slight smirk.

"From the little bit I've heard on the news, not very well. He hasn't given me any details. He's been rather distraught and well, distant lately," Emma said casually.

"Well I've had my ear to the wind, and it seems some of his big ticket contributors have backed out on him," Olivia said with a devious chuckle.

Emma sat staring at the small chlorine container bobbing in the pool.

Olivia stiffened, almost stunned and outright disappointed in Emma's indifference.

"It really makes no difference to me, he always gets his way," Emma said, entranced with the water.

Olivia crossed her arms on her chest watching Emma, so elegant, poised, and well-trained. But the vague air of emptiness smothered Emma, lying heavier around her than it had before.

"I'm too late..." Olivia whispered, staring at Emma.

"Too late for what? You have plans?" Emma asked.

"He has finally broken you, hasn't he?"

Emma spent years sobbing with Olivia in moments of desperation, in need of understanding, but life always flickered inside her glassy eyes. But as Olivia bore a frightened look into Emma's empty eyes, nothing seemed to look back at her.

"He's truly made you empty, hasn't he?" Olivia said, touching Emma's cheek like a delicate porcelain doll. Olivia went pale like a crisp, bleached sheet.

Emma's gaze drifted to the smoldering cigarette butt at the edge of the grass; she sank back in her chair and let the calm breeze blow against her hot face. Emma tried to take quick stock of the last few months. She thought she had been fighting, rebelling his demands and plotting escape.

"I suppose I feel...empty," Emma said, raising her eyes to Olivia's. "Not sad that he doesn't love me, doesn't care, but, like I've missed something, or lost something somehow?"

"I'm so sorry..." Olivia said in a whisper.

"Of course I wish things were different, but I'm surprisingly not torn up over our marriage like you might think," Emma said with an empty stare. "It's like I've lost someone, but not him. Does that make sense?" she said and turned to face Olivia.

"I'm so sorry, darling. I've waited too long."

"Too long for what?"

"To do something. *Anything.*"

"There's nothing you could do. He is who he is, there's obviously no changing that."

"I should have stopped him years ago!"

"Olivia, there's no changing him or the choices I've made—"

"I know that!" Olivia barked, shoving her glass away from her.

"Then why are you so—"

"Stoop to his level…low down…ugh," Olivia muttered to herself as her face flushed with anger.

"Olivia please, calm—"

"I have to go, I'm sorry," she interrupted, suddenly standing and jamming things back inside her oversized red leather purse.

"But you've just gotten here, please don't go yet," Emma said, standing and grabbed Olivia's arm. "I need to go over ideas with you, please."

"I'm sorry, there's something I have to do," she said and slid Emma's hand off her arm.

"But you can't leave—"

"I'm sorry, darling, I have to," she said with a quick glance of remorse, then left Emma on the patio behind her.

The giant metal handles on the front door clinked like chains as Olivia left. Olivia felt the house swallowing everything inside it, consuming the air from those who tried to breathe within it. She climbed into the comfort of her limo outside the cold, stone beast, and pressed a hand to the window as she whispered a promise to Emma in her heart. "I won't let him win," she breathed to herself. The dreary home seemed to flush all color from itself, mangling the beauty of the landscape around her into lifeless gray shrubs. She could hear the daisies crying as they choked under the hateful shadow of the house. The secluded mansion seemed to curl up into itself in twisted agony, feeding off the venom Craig poured into it, slowly killing everything inside.

She wiped tears from her face and reached inside her purse for a compact mirror and powder. Damaging him wasn't going to be enough, it was too late for that now. She had done it before, to easier targets, but she was determined to give him what he deserved. "Drive," she said to the driver, taking one last glimpse of the tortured mansion as the car pulled away.

Prudence peeked out on the patio. "Everything ok?" she said, stunned how Olivia stormed out of the house.

Emma sat paralyzed, staring at the empty seat as if Olivia still sat there. She didn't blink or move when Prudence called out to her.

Prudence took a cautious step forward. "Emma?"

"I, Prudence..." Emma said, bent her head and rested her forehead on her palm.

The weight of the air felt thick and hard to breathe, like a bulky scarf wrapped too tightly around your face. Fear and change swirled around them, like the stiff wind that tries to funnel into a tornado.

"Do I seem, different, to you?" Emma asked with angst-ridden eyes.

Prudence took a deep breath as she thought. "Different how?"

"Empty, or broken, oh I don't know really, I must sound crazy," Emma said, closing her eyes and rubbed her forehead.

"Oh gosh, Emma I don't know really. Everything is so weird lately."

"I, this is all so..." Emma's ribs squeezed her lungs. She was almost angry with Olivia for bringing this up and then deserting her. She let out a painful breath and fell back into her chair.

"I'm sure it's mostly because of Mr. Beckett. You know, with how he's been lately things not working out," Prudence said. "But we're working on that, right? Life will get better," Prudence said, leaned forward and patted Emma's knee.

Emma put a hand to her chest to calm her pounding heart. "I, I thought I was fighting him," she said to herself. "Trying to leave, but..."

Emma flushed a peachy hue as the rush of James' face came poring into her heart, his bright smile hammering through her protective shield like an untamed fire. "James..." she whispered, her eyes wide with remembrance. "God, the look in his eyes...but it doesn't make any sense."

"What?" Prudence said, cocking her head in confusion.

"James..." Emma breathed, closed her eyes and let her skin remember the soft touch of his hand caressing her back. A fire started to boil inside of her as she let his memory overwhelm her.

She craved more than anything to be with him. "But I don't even know him," she said, opening her eyes.

"Oh, that guy! Wait, what are we talking about, exactly? Did Olivia do something to him?"

"Nothing like that," Emma said, her eyes still unfocused. "It's impossible to feel so connected to someone you don't know, isn't it? I mean that love at first sight stuff, that's not *real*, right?"

"I've heard stranger things before. Maybe you should just go see him to, you know, see if that spark thing or whatever is still there?" she said and shrugged.

"But I'm married, can I really be that—"

The idea was complete insanity, risking so much for a stranger. But she couldn't ignore the intensity, that connection between them. It was beyond a simple desire or yearning. The connection she felt with him made life right, offered real love. *What would I even say*, she wondered. *Would he even remember me?*

Emma whispered in secrecy, "How would I even find him? I don't know anything about him. God, I couldn't possibly—"

"You don't know anything about him?" Prudence said in disbelief.

Emma sifted through every gesture, every word of their conversations she tried to forget. "Blue shirt…he didn't attend parties…" she said to herself, quietly mouthing words to their conversation. "Crystal Lake," she almost shouted. "His shop is in Crystal Lake," she repeated softly.

"Crystal Lake, hmm," Prudence repeated with a small, sneaky smile. "Well, looks like you'll be going for a drive," she grinned.

"I can't do that. What would Craig do?"

"You think he'll find out?"

"I can't be, be like him. Cheating."

"Just seeing someone doesn't make you like him."

"Prudence, I can't—"

Emma's heart pounded in her ears. She was cautious to trust in hope. Hope had failed her so many times before. But she couldn't help it. The thought of seeing James surged blood through her veins and flushed the color of life back into her soul. She could almost hear a voice pushing her to him, urging her toward this crazed idea of love with a stranger.

Fourteen

Emma stayed cooped up in Prudence's room all afternoon, plotting how she might see James again. They sat on the bed, the room being too small for extra chairs. Prudence traced her finger along a map while Emma flipped through the Yellow Pages for antique shops in Crystal Lake. Emma sat up and looked away for a moment, letting her heart take a break from its feverish pounding and giving her lungs a chance to catch her breath.

Emma scanned the cramped ten-by-ten foot room and almost felt as if she was infringing on a world where she didn't belong. She felt bad for Prudence, realizing no family pictures or trinkets sat in the room, just one lonely, blurred Polaroid of a black, fluffy dog propped against her alarm clock.

"Well, it's going to take a least an hour to get there it looks like," Prudence said, reaching up to stretch her strained spine.

"An hour?" Emma said, cringing at the distance. "That's two hours just in travel."

"He hasn't really been around much, you know," Prudence offered, nodding toward the mansion in the distance. "So it really won't be all *that* hard," she said with a timid smile.

"I suppose. I could probably vanish for a week and he wouldn't notice," Emma said through a nervous laugh. "Or care…"

"Did you find the name of the place?"

"I'm not sure. There are a few listed but none are actually in Crystal Lake. They seem to be dotted around it in small towns. Hopefully it won't be that hard," Emma said and crossed her fingers for good luck.

"Wouldn't that be awful if you get recognized or something."

"Oh, God, I hadn't even thought of that!"

Prudence placed a calm hand on Emma's arm. "I'm sure that won't happen though. A small town like that, what do they care about rich people in the city, right?"

"I can't do this, it's too risky!" Emma nibbled a fingernail. It terrified her, the great risk of getting caught, and the notion of adultery. But she needed to see him, just to be in his company. "No, I'm going to see him. Who cares about risk, right?" Emma said, turning to Prudence with apprehensive courage.

"Absolutely," Prudence said and patted Emma's shoulder. She leaned across the bed and pulled a soda from the tiny fridge, cracked it open and leaned back against the wall. "Now, for the important stuff. What are you going to wear?" she said, laughing to ease the tension.

Emma's eyes widened to superficial worry. "Oh, I don't know. I haven't done this sort of thing in a long time," she said with a light laugh, raising a hand to her cheek and tried to remember the habits of dating.

"We'll have to raid your closet for something sexy," Prudence teased.

Emma leaned back and crossed her arms behind her head while she surveyed the room. "Can you look sexy if you don't *feel* sexy?"

"I think you can fake it, sure," Prudence said.

"And I call Craig heartless. God, look at me," Emma said, disgusted by her behavior. "Hiding in my maid's room and talking about being sexy for a strange man."

Prudence cringed. "Sounds kind of bad I guess." She bit her lip. "But it makes sense when you hear the whole thing."

"You think so? I think it all sounds like madness," Emma chuckled, then a twinge of worry scraped her nerves. She checked her watch and eyed the door. "I should head back, just in case."

Prudence nodded, gave a sweet smile and folded up the map. "I'll sneak this into your purse in the morning," she said and gave the map a gentle tap as she tucked it in her pocket.

"I must be crazy…" Emma said and put a hand over her mouth as she eyed the map.

Prudence wrapped an arm around her and gave a gentle squeeze. "Don't worry."

****

Olivia looked stunning, yet exceptionally ordinary. She wore a knee length black, sleeveless dress, and a dark purple belt with matching heels. Her satiny hair pulled up into a French twist and simple gold hoop earrings were the perfect, dainty touch. She had never been known as an early riser, but this morning she climbed out of bed with no complaints or whining about the glaring, rising sun.

Her confident stride led her through the crowded halls of the impressive building. Young assistants and interns gave snide glares at the striking stranger. Olivia smirked; their jealousy only fed her cockiness. Conversations between small groups of men came to a sudden halt as the sultry beauty glided by. She eyed them from behind her sunglasses, ignoring their flirtatious grins and charged ahead.

"May I help you, ma'am?" Sheila asked with a welcoming smile.

"I've come to see Craig," Olivia said.

"Do you have an appointment?" Sheila asked with an odd look.

"I don't need one," Olivia answered, annoyed by the apprehensive secretary.

"I'm sorry but—"

"Olivia Child. I'll be waiting in his office, if you don't mind?" Olivia said sarcastically from over her shoulder, with her hand already on the doorknob.

"Oh, Child, yes, of course. Would you care for some coffee, Ms. Child?" Sheila asked.

Olivia slammed the door behind her, not bothering to answer the stupid assistant.

Sheila let out a huge breath of relief when Craig arrived from court proceedings an hour later.

"Craig!" she said and ran toward him.

"Sheila, don't cause such a scene."

"I'm sorry but, well, Ms. Child is in your office. I tried to—"

"What the hell is she doing here?"

"I'm not sure, she wasn't very forthcoming in conversation," she said and cast her look to the floor.

Craig rolled his eyes as he pushed Sheila out of his way. He held his hand on the knob and cracked his neck before opening the door, as if preparing for a street brawl behind a bar.

Her long, sexy crossed legs peeked around the side of a chair, with one foot casually tapping as she waited.

"Good afternoon, Olivia. I hope you didn't wait too long."

"Ah yes, afternoon, Craig," she said with a charming smile.

"To what do I owe this great honor?" he said as he settled at his desk.

Olivia stretched out her legs and re-crossed them, taking a deep pleasurable breath soaking up every minute of what she was about to delve out.

"Oh Craig, Craig, Craig…can't a dear friend of your wife come by for a visit?" she said, smirking at him from the oversized leather chair as she pouted.

"You, my dear, don't typically roam the halls around here."

"I thought I needed a bit more culture."

"Someone of your stature can't possibly *need* anything else."

She forced a laugh in reply, shifted in her chair and settled in for a while.

He thought for a moment that she might even kick off her shoes. "So?" he said, somewhat impatient as he flipped open his briefcase.

She still hadn't received everything from Johnny, and merely came here on a whim in hopes of making Craig squirm. "There's some awfully troubling information going around about you, isn't there?" she said as she glanced at him from the corner of her eye.

He dared not give her any type of reaction. It would be like throwing himself into a shark feeding frenzy. He managed to smile. "I'm sorry. I'm not sure what you mean."

She erupted in laughter, stood and sauntered through his big stuffy office. She stopped at a small table by the windows and helped herself to the array of liquor.

"Oh come now, Craig. Do you take me for a fool? Who else did you think could produce something so beautiful?" she said, cupping a glass in her hand. "Alan? Richard?" she said as she laughed.

He grunted, rubbed his moist hands on his pants and cracked his neck again. "It was quite the display, my life so neatly packed inside that envelope," he said, instinctively clenching his fists.

She saw his jaw tighten, his big hands gripping the armrests, and his temples throbbing in anger. With her back turned to him, she took a gulp of her drink and let it pour down her throat. She hadn't a clue what he was talking about and wondered if someone had beaten her at her own game.

"Pray tell, why would someone like me stoop so low to your level like that?" she asked with a smile.

"My level, huh?" He chuckled, leaned back and crossed his arms. "You're too good for blackmail?" he laughed. "I highly doubt that!"

"Blackmail," she said and laughed, almost choking on her drink. "You're dumber than I thought!"

Craig turned a brilliant shade of red and shot up from his seat sending it slamming into the wall behind him.

"Oh come now little Craig. Let's not throw a tantrum like a spoiled child just because I found all of your dirty little secrets so easily." She smiled and walked back toward the stiff brown chair. She sipped the whiskey and set the cup on the armrest. "But I must say, that little girly of yours…" she waved her hand in disgust toward the door. "She can't hold a candle to Emma. Really, just, ugh…"

"Did you really come down here to comment on my taste in women, Olivia? What do you want?"

"Money dear, Craig, I have too much of already," she said with a calm voice while swirling whiskey around in the glass, then scowled at him above the rim while she sipped.

"If not money, then what? You want to stick your claws into this? You want your piece of the action too?"

She laughed. "God, of course not. I despise you people. I want one thing, one simple, sweet little word…" she said, sitting up and leaned in toward him. "Consequence," she whispered. She smiled at him squirming in his seat.

"What do you want then? Want me to step out of the election? Promote one of your stupid charities?"

"I don't want your filthy hands touching anything of mine! And I don't care about your *precious* election. You're just as corrupt as the last Senator and the guy behind you will be just as corrupt as you," she said, and then finished off the rest of her drink. "None of the things you think are important have anything to do with what I want."

"Would you just get to the point for—"

"Sh, Craig. Patience, my darling. What I want is for the thing you neglect the most," she said with a devious little smile, almost giggling at the confusion on his face.

He rubbed the bridge of his nose, sighed and held his arms up. "I, I have no idea what you're—"

"Emma."

"Emma?"

"Yes, Emma."

"What does Em—"

"She needs something only you can give her. And until you do, there will be many more pretty little packages finding their way to your desk. As well as any other desks that might be interested in such titillating information," she said with a confident smile, stood and started to walk toward the door.

"Wait, what, what do you want me to do?" he asked, almost begging as he jogged behind her.

"Oh, no," she chuckled, "seeing you like this is far too fun. I think I'll let you stay like this a while."

Her Armani dress moved beautifully as she strolled to the door, turning back for a victorious snicker at the sad, slumping lawyer behind her.

His wide, glassy eyes filled with confusion watching the stunning woman saunter down the hall. He had no idea why his worthless wife was the cause of his dismay.

"Emma?"

Fifteen

"What about a dress?" Emma asked, holding up a red, strapless cotton dress.

Prudence curled her lip. "It's pretty but seems a little—"

"Too much?"

"Yeah. Something simpler," Prudence said, eyeing a mound of clothes on the bed. "Something classy, but not boring..." she said to herself, tossing skirts and shirts on the floor.

"Wait, what about that one?" Emma said, rummaging through the discarded clothes.

"Yes!" Prudence replied, snatching the clothes out of Emma's hands.

Emma stood by the bed, her head and chest halfway inside the tight chiffon blouse, arms straight up and struggling to make it through the tiny sleeves. Prudence pulled down on the sides of the blouse. "Okay, now wiggle your shoulders through."

"I don't think it's going to work," Emma muffled through the shirt. "I think it shrunk."

"Good morning, ladies," Edward said, almost smiling at the sight of the two women.

Emma spun around, not sure where his voice came from inside the suffocating top.

"Don't you ever knock?" Prudence said as she stretched her arms to cover Emma's exposed chest.

"Morning tea?" he asked, disregarding Prudence.

"I need my car," Emma shouted through her blouse.

"Shouldn't you use the driver, ma'am?"

"She'll drive her damn car if she feels like it. Go away," Prudence said.

"Can we get me out of this now?" Emma asked, her arms dangling in the air as she wiggled around in the shirt.

"Sure," Prudence laughed.

"Is it too frumpy?" Emma asked with a dismal, sideways snarl at her reflection. Despite Prudence's insistence, Emma opted against a mini-skirt and decided on a knee length, sea foam green, a-line skirt. Emma couldn't remember the last time she had to dress with the sole intent to gain the attention of a man. She found it nothing like riding a bike and had no idea what to do.

"I still say the mini-skirt, but that looks great. Casual but not Mom-like, but not slutty either," Prudence affirmed.

Emma slumped on the oversized foot stool next to Prudence and let out an anxious breath. "I don't know if I can do this."

"Of course you can. I mean you think this guy was something special, right?" Prudence said, nudging Emma's shoulder. "If life gives you a chance at something, you just gotta take it, you know."

Emma closed her eyes. The sheen of his tender gaze overwhelmed her. "He's worth it, he is," she said softly. "I'm not sure why, but it just felt like...like I was pulled toward him. That sounds so stupid and cliché I know!" she laughed and covered her face.

"It's fate," Prudence said in all seriousness.

"Fate, I wish there was such a thing." Emma chuckled. "Maybe I wouldn't have ended up here," she said, shrugging as she slouched.

"Well, you're as beautiful as anyone can get!" Prudence said with an excited, girly smile, stood and pulled Emma toward the door.

Emma stopped by the full-length mirror. "You really think it looks ok?"

"You're gonna stop the man in his tracks. Now get out of here before you drive me nuts!" Prudence giggled, shoving her out of the room.

Emma's hands trembled when she reached for the shifter, *I can't believe I'm about to do this,* she thought as she stretched her trembling hands. "Oh my God, I must be out of my mind," she said to herself, resting her hands on the steering wheel and tried to take a few calming breaths. She clung to the sweet remembrance of James' warmth, and concentrated on keeping her hands steady as she put the car in gear.

"Oh God, what am I doing?" she whispered as she pulled out of the long driveway.

The farther away from the hustle and bustle of the city she drove, deeper into rural areas she didn't know existed, the calmer her mind became. She found herself rolling down the window, letting the warm morning air tousle her hair as she drove through the California countryside. Lip-syncing to John Cougar Mellencamp, she turned up the radio and drummed her fingers to the beat on the steering wheel. She drove through strange towns in search of a man she had known for only minutes, leaving behind the scars and stresses of her overbearing, hateful husband. Despite the ramifications if she were to get caught, the forbidden journey sucked her into the undertow of freedom. She was simply Emma, driving down the road.

The last town on the list was something out of a 1930's old photo, with narrow brick roads and white picket fences. Dozens of quaint little shops crammed together stretched along Main Street. Big canvas canopies in hues of forest green and midnight blue hung proudly over tiny windows and solid oak doors. Carefully crafted, hand carved wood signs swayed above the small entrances.

Emma decided to pull over to stroll down the old time street, and peered in windows as she searched for the only antique shop in town. There was something classic and timeless about this town. People smiled and greeted her as they walked down the street. Dress shops displayed hand-sewn gowns and pant suits in the window, and shop owners chatted with the town folk. No one seemed to know her, but welcomed her just the same. She could see why James stayed in this picturesque little town.

Halfway down the fourth block she spotted the store. J&H Antiques was printed on the window in big, swirly gold letters. She stopped and held a hand to her chest. Her heart thumped hard against her fingers. She could barely breathe as she stared at the oak and glass door.

She waited, contemplating if the slightest chance of that same connection was worth the risk. A small bell rang above the wooden door as she stepped in the antique shop.

"Be right with you!" a man's voice called from the back of the store.

She swallowed hard. "Okay," her voice squeaked.

She roamed through the tiny shop as she waited. Every nook was filled with forgotten possessions; Great Grandma's treasured Hummels, and beautiful paintings and photographs hung on every space on the walls. A crackling paint-covered Victorian banister rested against gorgeous bedroom furniture with rich cherry tones and Craftsman detail. She wove her way through the makeshift aisles ways and came up to a long jewelry case along the main wall in the store. She admired the stunning earrings and necklaces, tarnished silver pocket watches, and old coins carefully wrapped in plastic baggies. She came to the last case, pressed sweaty palm against the glass and hunched over in bewilderment.

Toward the back, resting on soft bunched up satin cloth sat the gorgeous brooch that brought them together months ago.

"Can I take something out for you?" said a gentle voice.

He seemed more handsome than she remembered. The flecks of gold in his green eyes contrasted against his pink skin; wispy strands of brown hair curled over his forehead and matched the blotchy stubble covering his strong jaw. He looked neat, but rugged, in a dress shirt and loose striped tie. An instinctive smile lit up his slender, handsome face. Her heart bellowed for her to say something profound before he slipped through her grasp again but no words could make their way through her lips. They stood in silence, staring in each other's eyes in the stolen moment.

She blushed, smiled coyly and shifted her stare to the ground. She tried to clear her throat but nervousness made her voice squeak. "I, do you—"

"Emma…" he said, taking in every feature on her flushed face.

She wanted to tell him of the crazed, unexplainable yearning for him that drove her to track him down. But she feared she sound like a loon, and her feet firmly planted themselves on the dark gray carpet like boulders. She heard nothing but rapid thumping in her ears, begging her to step forward and sample his sweet lips. After months of forcing his warmth out of her heart, there he was but a few feet away.

"You remember me?" she whispered.

"How could I forget?"

Her dimples dug deep into her sun-kissed cheeks as her trembling body calmed itself. Her fingers traced tiny, desperate circles on the glass case hoping he felt the same temptation and would reach out to her. Her eyes locked with his, begging him to caress her as he did in her dreams. She grew flushed and quickly shifted her focus to an odd cuckoo clock on the wall beside her.

He tucked a few strands of loose hair behind her ear, and she nearly melted from the teasing touch against her skin.

He paused for a moment, took a shaky breath, and cupped his hand over hers on the counter.

Her whole body sighed in relief, every muscle giving in to the relaxation of love. "Would you like to go out to lunch?" she asked.

"And dinner too?" he said with a shy, fun-loving grin.

The Corner Diner smelled of french fries and hamburgers. Frank Sinatra sang sweet tunes through the crackling speakers from the jukebox in the back corner. The booths and seats along the counter were filled with regulars, chatting with waitresses about their kids and grandchildren, or who they were rooting for in the election in the fall. Everyone knew each other by first name. Being surrounded by comforting, small town living gave Emma the sense of being home again.

It stunned her that she would even contemplate breaking her wedding vows, no matter how wretched her husband was. She was still married. Yet in this moment with James, seeing his smile, feeling the warmth of his touch, his comforting familiarity; the connection was undeniable.

She fidgeted with her wedding ring underneath the table. Twisting it, pulling it off and pushing it on her restless hand. It hadn't occurred to her to think about what she wanted to say once she was with him. Her pulse soared, and she clumsily bumped condiments on the table as she struggled for words.

"I, ugh…" She chuckled, rolled her eyes at herself and took another sip of her water. "I, well, I'm not really sure what I'm doing here," she said with an apologetic grimace. She took a deep breath with eyes. "Truth is, I didn't actually think about that part."

James thought it was adorable the way she kept tinkering, spinning the straw in her water and tapping the spoon on the table. It took everything in him not to stop her stammering with a hard kiss. He sat up straighter and placed a hand on her twitchy fingers spinning a spoon.

"What part did you think about?" he asked.

Lost in his emerald gaze, she felt herself breathe for the first time. "Forgetting you, actually."

"Oh great!" he said, playfully throwing his arms up in defeat.

"I spent hours reliving that night we met, but was just…" she shrugged. "I couldn't live in a daydream, you know? So I tried to forget about you. I'm not even sure what I expected coming here like this."

"I tried to forget about you too. Being a married lady and all. To that Beckett guy, no less. Took me a long time to get my life settled down again," he said, pausing to stir coffee creamer. "But everything reminded me of you. Harvey thinks I've gone whacko," he said through a chuckle.

"I'm, I'm not really the type, the kind of woman who." Frustrated with her stammering she took a second to breathe. "I'm not the kind of woman who does this sort of thing."

"I know you're not," he said, and let his thumb feel the silkiness of her skin as it caressed her cheek.

The moment James touched her, a rush of warmth and tingles surged through her body. "How do you know that?" she asked, trying to tame the flush climbing up her neck.

"I don't know. I just kind of do, I guess. You know, since we already know each other, somehow," he said with a grin.

Emma laughed. "We don't really know each—"

"Sure we do," he said with a confident nod.

"Oh, and how's that possible?" she teased, crossing her arms.

"I have no idea," he said as he laughed. "Maybe another life or something? What is that called, fate, Karma?"

Emma laughed and playfully rolled her eyes.

"No, that's not right. Re-re-reincarnation, that's it!" He snapped his fingers and wore a goofy grin as he nodded in agreement with himself.

"You're just full of it—" she chuckled.

"Kind of crazy now that you mention it, isn't it?" James grinned, let his hand run down her arm and interlaced their fingers.

Emma looked down at their hands clasped together and rubbed her thumb along the top of his hand.

"What is it really like?" he asked, nodding to the obnoxious ring on her left hand.

Self-conscious, she tucked her hand underneath her thigh. "Not how everyone thinks it is." She tried to chuckle before looking away. "He's rough, cold. He despises me, really," she said, ducking her head down. "We're on the rocks I guess you could say. Or we were always on the rocks, I'm not sure."

Without thinking Emma scooted toward him and nuzzled under his arm. A shaky breath escaped him as she laid her head on his chest. He closed both arms tightly around her and kissed her forehead.

"Don't you think this odd?" she asked, cocking her head up. "That this feels so comfortable?"

"I guess I should," he said, scratching his head at the strange encounter. "Not my best idea being with you I'm sure. Probably all kinds of trouble coming my way. But, I, well—"

She sat up, her ocean colored eyes encouraging him through his stammers.

"Can't say I've ever felt something so, natural, I guess." He grinned watching her expressive eyes, then glanced down at her plump, soft lips. He slid his hand behind her neck and slowly pulled her forward.

"Saved room for some pie?" the waitress asked.

His arms dropped as he looked over at the waitress. "No thank you," he said with polite frustration.

Emma offered a sympathetic chuckle and patted his knee.

"All righty then, have a good one, folks," the waitress said, tossing the check on the table as she walked away.

James peered out the window to his locked up shop three blocks down, then anxiously checked his watch.

Emma's heart sank into her belly. "You should get back."

"No. I mean yes, I should, but—" his brows contorted in agony. "I don't want to leave, but I can't leave the shop closed for much longer. Harvey, he'll—"

"I, well...I could come with you?" she said.

They strolled back to the shop with their arms comfortably intertwined while they slipped into light-hearted, easy conversation.

"An Army brat, always went from one place to the next," James said, flipping the plastic window sign back to Open. "Guess that's when I started looking for antiques and such. Never stayed no place long enough to get attached to people," he said. "Will you excuse me," he said, nodding to the back. He wanted to hide the remnants of his half-eaten lunch on the desk. "Feel free to wander. I'll only be a minute."

Emma loved the aromas in the store. It filled her with the scents of libraries and grandparents' attics, bringing to life blurry memories of lazy Sundays and family dinners of the past. She ran her fingertips across bumpy carved daises on an old wooden rocking chair, *so much like home.*

"This is going to be nothing but trouble," James whispered to himself, stuffing a Styrofoam container into the overflowing trash bin. "A married woman..." he said, shaking his head. "Nothing but trouble. Stupid, stupid, stupid."

James stopped halfway through the doorway struck by admiration. He found her intoxicating, the way her simple white shirt hugged the curves of her long torso, how her eyebrows crinkled when she was concentrating, or how she tugged on her earlobe when she was nervous. There was something instinctively familiar about the urge to love her.

Emma turned and flushed at his awed gaze. "How long were you standing there?" she said with a bashful smile.

He drifted toward her and shrugged. His white teeth peeked through a boyish smile as he wrapped his arms around her waist and pulled her toward him.

"You shouldn't be here," he said, brushing his cheek against her wavy hair.

"Do you want me to leave?" she said, swallowing her worry.

"I should tell you yes. You're married, and I won't date anymore."

"Oh, I understand," she said, turning to get her purse off the counter.

"You don't have to leave though."

"I shouldn't be here, you're right. I don't know what I was thinking doing this," she tried to tease.

"I'd like you to stay," he said and reached for her arm.

"I shouldn't, James," she said, brushed his hands off and tucked her clutch bag under her arm. "It wasn't logical to come here. It was whimsical and silly, I'm sorry," she said, seeing the hesitancy in his stare.

"I'd like you to stay," he said again, stepping closer and slipped the purse from under her arm and set it back on the counter. "I know it's not the right or moral thing to do. But I like your company."

"I can't believe I'm doing this," she said to herself, and then raised her eyes to his. "I don't know what I'm dragging you into, what my husband would do if—"

"You don't belong with him, don't you see that?" he said, and gently pulled her into his arms.

"But, James I—"

"He doesn't deserve you, and you know it," he said. "He doesn't love you. Not the way I—"

She knew what was about to happen, and that she should leave before it did. But her feet refused to move. Her heart threatened to stop beating as he leaned in, their breath slow and hot as their lips hesitated to touch.

She savored the taste of his lips, letting the rush of passion consume her as their tongues twirled around one another's. She grabbed a handful of his shirt and pulled him against her body. He wrapped his arms around her and slid a hand underneath her shirt. Her chest beaded up with sweat as his brawny arms squeezed tighter.

"You're so beautiful," he breathed, stepping back and ran his fingers down her chest.

"Oh, James, I," she said, tipping her head up as he bent to kiss her neck.

"I've never needed someone so badly," he whispered.

"Oh, James," she moaned, succumbing to his euphoric touch and reached to unbutton his shirt.

They fumbled with buttons and sleeves. Feverish fingers yanked on clothing in gripping rapture. Their lips and tongues tangled and twisted, and she moaned in unbound ecstasy struggling to loosen his belt.

He stopped and took a step away.

"What, what's the matter?" Emma panted.

"I, I can't…" he said, pulling the shirt back over his shoulders.

"Can't?" she said, suddenly embarrassed and tried to cover herself back up.

"I can't have it be, be like *this*," he said, nodding to their surroundings. "This is wrong," he said with eyes begging for forgiveness.

Emma thought for a moment he meant being with her was wrong. *Being married, I can't blame him.* But seeing the raw warmth in his eyes, feeling the gentleness of his touch, *not in a store*, she thought, silently nodding.

"Not like this," she whispered, bending her lips to a sweet smile.

"I want to, I really do," he said. "But it's wrong like this, here. I don't want to—Ah hell, I don't know what I'm trying to say," he said as he rubbed his forehead. "Please don't think it's you, okay?"

"I shouldn't even be here at all," she said to herself.

"I know," he said, mostly to himself.

"Do you have someplace I can, um, straighten myself up?" she asked with a timid smile and trying to button her shirt back up.

"Sure, over here." He led her to a small bathroom in the back of the store.

"God, I must be out of my mind," he said to himself after Emma closed the bathroom door. "She's married, what are you doing?" he muttered, tucking his shirt back in. "Probably won't see her again now either, dumbass." James closed his eyes and took a deep, hopeful breath that she would return to him. "Oh I'm never gonna date again," he mocked himself as he yanked on his belt. "Then just go right for a married woman. Jesus—"

Emma came out of the bathroom looking as breathtaking as she had when she arrived.

She pulled her hair up and pinned it in place. "It's getting late."

He turned to the setting sun through the front window.

She stood in front of him and wrapped his arms around her waist.

"When will I see you again?" he said.

She looked up at him. "I don't know."

"I want to see you again. When—"

"Soon, I think. Craig doesn't much care for being around me lately, I think."

"Can I come to you? I can drive there, we can go out."

"No! That's the last thing I need, you coming to get me. I can let you know, somehow," she said, reaching for his business card and slipped it into her purse.

"Soon?" he said again.

"Soon…"

Sixteen

Craig looked at the inch of whiskey in the glass, held it to his lips, and then gulped the last sip.

"Get ya another one?" the bartender asked.

Craig slammed the empty glass on the counter. "No, that'll be all." He grabbed his jacket and threw a twenty on the counter.

He had heavy, drunken feet. The heels of his shiny shoes scraped along the ground as he walked through the parking lot.

"Shoe shine, mister?" said a young boy with his filth covered face looking up at Craig.

"Not today, kid."

"Got a car? I'll wash the windows," he said, showing Craig a rag and filled spray bottle.

Craig stopped and looked down at the boy. The tattered shirt was big enough to be his fathers. His worn-out sneakers were covered with duct tape to patch holes on the torn leather. *He must be about nine*, Craig guessed.

The boy inched the rag and bottle closer to Craig. "Wash?" he asked again.

"Nope, don't need it."

"I, I can carry your briefcase. I'll be careful, I promise," he said, rubbed his dirty palms on his jeans and held his hands up for inspection. "See? Please, mister?"

Craig heard a gurgle from the thin stomach and looked down at his small, dirty palms. "You got something to eat?"

"I'll work, I work good. I'll show you," he said with bright eyes.

"I don't need work," Craig said. "You got food?"

The boy ducked his head, stuck his rag back in his pocket and shuffled a foot around.

"A working man, huh?" Craig asked.

"Yes sir! I'm no bum, I work hard," the boy said, standing proud.

"Here's what I want you to do, kid," Craig said and thumbed through his money clip. "I want you to go down there, get some dinner," he said, pointing to a diner two blocks down the street. "Then, I want you to go to the shelter on 5th, you know where that is?"

The boy nodded.

"Stay the night there. Then tomorrow, get some breakfast, maybe get some new sneakers, too, okay?" Craig said, stuffing a wad of money into the boy's breast pocket. "The ladies there can get you settled, with work and all that," he said and winked.

The boy gaped staring at the money puffing out his pocket. His bark colored eyes grew huge and lively. "Oh thank you, mister!" he squeaked.

"I like a working man," Craig said and patted the boy's shoulder. "But you need a break," he said and continued walking. "Kind of like a vacation, okay?"

"I won't waste it, I promise!" he hollered after Craig, jamming the money deep into his jean pocket and ran down the street with a grin on his grimy face.

Craig looked up to the clouds; his glassy, empty eyes pondering the approaching evening hours. "Fuck it, doesn't matter now. She'll still be up," he mumbled to himself and kept staggering toward the parking structure.

It only took ten minutes to drive there. He flung the door open and paused, eying her alluring body from the doorway. Startled, she jumped as she spun around toward the commotion. He licked his lips and loosened his tie.

"I wasn't expecting you," she said, arms braced against the desk behind her.

His hunger consumed him. He tugged his jacket off, flung it on the floor, and stormed toward her. He scooped her up and slammed her on the desk, pausing a moment to marvel her beautiful face, then ripped her shirt open to expose her breasts and furiously kissed her neck.

"Oh, Craig," she moaned, and yanked his belt loose.

"God, baby, I need you so bad," he said, sliding her bottom to the edge of the desk.

"But the door, Craig, someone might see us," she said through an exhale.

"It's late, no one's here," he said, pulling her toward him as he clenched his hands around her inner thighs.

"Oh, God!" she squealed, digging her nails in the edges of the desk as he thrust himself inside her.

"Oh, Sheila baby…"

Sheila sat in the big leather chair wearing his shirt, with one leg dangled over the edge of the armrest while the other twirled her around in a circle. She puffed on a cigarette. "So, what are you going to do about it?" she asked, stopping the chair when it faced him.

"How the hell am I supposed to know what Olivia wants?"

"You sure it isn't money?" she asked as she got up and sauntered toward him.

"Bitch has enough money, it's something else." Craig shrugged and leaned forward to sip from the vodka bottle clutched in his hands. "Something to do with Emma."

She grunted with and rolled her eyes. "Well, what are you going to do about *her*?" she asked with a curled lip, stopping in front of the leather sofa he was sprawled out on.

"I should just divorce the damn bitch."

Her eyes flickered excitement as she dropped to her knees. "Yes, yes you should!"

"You know I can't do that," he said, brushing her hand off his stomach as he sat up. She sighed and grabbed the bottle from his hand and took a big swig as she glared at him.

"I'll have to…have to win her over somehow. Be nice to her, all that sappy shit she likes."

Sheila gagged on the vodka, coughed and scowled at him with bloodshot eyes. "You already tried that, and she didn't appreciate it," Sheila said as she cleared her throat.

"She doesn't believe I *love* her," he said, rolling his eyes.

"Well do you, love her?"

"I have too much going for me to worry about love," he said, turning back toward her.

Her wounded eyes rose to his as they started to water. She bit her quivering lip and tucked her legs up inside the button-down shirt.

"You know what I mean," he said, brushing his hand along the side of her face. "I'll just have to be more convincing, win her over."

"She doesn't deserve the attention you waste on her," Sheila said, glaring at Emma's photo on his desk.

"It's my only option, Sheila. I can't piss Olivia off when she's on a rampage. She's obviously gone to great lengths to get information on me from somewhere," he said with impatient force.

She huffed and threw her arms across her chest in a pouting fret.

"Awe, come on, baby, don't be like that. You know I'll only do it because I have to," he said with a charming smile. She let an evil look pierce him for a moment, but a faint smile crept out and she relaxed her arms. She slid her hand down her chest, flashing a flirtatious grin as she slowly unbuttoned her shirt.

"I don't want to talk about them anymore," she said with a smirk.

"No?" He grinned as she sauntered closer. "What do you want to do then?"

Sheila licked her lips as she let the shirt slide from her body and onto the floor. "Let me show you."

****

By the time Emma arrived home the sky had grown black. The solace of her forbidden afternoon with James vanished the moment her hand touched the gold knob to the front entry. The stress of finding Craig on the other side of the door overwhelmed her, but her only choice was to step through and see what waited for her.

She tried to be weightless as she tiptoed through the hushed halls and strained to listen for sounds of his presence. She heard light clicking of heels and muffled talking by the kitchen; she peered down a hallway but didn't see the light from his office. Relief wouldn't set in until Prudence could ensure that he wasn't home waiting for her. She fidgeted with the key ring dangling from her hand and attempted to form a clear thought.

Well, the best way to get attention is to do something, she thought, and re-closed the front door with a bit of force. The big metal handle clanked and stirred a scurrying throughout the house. Lights in rooms flickered on or off as the bustling sound of busyness smothered the silence. Seconds later Edward came trotting across the marble floor as she had expected.

"Evening, ma am'. You were gone for quite some time today, weren't you?" he said.

"It was a pretty busy day," she said, struggling to appear casual.

"What could possibly take up that much time?"

Her feet hesitated, *what's my excuse,* she thought and cursed herself for her careless planning. "I was browsing areas for a winter cottage," she said, surprising herself with the quickness of the blatant lie.

"Oh..." he said and popped out in front of her. "And whereabouts did you look?"

"In Bethel County, I love the mountains," she spouted. She wanted to scream at him to leave her alone, but that would only entice greater curiosity. She walked around the long, granite counter in the lounge, popped the cork on a wine bottle, and filled a glass for herself. *God, where's Prudence,* she thought and eyed the dark red liquid.

She brought the glass almost to her lips. "Oh, shoot," she said as she let the wine spill down onto her white blouse. "Would you fetch Prudence for me please, Edward," she said and dabbed her shirt with a cloth. "Look at this mess, seems I'm all thumbs today." She turned back toward the staircase and bit her lip to hide a mischievous smile.

"Of course, ma am'. Will that be all?"

She paused and looked back over her shoulder. "Come to think of it, is Craig home yet? I found a darling little spot today."

"I'm sorry he's not."

"Pity. Any word from his office on when he'll be home?"

"There have been no calls."

"All right, that should be all then."

She took purposeful steps up the stairs, concentrating on walking as poised as her wobbly legs would allow.

Prudence knocked as she came in, closed the door and ran across the bedroom. "I have been dying to find out what happened today!" she said, pausing as the red dribbles on Emma's shirt caught her attention. "Eww, what happened?"

"What? Oh, nothing I just had to—" Emma said, looking down and wiped her stained shirt. "I needed an excuse to send you up," she said, sat on the bed and pressed a hand to her cheek. "Oh, Prudence…" Emma exhaled. "I don't even know where to start, everything happened so fast."

Prudence clenched her hands, shaking them with a bright girly grin. "Was he everything you remembered? What did he say? What did you guys do?" she spouted in one breath.

"Oh, wow, let me think." The day was a whirlwind of a dream. "He was definitely much more handsome than I remembered. And the afternoon, it was just so…it was all so, so strange, but so…."

"So, so what?" Prudence squeaked, grabbed Emma's hands and squeezed them while she giggled.

"Natural," Emma said, turning back to Prudence with a love-struck smile. "It was so, easy. Like I've known him forever."

Prudence clapped her hands and bounced up. "Oh, I knew it, I knew it!" she said, and then jumped back on the bed nearly knocking Emma over. "Did you, you know?" she asked, nudging Emma's shoulder as she winked.

Emma laughed as she blushed. "No, we didn't."

"You lie, look at you!" Prudence teased and slapped her hand. "You can tell me! Oh…" she said as her smile fell. "Was he no good, or really teeny weeny?" she asked with pinched fingers.

"Prudence!" Emma chuckled. "You're just as bad as Olivia! For your information," Emma said. "We, well we *almost* did—"

"Almost! What happened? Did he get stage fright?" Prudence laughed.

"Would you stop it. No he didn't get stage fright. He changed his mind—"

"What!" Prudence shouted.

"He changed his mind. He wanted to but we were in his store, there's a big window and," Emma said, covering her face as embarrassment set it. "So it was kind of bad timing. It was nice though, him wanting it to be, um, more special than that, I guess."

117

"Awe..." Prudence squealed. "Do you think he's, well, the one—"

"Yes." Emma said, then her head jerked back, surprised by words she blurted.

"Oh, oh, I knew it!"

Emma bit her lip, but her mouth stretched to an ecstatic smile with glistening eyes.

"When are you going to see him again?" Prudence almost begged, turning her attention back to the basket of laundry she came in with.

"I don't know," she whispered and turned to Prudence with a bleak look.

Prudence brought her mouth to an encouraging smile and gently bumped Emma with her shoulder. "We'll figure something out."

"I was so lucky to get away with today."

"Its fate, I already told you that," Prudence insisted.

Emma rolled her eyes at the silly notion. "Fate, right," she chuckled.

"Stop that," Prudence said and lightly smacked Emma's arm with the folded shirt in her hand. "My mom spent most of her time mumbling drunken nonsense, but the one thing she did teach me was that everything happens for a reason—"

"So my making all the dumb decisions I have are for a good reason, is that what you're trying to tell me?" Emma smirked as her brows rose, and playfully crossed her arms as she stared at Prudence.

"Well, yeah but, you make it sound stupid when you say it like that," Prudence teased.

"Then maybe my stupidity was really great, inner genius!" Emma's chuckle grew soft as she tipped her head back against the wall, watching the slow motion fan blades of the ceiling. "God, Prudence, what am I doing? Really?"

"Having a little fun," Prudence said with a grin.

****

Edward set the wine he stole from the cellar on his dresser, locked the door, and retrieved the striped hat box. He staggered to his writing desk, fell into the seat and let the stolen wine tickle his senses as he haphazardly settled at the desk. He rubbed his hands together as he peered into the big box. "Hmm, let's see." A conniving smile stretched his hamster-like face. "Yes, yes these should indeed do the trick," he said with a soft, calculating chuckle.

He sloshed the wine around in the glass as he surveyed the goodies, took a sip and licked his lips. "Delicious…" he mumbled, then pulled from a drawer a red envelope and matching piece of paper. With his head cocked toward the ceiling, he tapped a pen on the tip of his pointy nose. "Ah, yes!" he said and began scribbling on the paper.

With the last bit of the letter finished, his craftiness produced a grand smile as he sealed the envelope and leaned back to appreciate his work. He sipped the wine, nodding his head as his mind wandered. He patted the red package as he chuckled to himself and shut off the light. "Dense little twit…" he whispered through a laugh, pulled back the sheets and climbed in bed.

****

Main Street had been barren of traffic for hours, except a lone car parked outside a shop. James sat on the floor in the middle of his office, with stacks of old photographs, letters and random papers scattered around him. His forehead was scrunched and taut with tension as he slid his fingers from his head to the nape of his neck. An empty cheeseburger wrapper lay on the floor beside the mostly empty six-pack of beer. He leaned back and took a swig.

Emma overran his thoughts and he closed the shop early after a moment of frantic thought. "The brooch…" he mumbled to himself and ran to the office. Five hours later, he had nothing to show for his efforts but an ungodly mess.

"There's a connection, I just have to find the paperwork," he said to no one. It felt stupid such a trivial piece of jewelry tormented him. "That has to be it, it has to," he said, vigorously ruffling his hair. "God—this doesn't make any sense!"

James's partner, Harvey, stepped in the doorway and surveyed the chaos encompassing James.

"Bill called me, said the shop lights were on."

"Yeah, I'm uh, I'm just trying to find something," James said as he flipped through a file.

"Here I thought we got broke into or something," Harvey said with a glare.

"I'm sorry man, I'm just looking for..." James mumbled, turning around and started sifting through another pile. "You wouldn't understand."

"I hope you don't plan on leaving it like this," Harvey said as he nudged a teetering pile with his foot.

"I'll take care of it," James said, dismissing Harvey with a wave of his hand. "I just have to find something Harv."

"I hope so, because this looks like complete insanity to me," Harvey said, then turned around and left without another word.

James glanced at the clock. "Jesus, 11:30. This is ridiculous, what the hell am I doing here?" he said and turned back to the pillaged documents. He held only a fragment of memory about the brooch, but remembered once refusing to sell it, even though the woman offered twice its worth.

"Insanity..." he said to himself, taking another gulp of beer. "What the hell do I think I'm gonna find here?" He tossed a stack of papers to the side and looked at the mess he created. "It's going to take hours to clean all this up." He closed his eyes and saw Emma's brilliant blue stare. His eyes jolted open; he stood and jumped over a pile of papers to the other side of the room. He tossed things around him as he sifted through the documents and then froze as he came to an old photograph.

The photo entranced him; a stunning young bride stood proudly on church steps with her parents and new husband. The brooch sparkled on the bodice of the dress. He examined the brides' jovial face. Her golden hair was pinned into a loose bun, but the face was an exact match to Emma. "That can't be possible," he said as he squinted and brought the photo closer to his eyes. The tall, slender groom beside her was his own face staring back at him. "This doesn't make any sense..." he said as he flipped the picture over. The yellowed, aged paper backing had dainty, women's writing. Carol and Ted 1954, it read. He flipped it over and looked at the couple, Carol and Ted, or Emma and James as he saw it. "It's us," he whispered. "But that can't be possible..." His arm dropped and the picture fell to his lap.

Seventeen

Specks of dust floated through the streams of light drizzling over the shelves stacked to the ceiling with books in the library. Emma's slow meandering echoed the sense of peace that had been her mood for the morning. The night passed with silence and images of James floating through her dreams. She woke with bubbling eagerness to plot another afternoon escape.

"Found something that's pleased you I hear?" his voice called out from across the hall.

Her heart dropped and skipping a beat at the sound of his voice. She turned and cautiously walked to the dining room. Craig sat mulling over the morning paper, nibbling on a croissant with half-eaten grapefruit on his plate. He glanced at the door waiting for her reply as he slid a spoonful in his mouth.

Emma rubbed her nervous hands together behind her back. "Pardon?" her voice cracked.

"I hear you found something of interest yesterday, a piece of property in the country?"

She blinked and stared at him until the lies dribbled into memory. "A few possibilities maybe." She stepped toward the table. "Is that all right?'

"Of course, my love," he answered with a smile, set the paper down and motioned to the empty seat across the table. "Sit with me?"

"Of course," she said with a forced smile.

He bit off a bite of pastry, and then put it down as he asked, "What have you found there? I don't recall our realtor calling me about this."

Her heartbeat sped to full panic. "I used someone out there," she blurted out as her eyes flickered in worry.

"Oh, really, and why is that?"

Breath escaped her as he walked toward her. *Oh God, he's coming at me*, she thought. "Well, you know…they, they know the properties so much better than someone from the city," she said, almost proud that she managed to pull it off.

"True," he said, taking her hand in his. "Will you be going there again?"

She resisted the urge to jerk her hand away in disgust. He raised her hand to his lips, kissed it softly and gazed into her eyes.

"Hmm?" he pressed.

"I was thinking I would look at a few more places. If that's all right?"

"A cottage in the country would be a fine piece of real estate, I think," he said and pressed a hand to her cheek. "It's a wonderful idea you came up with. A place to get away from it all would suit us well." He smiled and slid a hand into his pocket. "You'll have to tell me about it tomorrow though I'm afraid."

"Why's that?"

"Meetings, and I have a deposition that will probably go through the evening."

"All right—"

"If I make it home, I'll not sleep in the room. I don't want to disturb you," he said, kissed her on the cheek, and turned to leave. He stepped out in the hall, grimaced, and wiped his lips off with his sleeve.

Emma crept to her room to peek through the curtains, and as the car left the courtyard, she turned and sprinted for the phone. She coiled the cord around her finger waiting for someone to pick up, *maybe they aren't open yet*, she thought, listening to the unanswered rings.

"J and H anti—"

"Oh it's you!" she exhaled.

"Emma is—"

"Can you meet me in Bethel County?"

"Bethel County?" James asked, thoroughly baffled.

"Today, can you make it there today?"

"I suppose I can, why so far away?"

"We need to look at cottages."

A moment of silence filled the line. She called before thinking how the request might sound.

"Cottages?" he finally said. "Is this some twisted joke?"

"I'll explain when we get there," she said through a chuckle. "How soon can you meet me there?"

"It's going to take me probably about an hour, maybe a little more."

"Meet me at the visitors' center off I-37, okay? I'll see you in a few hours!" she said and hung up. The sound of his voice washed a fresh calmness over her.

She took her time sifting through the array of clothes. The large walk-in closet was like a rainbow of silk, satin, and chiffon elegance. She hummed "At Last" and let her fingers glide across the soft dresses and blouses as she floated around the room. As she turned something caught her attention. Standing there, staring at the clothes from her past and contemplating the bold move of digging them out felt like exposing a secret she was sworn to bury. *Do I even have the guts to try it?* She bit her lip and looked around to be sure she was alone, then pushed hard to slide the clothes down the clothing rod.

She held the hanger far from her body as if she held a ghost in her hand.

"Where have you been?" Prudence asked barging into the dressing room.

Emma screamed, dropped the clothes on the floor and held a hand to her jittery heart.

"Wow, you're jumpy!" Prudence said, bending to pick up the hanger. "What are you doing?"

"Nothing, I—" Emma snatched the hanger and tried to jam it back into the packed closet.

"What's that?" Prudence said as she pulled the hanger from Emma's hand.

"It's nothing really, just—"

"Jeans?" Prudence said in amazement. "*You* own jeans?"

"It's not what—"

"Well holy shit, you were normal once weren't you?"

"I was just looking at them," Emma said, yanked the old pair of jeans out of Prudence's hands and clutched them to her chest.

"No you weren't. You were thinking about wearing them, weren't you?" Prudence glared with a sisterly, mocking grin as she poked Emma's shoulder.

"I was just looking—"

"I bet you'd look pretty cute wearing them." Prudence picked up a dangling pant leg to examine the dark-wash denim.

"I couldn't wear something like that, are you crazy?"

"Why not?"

"Well, because—" Emma scratched her head. "Well I know there's a good reason, give me a minute."

"Decision made, you're wearing them," Prudence smiled.

Emma gaped, as if she had asked her to go streaking through the streets of Beverly Hills in mid-afternoon.

Prudence squinted as she eyed Emma from head to toe. "You're already dressed," she said, shaking a finger at her. "Why are you even in here like you need to get dressed?"

Emma blushed and her dimples appeared with a huge, delighted grin. "I'm going to see him."

"Today? Now?" Prudence squealed, grabbed Emma's hand and spun them around in a circle.

"Yes, but I—"

"Where are you meeting him this time?"

"Bethel County, I'm meeting him there in about an hour."

"Bethel County? What the hell is out there?"

"We're going to go look at cottages," Emma said.

Prudence stopped in mid-spin.

"I'll tell you about it later," Emma chuckled. "Now help me find something to wear," she said with a smile and grabbed Prudence to pull her to the appropriate clothing.

"Sure," Prudence said, tossing the jeans back in Emma's arms.

Emma arrived at the visitors' center earlier than James would be able to meet her. She paced outside of her car, jammed her hands in her pockets and looked down at her outfit. "Jeans…" she muttered as she shook her head.

Her heart jumped every time a car pulled in the lot. She couldn't believe she was doing this. Again. A dark-blue sedan pulled in a few spots down from her. She took a deep breath, rubbed her sweaty palms on her pant legs and walked toward the car without having seen the driver. James climbed out of the car and looked right at her. Emma's lips stretched to a stunning smile and she quickened her pace to a slow jog.

He picked her up and held her so tight she nearly lost her breath.

"I wasn't expecting you this early," she said.

"I drove a little too fast. Want to see the speeding ticket?" James laughed, squeezed her tighter and lowered his voice to almost a whisper. "You're really here," he said, and set her down as he stepped back to give her a good look.

She blushed and held a hand over her eyes. "God, I know I look just awful—"

He smiled playfully. "You look amazing."

She self-consciously cringed and tugged her Tom Petty t-shirt. "Oh, I don't but—"

"I think I like you better like this," he grinned. "Not so stuffy and uppity," he said, brushing off the shoulder of the worn t-shirt.

She chuckled and tapped him on the cheek. "You're a terrible liar, Mr. Dover."

"So, why are we looking at cottages, exactly?" he asked, wrapped an arm around her waist and escorted her back to his car.

"It just sort of popped out of my mouth. I'm not used to," she cocked her mouth to the side and shrugged. "To lying like this, I guess," she said, shifting her look to the floorboard. "I told Craig I would be going to see more. So I kind of *have to* go look at some now," she said, twisting her feet around as guilt set in.

He tugged on her forefinger and said, "So let's go check out some cottages. I'm already knee-deep in a really bad situation. Besides, it'll be interesting to see how the other half lives." He chuckled and put the car in reverse.

"No," she said.

He stopped the car and looked. "No what?"

"I mean, I want—*need* to look at ones he might like. But that's not what I want to look at. If I have to go through this charade, I want to look at something *I* would like," she said with a false sense of determination. "Something like, like back home. Something cute and country."

It was something about her unadorned manner, this hidden desire to be simple, normal, that made her even more appealing to him, each moment with her solidifying the faith that they belonged together, even though she was already married.

"I take it California's not home then?" he said, rolling down the window as they started to drive away.

Emma laughed. "God, if you saw what I was like growing up! No, no, that little town you're in, *that's* more like home than my home will ever be."

****

Emma told the realtor they were tired of city living and wanted something quieter and more private. 'Something with a nice porch and a lovely view,' she said.

She remembered the huge wraparound porch at her parents' first house and how she ran laps around it with her friends. And when Daddy collected boxes for her to draw on and she lined them up to make the world's best cardboard fort. She ached for something so comfortable and welcoming like that again.

They barely walked through the first home, only stepping into the great rooms out of obligation. The grand home was tucked up on the edge of a mountain side, with a breathtaking view overlooking a lush valley with a hidden river flowing through it. It had huge cathedral ceilings, striking marble flooring, and bedrooms larger than her parents' entire first home. Craig would think it perfect. But the moment they were back in the car Emma tossed the flyer in the back seat. "That place doesn't feel like a home at all," she said.

They made their way through secluded dirt roads, much farther south than she had ever been. It almost felt as if she had crossed state lines they drove so far. James didn't seem to mind the driving and pretend home hunt, and didn't notice that he too had gotten sucked into the idea of it all. He commented on poor foundations, outdated plumbing and no space for a workshop. They held hands as they strolled through homes, peered into tiny bedrooms and said how 'It wouldn't be enough room for all of the books,' or 'It's sweet, but there's not enough natural light.' They slipped into this imaginary world, where they were married and looking for a new home; they fit the roles perfectly.

As the car crept up to the seventh house, she gasped and squeezed his hand. A rustic old cottage with chipping white paint, neglected eight pane windows and a tattered roof sat veiled behind a line of Weeping Willows and regal looking Muskogee Crape Myrtles with their beautiful lavender flowers in full bloom. Two old, wooden rocking chairs still sat side-by-side on the wraparound porch.

James' slight grin grew to a full smile. "It's perfect," he whispered, turning to Emma as she pressed her face against the car window. She looked at him from over her shoulder, her face glowed with excitement. She barely waited for the car to come to a full stop before jumping out.

They strolled through the house with hands clasped inside each other's, silently admiring every outdated room. The living room had a sweet fireplace, with a big carved log for a mantle. Sun-faded white lace curtains flapped in the southern breeze creeping through a window that wouldn't latch. The realtor hid a grin as she watched the quiet couple, then silently backed away certain she had made a sale.

The dining room was to the left of the living room, a simple room with a round, wooden four-person table. Yellow paisley curtains hung on the only window, adorned on either side by tarnished bronze sconces. At the kitchen Emma paused in the doorway with a silent breath. It looked exactly like her Grandma's old kitchen. She stopped at the sink and gazed out the window overlooking a large pond with a crooked, crumbling dock and broken boat. She ran her hand along the cracked black-and-white tile counter, chuckling to herself how she once hated her Grandma's kitchen. Now it never seemed more inviting.

They went down the hall off the living room and came to the only bathroom, a bright pastel green and yellow tiled room with an ivory pedestal sink. She grinned, *it's just like home*. One bedroom was big enough to be a small study, or perhaps a sewing room. Emma had always wanted to pick up some crafty little hobby, but Craig would never allow it.

The second bedroom would make a quaint guest room, with two windows looking out on the beautiful Myrtle blooms. The master bedroom was a decent size, big enough to serve its purpose. In the middle still sat an old bed with a gold, curvy metal headboard from the fifties. The centerpiece of the room, opposite the bed, was the French doors. James gave the painted shut doors a yank as he jiggled the wobbly knobs to crack the doors open. As they stepped out on the back porch, and were surrounded by a mass of willow trees stretching beyond the cottage's property line. He squeezed her hand, their eyes locked, and they smiled. "It's perfect," she whispered.

The realtor cleared her throat announcing her presence. "You can borrow it for a few hours if y'all like. Get a feel for the property and how much work it needs," she said smiling, dangling the keys from her hand. "It's the biggest lot of the ones we seen, take some time to survey it all."

"Oh, no we couldn't—"

"Not a problem at all really. Just lock up behind yourselves and bring the keys back to my office when you're done. Ain't like you can steal the thing!" she laughed through a snort. "You can't do any damage, it's already in shambles."

They looked at each other, and then James turned back to the realtor. "If you're sure it won't be a bother—"

"Not in the slightest!" She smiled and tossed the keys to him.

They stood on the creaking, wavy porch and gave a polite nod goodbye to the realtor, and then turned toward each other as she pulled out of the driveway. For a few minutes they just stood there, taking in the sweet silence, the gentle breeze, and soft scent of the flowers around them. He bent his head down and rubbed his cheek against her silky hair.

"Well, what do we do now?" he asked.

"Let's explore."

They stepped into the dusty living room and surveyed the empty space.

"That fireplace is really something, isn't it?" he said, walked over and slowly ran his hand along the varnished log mantle.

"That cute little roll-top desk at your store would look great right here. The maple one, with the cherry finish?" she said, standing in front of one of the windows that looked out onto an overgrown garden.

"And that rocker you liked, with the daisies? It could go over there maybe?" he said as he walked over and slid his hand around hers. "Be nice there, with a fire going in the evening."

She imagined curling up by the fire in his arms. *I can't ever have this*, she thought as her face went pale.

James felt her go stiff in his hand, turned and saw her heavy, welled up eyes. He gave her fingers a gentle tug.

"It's not completely impossible, you know?" he said in a low, soft voice.

Her pain-filled eyes looked up at him. "I can't yet," she whispered.

"What do you mean *yet*? You're not staying with him, right? Tell me you're leaving him," he said as he stepped toward her. "You can't stay with him. People get divorced, isn't that your plan?"

"I can't, James, it's not time yet." Tears trickled down her cheek. She spun away from him and bent her head toward the worn-out hardwood floor.

"Not time yet? You hoping to bleed him dry and drag me along for the ride?" he asked, taking a hesitant step away from her.

She snapped around. "How dare you!"

He stepped back, hurt and confused.

"I'm sorry, I shouldn't have snapped like that. There's just so much I still need to plan. If I miss a step, he'll find me," she said softly, took a step toward him and attempted to reach for his hand.

He jerked his hand back. "Then what? What is this? What are we doing? You just want me as some, some boy toy or something? Is that what you rich people are into?" he snapped with his wounded eyes locked on hers.

"No, I would never treat you like—" She took a tentative step closer. "I'm not like that, not like those women."

"He won't ever love you, Emma, you know that. Not the way I—" He breathed hard through his nose. "You're just a trophy wife, can't you see that?" he said and turned back to the fireplace. He stretched his long arms, resting his palms on the mantle as he dug his nails in.

She lifted her head. "Why are you so angry? I can't just walk away."

"What do you expect me to say?" he said, turning around and threw his hands up. "I'm taking a huge risk here—"

"Like I'm not?" she snapped, resting a hand on her hip.

"I see the *real* you, the one he'll never see or appreciate. If he did I doubt you'd be standing here with me."

Emma crossed her arms but was ashamed by the anger she felt at James truthful words.

"This is damn near the craziest, dumbest thing I've ever done, being here with you," he said, walking toward her and slipping her hand inside his. "But I can't say I've ever felt such lov—"

Emma started to cry and tipped her head up and away from his bruised stare.

He put his hand on her cheek and guided her back to him. "Say it, Emma. Trust it. I know you feel it too, don't you?" he begged.

"I, I…God I don't know why or how…" she sobbed and panted trying to catch her breath. "But I do," she whispered, her face contorting in anguish. "This is so stupid and wrong, but I—"

"I'm willing to do what I swore I'd never do again for you, please tell me you think I'm worth the risk too."

"You're worth the risk, but I—" Emma put a hand over her mouth and shook her head. "I can't, it's too soon. There are too many loose ends. He'll find me and…" Unable to hold back the twisted pain, she covered her face and ran outside toward the pond. James stepped forward in a half-hearted attempt to stop her, but stopped at the porch as he watched her run through the weed-filled grass.

Eighteen

Craig's ruffled hair, crooked suit jacket, and heavy feet bared no resemblance to the tall, proud walk he usually carried. Sheila saw him coming down the hall and desperately wanted to hug him, the poor thing, and curse that bitch wife of his for putting him through all this. She took a few deep breaths as he approached.

"Morning, Sheila," he mumbled.

"Oh Craig…" she said with sympathetic sweetness. "I—something came for you," she muttered, glancing up with a wince. She reached in a drawer and pulled out another red envelope and handed it to him.

His empty eyes sank as he stared at the stuffed envelope. He yanked the package from her hand, stormed to his office, and slammed the door.

Damn that bitch for sending another one. And damn Emma for putting me through this shit. He plopped in a chair, eyeing the red affliction before he ripped it open. First was an old planner, leather bound with his family crest embroidered on its center. He could only imagine what incriminating tidbits were in there. He sat up, flipped it open, and in the front page found a letter written on red paper.

Dearest Craig,

It's such a shame, that someone with as much potential as you once had, would let yourself go down such an ugly path as you have chosen. So careful in your planning and plotting, yet so foolish in not taking notice of the ones you hurt around you. You storm through people's lives, taking and changing what you please without the slightest care of what you destroy. It's all for a good cause, I'm sure that's how you see it. But soon you will see. Every nasty step you have taken to climb so high, become this grand thing you think you are, can easily be taken from your wormy grasp. Tsk tsk boy, for not being wiser about the lives you crush.

Craig ground his teeth until they squeaked. His face dotted with red blotches of flushed anger as he crumpled the letter and threw it across the room. He cracked his neck as he flipped through the assortment of photos with his mistresses and receipts of their time together. All paid for by the firm's expense accounts. The following pages would contain more of the same. He knew what he had done, but he turned the page anyway.

Page after page was filled with notations and appointments he should have never written down, and receipts for things he should have paid for in cash: a sloppy trail of his corrupt path up the ladder. Craig set the planner down and grabbed the next stack, sighing as he flipped through it.

"What have I done...' he whispered. "I'll never be able to hide all of this. How could I have been so stupid?" he shouted as he smacked the pile of papers and sent them flying off the desk like confetti.

Sheila jerked at the sudden clatter, stood and pressed her ear against the closed door, wary if she should enter. She took a deep breath and turned the knob.

"Is everything—"

"It's you!" Craig screamed, glaring up at her from his desk. He stood, palms flat on his desk, and his back arched as if he were about to pounce. Sheila stumbled and stepped backward as he came around to the front of the desk.

"It's you, you worthless..." He knocked a lamp off the desk, and then flipped a chair over as he stomped toward her. "Worthless whore!" he bellowed and rushed for her. Sheila's eyes widened with fear as she backed into the wall, turned her head, and cowered in the corner as he sprang to attack.

"You'll ruin me!"

"Craig, I'm sorry!" she cried, covering her face with a hand.

"It's your fault," he yelled inches from her pale tear-covered face.

"Please, Craig, I didn't do it." She sobbed as she ducked her head against a bookcase, trembling as his hot breath threatened to devour her.

"You all will ruin me," Craig hollered. "Get out!" he wailed in her ear. Sheila flinched and crouched low. "Get out, get out!" His voice filled with insanity as he pointed to the door.

"I didn't do—"

"I can't stand to look at you." He pressed his face into hers. She screamed, eyeing the door as she bawled, then cautiously ducked below his arm as she scooted out and ran for the door.

He slammed a fist into the wall, then spun around and looked at the papers on the floor, grabbed his jacket and stormed out behind Sheila.

****

Deep into a soothing, hangover induced catnap, Olivia stretched her long limbs as she waited for Johnny to return her call. The thought of someone else tormenting Craig delighted her; she settled into a carnivorous grin and took a breath of satisfaction imagining his demise.

The deliciously evil daydream was halted by clamoring and shouted Spanish insults. She turned and peered over the chaise at the commotion behind her.

"Ms. Child, I sorry—" her maid said, trying to brace the door with an arm but Craig charged through the old woman's grasp.

"Damn you, Olivia!" he screamed.

The poor old maid stumbled after him and pulled on his huge arm trying to drag him back. But he swatted her off like a pack of gnats.

"You worthless—" he screamed through clenched teeth.

Olivia calmly stood and gestured at her maid. "It's ok, Sonya," she said as she raised a hand in reassurance. The frazzled woman hobbled for the safety of the house, mumbling prayers to the saints and giving the sign of the cross.

"Now, now, Craig—"

"I should kill you."

She slid her sunglasses on so he wouldn't see the glimmer of fear that flashed in her eyes. Her manicured fingers started to tremble as the silver lighter shook in her palm.

"You'll have to come up with something a bit more creative than that, Craig, if you wish to scare me," she said through a puff of smoke.

"You're all the same, you trash," he said, eyeing her stern stance. "You think you're just *sooo* smart, sending me another package like that." He pointed a finger in her face. "But I'll have you know, if you keep this up I swear I'll—"

"Package?" she said in casual confusion as she poured herself a new drink. "What *package?*"

He took a step back. "Don't play coy with me, it doesn't suit you."

"I'm sorry, darling, but I haven't the slightest clue what you're talking about," she said, sliding back down onto her chair.

"Don't toy with me anymore. You know exactly what I'm talking about. Your pretty little red packages."

"I must say I'm rather intrigued, but I'm sorry, darling, red simply isn't my color."

He paused for a moment, pouring bewildered rage into her eyes. "It has your stench all over it."

She shook her head. "My packages aren't fully assembled yet, but you'll get them soon."

"I...I don't—" He pinched the bridge of his nose and said to no one, "But then—" and then turned to leave.

Olivia leaned over the chaise and watched him walk away. Once out of eyesight she let herself breathe, brought the cigarette to her lips and choked on the deep inhale as the phone rang.

"Yes?" she said through a cough.

"It's ready," he said.

"Oh, thank God, not a moment too soon."

"You're not big on patience are you?"

"If you only knew what I've just gone through, Johnny, you'd not take it so lightly."

"Having some problems with your game?"

"Problems? He's getting terribly vengeful." She took another sip in hopes of calming her nerves, sat back, and tucked her feet up on the lounge chair. "Did you find anything good? I really need to bring this bastard down, hard."

"He's probably one of the messiest I've seen. Still took a bit of digging and I used up a lot of favors for you. So you owe me, believe me. But I found more than you can handle, honey," Johnny chuckled.

"Good, makes it easier. It won't take long to finish him off then. I fear he's going to be a threat soon."

"Is this a secure line?"

"Do you think my father would have me using anything else?"

"I know someone, who could take him down—"

"What do you think I'm doing, darling!" she giggled.

"For good, sweetheart. Like a vacation he doesn't come back from, freak house fire, you get me?"

"Really?" she said, flipping through Vogue. "Would it be messy?"

"He's very discreet. It could even be open casket."

She paused for a moment, stamped out her cigarette and said, "How much for something tasteful?"

******

Edward sat in the library, perched on the scratchy plaid sofa in front of the six-foot fireplace. He relaxed into his thoughts, more than certain neither of his employers would be home for hours. With Emma off doing whatever had caught her attention, and Craig hopefully wallowing in self-pity, the afternoon was his.

A bottle of Craig's favorite wine sat half finished beside him while he sifted through a stack of pictures from his hat box. He caressed her young, fresh face in the photograph with his thumb. Both so in love, so naive as to what their future would truly hold. It seemed forever ago they were like that, before Craig destroyed everything. He flicked the photo in the fire, watching its blue and green flames dance around on the logs.

Edward glowered at the rainbow flames in the fireplace as the chemical stench filled the room. He grabbed an overflowing handful of pictures and threw them into the fire, sat back, and watched the swirling heat encompass the unforgiving memories.

If not for her insatiable desire to have a bigger life, she never would have met him. He closed his eyes and tipped his head back. "Why?" he pleaded to the air. "Why did he have to have her?" He rubbed his eyes trying to hold back the pain and hold onto the anger. He had spent enough time in pain from the things Craig did, and where did it get him? Being the nice guy gets you cheated on, belittled, beaten and forgotten. Greed, lust, pride, and wrath, the best of the seven deadly sins took people like Craig and placed them on a pedestal. It was time to act as Craig did, take everything he wanted.

"Come to think of it," he said with a slick smirk, sat up and dug through the box in search of Emma's journal. "She must have something in the works, or else why would she say that?" he murmured, his beady eyes skimming the recent pages. "Now there's an interesting idea, but how could I get to her?"

He tapped a finger to his chin as he thought out loud. "She could expose me, but it might be well worth the risk..." he ran a fingertip along the white lily on the journals cover, and then threw it in the fire with the photos. He chuckled to himself. "It's beautiful," he said with a giggle, stuffed the hat box under his arm and headed for the garage.

Nineteen

In the rotting, wooden boat by the dock, Emma sat sniffling and wiping her nose on her sleeve. James gradually walked toward her and stopped a few feet away from the boat. Still wet from crying, her red, swollen eyes looked up and locked with his. She attempted a welcoming smirk, and then motioned to the empty spot across from her.

"I don't know what I'm doing, James."

"Neither do I," he said, resting a hand on her knee.

"I don't want to be a cheater," she said as she sniffled.

"I can't share you, Emma," he said. "I can't share you with him. I can't be the *other* guy," he whispered.

She pressed her hand to the scars hidden underneath her bangs. "I have this plan, and it's starting to work but—it's complicated," she said through a sob.

"You just walk away, what's complicated about that? Walk away, and don't look back. From me, or—" He rubbed his forehead. "You can't have us both. I won't be used. I won't be left or deserted."

"I need a fake identity, things his people can't track. Don't you understand that? I wish I could just leave, be free and be with you who—" She bent her head with tears dropping onto her jeans. She sniffled, wiped her nose again and looked back up at him. "Whom I barely know."

"Look, I know we've both got some pretty heavy baggage here but—" James crouched to his knees and held her hands. "You know this," he said, pressing her hand to his pounding heart. "I swore to myself I would never love again, never marry again," he said, locking his eyes on hers. "But you have to feel this is worth the risk, don't you?" He pulled her into the warmth of his hold, letting her silent tears soak his shoulder.

"I need more time," she whispered. "Please say that you'll wait."

"I can't keep going on like this, you don't know what this is doing to me."

"James..." she said, sobbing as she caressed his face. "I don't mean to put you through this—"

"This is going to sound crazy, but I need to show you something," he said as he dug into his back pocket. "I wanted to show you, but didn't know what to say, really. But I guess this is as good a time as any." He held the photo to his chest, took a deep breath, and then handed it to Emma.

She scrunched her brows as held the photo close to her face. She traced a finger down their images. "I don't understand, who are these people?" The photo of her and James on their wedding day made her heart pound against her chest. "They look just like," she said as she shook her head. "What is this?" she said, finally lifting her head to look at him.

James bit his lip, and then took a deep breath. "I know this sounds crazy, but." He ran his fingers through his hair and let out a nervous chuckle. "But I think that's us, Emma. You and me."

Her eyes squinted as she stared at him, and then looked back at the photo again. It wasn't just similarities, it was exact. Right down to her big, round freckle on her left cheek.

"I mean, that's us, you can't deny it," he said as she continued staring at the photo.

"I know," she managed. *The dress*, she thought as she stared, *I remember this dress*. "James, how did you find this?"

"When I bought that broach you love, they gave it to me. It was hers...yours."

As she looked down at their faces from before she was even born, flashes of her dreams began flickering through her mind.

"I know this sounds crazy. I'm not even sure I really believe it. But we're connected somehow, Emma. I mean come on, that's us!"

"James…" She slowly set the photo on her lap and raised her gaze to him. "I've seen this dress before, I remember now. I've seen this is my dreams."

They gazed hard at each other for a moment, and then James took both of her hands into his. "We're connected, Emma. We're meant to be together. You have to see that now, don't you?"

Emma's mind spun with images of her dreams, the photo, and how this was possible.

James stood and held out a hand to her. "Come on, let's go back inside, okay?"

Back in the cottage, they curled up on the old, musty bed together in the bedroom. This is how she secretly hoped they would spend the rest of their days. She let the guilt and fear fade away with the afternoon sun.

She opened up parts of her soul she thought died long ago, revealing bits of herself she tried to hide, even from herself. A barrage of confessions slipped from her lips to James. All the shrewd things she had done to help Craig achieve his selfish goals, turning her cheek to her morals for the sake of dead love.

"It makes me feel so dirty," she explained. "I try to figure out how I got to be like this. I hate myself for being like him," she said, snuggling her head into the crook of his arm.

"People abuse love, abuse trust, it's sad and disgusting, but they do. He used you," he said, stroking her arm with the tips of his fingers. "My wife—ex-wife, knew I trusted her completely. I didn't question if she came home late, or wondered if she was someplace she said she wasn't."

"I'm so sorry she did that to you," Emma said, rolling over and rested her chin on his chest. "I must seem like the same kind of woman to you. A cheater, deserter," she said, knowing its truth.

"No, you're not," he said. "I don't think you are. I hope you're not anyway."

"I wouldn't do that to you," she said, pleading for his trust. "I know you may not believe that, coming from a married woman," she said and tried to gulp down the lump in her throat. "It's different with you. With Craig it's cold, a disaster of misguided love. But I don't feel that with you. I feel like it's—"

"Meant to be?" he said.

"Yeah, I suppose so."

"What a soap opera we could make huh?" he said through a chuckle.

As the sky grew dark, they stayed cuddled up in the dust filled room and fell asleep wrapped in each other's arms. Emma awoke with panic and blind in the pitch-black house with no idea what time it was. Frantic, she fumbled through the empty house and toward the front door. "Hurry!" she called out from the living room, ramming her shoulder into the stubborn door trying to open it.

"I am! I just have to, damn it where are they?" he said, stumbling in confusion behind her, groggy and searching for his keys that fell out of his pocket while they slept.

She wailed on the horn so hard he thought she was trying to wake the dead. "I can't find them," he hollered, holding up his empty hands in the air on the porch. "Just hold on!"

"I'll never make it back in time," she said, eyeing the black country sky.

"All right, all right," he said, rushing to his car and rummaged through the trunk for the flashlight.

"Please hurry," she said, cringing and biting a fingernail.

"Got them!" he yelled from the house, slammed the door and ran to the car. "I wish you'd just be with me," he panted as he started the car.

"I will, when it's—"

"It's time, I know," he said and shook his head. Her worried eyes locked with his, he raised her hand to his lips and kissed her shaky fingers.

They dropped a letter of apology in the mail slot at the real estate office along with the keys, and then continued to weave around traffic on the highway to get Emma back to her car.

After a hasty goodbye, she sped off, leaving James behind her. James leaned against his car, watching Emma race to be with a man who couldn't stand her. He shrugged in confusion. "I don't get it," he mumbled, then grunted as he kicked his car. "What the hell am I doing with her?" he said to himself as he sat on the hood and crossed his arms.

Twenty

It was eerily quiet. Emma tiptoed through the halls, her heart beating too loud in her ears for her to hear his voice. She could barely breathe and almost gave into relief when she reached the staircase, so close to the safety of her room. With her feet on the steps and her hand on the railing she heard a swishing sound behind her.

"Another busy day?" Edward asked appearing from nowhere.

She should have expected to be greeted by his boorish curiosity. "Excuse me?" she said, looking down at him from the steps.

"I think this is your latest night in, well, it must be years."

"Are you keeping track?"

"That's a strange idea." He stopped a few feet in front of her, eyeing her from head to toe. "Now where could you have gone in such attire?"

She hated herself for wearing something so conspicuous. "Craig knows where I've been. Edward, I'll not have you—"

"It's of no matter really. He's already been here and left again."

She tried not to move, but fear rose up her insides and flushed her face a shameful pink. In the most casual tone she could muster, she said, "I suppose I'll have to update him tomorrow then,"

"He mentioned something about taking a few days off."

She swallowed hard, like trying to choke down a cue ball whole. She couldn't remember the last time he took days off. "I'm dreadfully tired, Edward, I'm turning in for the night. I'd suggest you do the same," she said, then continued up the stairs.

She left him on the landing, took a deep breath once in her room and then flicked on a lamp. An ominous pain reeled in her stomach at the sight of two-dozen red roses lying on her pillow. The flawless petals were tied with a delicate, lavender ribbon with a perfect bow. A little card with swirly, lavender hearts perched on her pillow beside the bouquet. She squeezed her hands into fists, pumping them as she looked down at the card so carefully placed on her pillow. Her name was written in big, loopy writing. The days of Craig's sweet romantic gestures were all but forgotten, tucked away in dusty boxes in the attic. Yet here sat the gorgeous arrangement, most certainly with a delightful promise inside the small card.

She flicked the corner of the card against her lip, heart pounding like a stampede of elephants as she considered the message inside. With the card almost open, she stopped. She tucked the card inside the bouquet, and then shoved the bouquet in the trash bin.

****

Emma could hear the clinking of Craig's spoon stirring cream in his coffee from down the hall. She wasn't sure if she should smile, be the cold, scorned wife, or crumple in guilt about spending the day with another man. She mustered a half-smile, nodding as she walked by him to her side of the table.

"Morning," she said while Prudence pulled a chair out for her. "Shouldn't you be in court already?" she asked, avoiding his look with pretend interest in the morning paper.

"I've got Martin filling in for me," he said, setting the sports section down. "Our arguments lately, I've been thinking about them," he said, dropping two sugar cubes into his cup. "You're right. We're not what we used to be, and I should have tried harder to fix it before it got this bad."

She looked up, fixing her wide eyes on him, hand frozen above her coffee cup with sugar cubes on the spoon.

"That's progress right, that I agree?" he said, letting a halfhearted smile flicker at her paralyzed body. "Well, say something, love."

"I," she said, looking down at her filled plate as confusion swirled in her head. "I'm sorry, Craig," she said, raising her eyes to his.

"Don't be sorry, love. I should have listened, *really* listened to you long ago. Maybe we wouldn't be so bad off now if I had—"

"No," she said, eyes shifting as her thoughts fumbled over each other. "I mean—" She raised her confused look back to him. "I don't believe you."

He cleared his throat and crossed his arms. "Well, I suppose I should have expected that," he said, raising a hand and scratched his brow.

A flash of anger whipped through his gaze, momentarily turning his dark eyes hard like coal. But in a blink he flushed it out, and raised his cheeks to a perfect, charming smile. "That's why I've taken a few days off, to convince you of it," he said, trying to soften his stiff posture.

She watched his mechanical eyes, *that won't work this time*, she thought. "Craig," she said, stiffening in her chair. "I think you've wasted vacation days then."

"Give me time, Emma, I'll show you I still care about you, about us," he said, grinning again and reached for her hand.

She pulled her hand onto her lap. "Say you love me," she said, facing him square.

Craig rolled his eyes as he turned his attention back to his paper. "Back at that, are we?"

"If you want to win me over, I mean that is what you're trying to do, right?" she said, putting a hand on his newspaper and pushed it down forcing him to acknowledge her. "Then say it, say you love me. Tell me how much you love me."

"If I didn't would I be wasting precious time at home when I have a huge case that's about to go to trial?"

"Then say it, it's only three little words," she said, refusing to let him distract himself. "Say it with me...I-love-you. It would change everything, I promise."

"This is ridiculous," he said, throwing the paper on the table.

"You're not going to, are you?"

"I shouldn't have to be subjected to this. I do believe I'm showing it to you now," he said, leaning away from her.

"But what a way to *show* it, by saying it. Don't you think?"

"This is stupid. I can't believe you're putting me through this," he said, tightening his crossed arms and looked away from her.

"All right then, Craig," she said softly, sliding his newspaper back toward him. "You don't have to."

"Finally," he said, sitting forward.

"Then lets work on saying what you're really doing here," she said and cupped a hand over his forearm. "Three *different* words."

He set his fork down and looked up at her.

"Ready? I'll make it real slow for you, come on, say it with me now," she said with a sarcastic grin.

He squinted an eye at her, hesitantly turning to face her.

"You're-using-me," she said, nodding to him with pretend encouragement.

His eyes clenched tighter, burning hate into her as he flicked her hand off his arm.

"Oh…" She pouted. "You don't want to say that one either?"

"This is ridiculous," he snapped, slamming his chair back as he stood. "I don't know why I even bothered—"

"Desperation," Emma said. "You need me, but I'm not your stupid, submissive country girl anymore."

"I don't need anyone," he said, turning back around.

"Sorry this whole, *pull the wool over my wife's eyes* thing isn't going quite like you thought it would."

"I should have gotten rid of you a long—"

"Perhaps all this doting would be better spent on your mistress?" she said, looking up at him as she slid her fork into her mouth.

He stopped in mid-step, casually turned to face her as he tucked the paper under his arm. "We have dinner plans tonight, dress nice," he said, abruptly turning out of the dining room.

Whatever his original intention for the day, after breakfast he seemed to abandon the idea. Emma heard his deep voice bellowing through the office door. Periodically the door would bang open as he came and went to retrieve one thing or another.

"Do you think he's onto us?" Prudence whispered, eyeing the closed office door from the sunroom.

"I think he's desperate, for some reason, and he needs me to be happy," Emma said, turning to look over her shoulder at his closed door.

They flinched at a sudden bang behind his door.

"Guess that's not working out," Prudence said, suddenly jumping to her feet and grabbed the vacuum that sat beside her.

Craig charged out of his office. "Edward!" he screamed, frazzled and fumbling with his briefcase.

Prudence flipped on the vacuum, scooting it around Emma's chair, appearing hard at work as she watched Craig from the corner of her eye.

Edward popped out from nowhere to hand Craig his suit jacket.

"Took you long enough," Craig scolded, ripping the jacket from Edward's hands.

"My apologies sir, but—"

Craig held a hand in front of Edward's mouth. "I don't have time for excuses," he said as he turned to leave.

As Craig slammed the front door shut the house skipped a breath, settling into the brief calm his absence brought. Prudence shut off the vacuum, Emma turned around to face the door, and Edward stood motionless in the foyer. They acknowledged one another, their eyes flashing the same confusion about Craig's behavior. Without daring to mutter a word, they let the moment pass; Edward vanishing, and Prudence sitting beside Emma again.

"Something isn't right," Emma said, still watching the foyer Craig stormed out of.

"I got more on Sunday," Prudence said, dug into her pocket and slid her clenched fist with a ball of money toward Emma.

Emma grabbed the money, tucked it into her pocket and whispered, "How much?"

"Another $300," Prudence said.

Emma pulled out a piece of folded up paper from her pocket, jotted down the number, then tipped her head as she doodled math in the air. "One more month," she said, tucking the paper back in her pocket. "I'll have enough to get the details paid for to really disappear."

Prudence nodded to the clock. "You should head upstairs, dinner reservations, right?"

"Can't wait to see how this plays out," Emma said as she stood. "You think he's with *her*?"

Prudence took a deep breath as she wound up the vacuum cord. "Does it really matter to you anymore who he's with?"

Emma thought for a moment, envisioning Craig wrapped up in another woman's arms, cursing his wife as they made love. "He can do as he wants," Emma said, turning back to Prudence. "Let me know when he's here, if you can," she said, then walked toward the staircase.

Emma ran the soft-bristle brush through wavy strands of hair, following Craig's reflection in the mirror as he dressed behind her. Craig started to pull on the tuxedo suspender to adjust them, then hesitated and let them drop back down to his sides. He came up behind her looking like a starved beast, gently pulling the satin strap off her silky shoulder.

"You do look lovely tonight," he said.

She wanted to distract him from the violating ideas that fluttered in his malicious eyes. "Where are we going? You haven't told me."

He ignored the question, slowly sliding a hand underneath the other strap, pushed it off, and ran his coarse hands down her smooth back. The room started to spin around her. Her stomach churned in violent protest. He bent over, slipped his hand into the cup of the dress and squeezed her breast with an evil smirk on his smug face.

The room flipped over on her, sending her running to the bathroom with a hand cupped over her mouth. Every time she thought of his touch another wave of nausea seized her, and she gripped the cold porcelain as she buried her face in the bowl again.

Craig stood to the side of the doorway, cocked his head and watched her with an odd curiosity waiting for her to finish. Almost an hour later, the relentless sickness began to cease. Emma propped herself up, gingerly stood, hobbled to the sink and hung over the edge as she splashed cold water on her face.

"Feeling better now?" he asked, leaning on the doorframe.

She bent her head toward him. "A little…"

"Such a pity for you to get sick like that. Have any idea why?" he said as he walked in, admiring his reflection in the mirror and tamed an uneven part in his hair.

"I think the oysters at lunch maybe," she whispered.

He seemed dangerously cheerful. She was certain now, *he's up to something.*

"Quite all right, I think I'll head out anyway. I presume you won't want to do anything tonight anyway?" He took one last glimpse at his handsome face, but didn't wait for her reply before he started to leave.

Emma heard the door slam, and then held her stomach as she walked to the bay window to peek out the curtains. She wouldn't dare blink. She had to be sure he was gone. Her knuckles turned white squeezing the curtains while she waited, when finally, his shiny silver Beamer pulled out of the garage.

Emma pulled herself into the fetal position and thought of James trying to convince her to stay. "Please wait for me," she whispered, hoping the wind would carry it to him.

****

Craig knew where she would be and that some twisted, demented part of her made her sit up and wait for him. He ran his tongue against the front of his teeth, shivering with disgust about having been so close to Emma. Her touch was like poison. He yanked the wheel hard to the right, cutting off three lanes of traffic to make the exit. He turned through streets without a thought; he could get there with his eyes closed by now.

The hallway was narrow, and the steps a bit too close together, making his long legs awkward on the clunky steps. Three floors up, fourth apartment on the left, he cleared his throat and knocked on the door. He heard the peephole swing open, but the door remained shut. He relaxed his shoulders trying to look as hopeless as possible, rested his hand against the doorframe and then tapped on the door again.

"Baby? Baby, I know you're in there," he called out to the shadow behind the closed door. "Baby, I'm sorry. I didn't mean to scare you like that. Can you just please open the door so I can explain?" he said, listening to silence as he waited. "Baby come on, I can't do this without you..." He hung his head lower, and then pressed his palm to the door. He heard the peephole shut, then smiled with victory as he waited for her to open the door.

Sheila's eyes were swollen and bloodshot from hours of crying, curled up on her couch with no one to talk to. She hung her head like an unhappy child, stood a few feet back with a mostly empty wine bottle dangling from her hand. One of his shirts draped her body, buttoned crooked and baggy over her slim figure.

Craig looked up at her with droopy, puppy-dog eyes, took a few cautious steps and closed the door behind him. "I'm sorry, Baby," he said, lifting her head to look at him. "You know I didn't mean to yell at you..."

She halfheartedly jerked her head back and looked away, her lips pursed to a full pout.

"She just makes me so damn crazy, and that bitch Olivia too...You know I wasn't mad at you, I would never mean those things I said to you," he said and stepped closer.

She glanced up at him as he scooted closer, playing the part of the scorned woman, but they both knew she would never turn her back on him.

"Awe come on, Baby, don't be like that," he said, wrapping an arm around her waist and pulled her closer.

Her plump lips pouted as she looked up with playful eyes. "You hurt my feelings," she said through a huff, but rubbed a finger on his arm.

He choked back a grin. "I'm sorry, Baby, I didn't mean to," he said, ran a fingertip along her collar bone, and slid the shirt down exposing a breast. She teasingly swatted his hand away and he chuckled. "Oh, come here." He picked her up and carried her to the sofa behind them.

****

Emma craned her neck around the corner of the house, lifted her robe and dashed across the large, open lawn. She looked around, panting as she tapped on Prudence's door.

"What the hell—" Prudence said, cracking the door open. "Emma!" She peered around the door, opened it and pulled Emma in. "What are you doing here?" she said, peeking out the tiny window in paranoia.

Emma huffed trying to catch her breath and collapsed on the bed. "I—" she panted. "I had to...talk to you."

"Oh God, Emma, this is a really bad idea," she said as she sat beside her.

Emma was the palest of white, looking up at Prudence with bloodshot eyes. "I don't know—" Emma breathed.

Prudence put a hand on Emma's back. "It's ok, breathe."

Emma took a moment to catch her breath, looked around aimlessly then shrugged. "I don't know what. But something is wrong, I can feel it," she said, glancing at Prudence with wet, fretful eyes.

"Has he been, you know?" Prudence said.

"No," Emma said with wide eyes. "That exactly what's wrong, it's the opposite." She shook her head. "I know he wouldn't do something like this without wanting or planning something."

"Maybe he's done something wrong, feels guilty?"

Emma looked at her as if she had uttered the strangest of insanities.

"I know," Prudence said, throwing her hands up. "I've got nothing. Nothing about this place makes a damn bit of sense to me. How did it go with James? I've been waiting to find out."

Emma took a deep breath. "Strange."

"Oh...I'm sorry."

"I cried terribly, and that doesn't usually mean you're enjoying yourself. But even still, it was okay," she said, and picked up the Polaroid off the alarm clock. "I know that can't possibly make sense to you." Emma wanted to tell her of the photograph James had shown her, of her dreams and this knowing in her soul that they were meant to be together. And maybe already have been. "He wants me to leave Craig," she said, staring at the fluffy dog in the photo.

"You will."

"I know but." Emma rubbed her forehead. "I don't know. His wife cheated, left him...I think he's scared too, you know?"

"Cheated on him? Yeah, I can see how he'd be scared then," Prudence said.

Emma's look cast down onto her fidgety hands and twirled her feet around. "I can't make sense of myself. I know it's stupid, it is—"

"What are you going to do about Craig? Do you think he knows?" Prudence said, nodding toward the main house.

"It feels insane that I would be terrified that my husband tried to be...attentive. I mean isn't that how husbands are supposed to be?" Emma said to herself.

"Well, he's not exactly the average husband, you know?" Prudence turned to face Emma square. "You know what he's going to do, he's going to kill you someday. Maybe an accident or something, I don't know, but—"

"God, maybe I am the sissy he thinks I am?"

"Abusive people can mess you up in the head, ain't your fault."

"My parents would be so disappointed in me," Emma said, shaking her head and wiping her teary eyes on her sleeve. "I guess it's good they're not around to see what I failure I am, huh?" she said with a pathetic chuckle and raising her shameful eyes to Prudence.

"I, I don't really know what to say. I don't really think your parents would be the type to think that sort of thing..."Prudence pursed her lips as she shrugged.

"I mean look at me, hiding in my maid's room, counting on her to pawn stuff to help me buy fake ID's." Emma raised her watery eyes to the ceiling. "I'm like a bad Lifetime movie," she tried to laugh, biting her lip as tears trickled down her cheek.

"Oh, Emma, uh," Prudence said, looking around her for tissues.

"I just want to be with James," Emma said through a sob and covered her face. "I want to leave."

Prudence wrapped an arm around Emma's heaving shoulders and rubbed her arm. "You're trying to."

"Who cares about money? I have to, I—"

Emma curled up into a ball and sobbed into her closed arms until exhaustion slowed her crying to a whimper. Without the comfort of James arms this tiny, ramshackle room was the safest place she could think of to hide. Prudence pulled the comforter over Emma's pitiful body and shut out the light.

****

Craig spent the night holding Sheila in his arms in her lush, king-size bed. Bright city lights beamed in through the huge window above them as horns honked on the street below. The thick, hot air blew in through the screens. Brief sanity came over him in the moment of relaxation, and he contemplated what to do with Emma. Showing affection proved to be useless, the stupid bitch cowering and vomiting on herself from his slightest touch. *So what to do with her?* With no more rumors flying around him, people were getting bored and moving on to the next scandal. *What would help the election,* he wondered as he slowly slid out of the bed, not wanting to disturb peaceful Sheila.

Stark naked in front of her windows, he grabbed the wine from her nightstand and took a swig from the bottle. He rubbed his hand on his bristly chin. "She's left me no other option," he whispered, finished off the bottle and nodded his head. He fumbled with buttons on the alarm clock, to get it all done he needed to be in the office early. Craig pulled his wedding band off his finger and held it up to the window, sighing as he twisted and turned it in the glowing light of the moon. *This is it,* he thought as he pushed the ring back on, slid back into bed and pulled Sheila against his chest.

Twenty-one

Prudence shook Emma's shoulder. "Emma, Emma. You have to go," she whispered.

Emma rubbed her eyes. An exhausting fog filled her head as she looked around. "What?"

"You have to go, people are starting to walk around," Prudence said, pulling the covers off of Emma.

Emma jolted up. "Oh my God, what time is it?"

"Quarter after five. You have to go before someone sees you."

Emma threw the covers off and ran to the door. "Thank you," she said over her shoulder, then cracked the door open and ran outside.

Edward stood in the shadows of the pool house, cupping his morning coffee as he observed the waking of the household. A strange sensation floating in the air promised a day full of pandemonium. Emma's figure dashed across the yard, her silk robe flapping behind her like a cape. *She must have come from the servant's rooms*, he thought as he blew on his coffee.

"What a peculiar thing," he said to himself. "Now why on earth would she be over here?" He slid a hand into his pocket, running the inner fabric between his fingers. "Perhaps she's taken up with one of the groundskeepers?" he said, watching her vanish into the house. "Interesting indeed..."

He slithered around the house in his usual fashion, silently observing, until an hour had passed and he wandered upstairs. "Good morning, ma'am, I trust you slept well?" he said with an unusually cheerful smile.

"Have you seen Mr. Beckett yet?" Emma said.

"I presume he's out for the day, and he hasn't left any orders for me," he said as he held up Emma's sweater and she slid her arms in the sleeves.

A terrible feeling swirled in the pit of her stomach. *Why would Craig just disappear? What is he up to?*

"Would you, would you call his office and check for me please?"

He cocked his head taking in her colorless image. The blood washed from her face, turning her peachy skin a dull, beige-gray, highlighted by dark circles encompassing her swollen eyes.

"Yes, of course," he said and nodded. "I'll do that right now."

Emma didn't have wits about her to notice his easy tone or soft demeanor, and sat simply nibbling her fingernail. In a daze and trying to sift through explanations, her exhausted mind only called out for James.

A few minutes later Edward returned. "He'll be out for the day with meetings, Mrs. Beckett."

"Are you absolutely certain?" she said, not thinking how the tone of her question might sound.

"Quite. I am placing a guess that he might be gone for the night as well ma'am."

She looked up at him questionably.

"Judging by his secretary's tone that is," he said. "Or perhaps, well, at least you should be."

Her brows scrunched. "Edward?"

"Please, it would be best," he said and took a step toward her.

"Edward, what do you mean?" she said, leaning away from him.

"Ma'am, I just ask that you trust me. Be home as little as possible, it's best for everyone," he said and then stepped out of the room.

Without cause, she trusted her enemy and picked up the phone.

"Hello!" he said, picking up on the first ring.

"Can I see you?" she said.

"Oh, thank God it's you," James said in a sigh.

"What? What's the matter—"

"I just, I've had this—I'm so glad you called."

Her head started to spin; nothing felt right. "Can I see you? Please, I need to."

"Where?"

"I'll come to your store, if that's okay?"

"Yes, please, hurry."

****

Although Edward had worn his best navy, pin-striped suit to trick himself into believing he was worthy to stand among them, the glares and snide whispers from customers around him devoured his false sense of confidence. As he wandered around the posh sushi bar trying to find her, he felt belittling eyes on him from all directions all wondering what someone like him would be doing in their restaurant. Glimpses of evil amusement and curled lips caught his attention as he circled around the smoking section one last time.

He heard her obnoxious giggle coming from the patio. He peered around a pillar and saw her slender silhouette surrounded in a cloud of smoke, flirting with the bartender at the bar.

He came up behind her, cocked his shoulders back and raised his chin as he cleared his throat.

She spun around on the barstool. "I don't want a menu," she said, shooing her hand at the strange man.

"Ms. Child, I am not your waiter."

She eyed the gangly looking man as she shook a finger at him. "I know you, don't I?"

"Yes, although not formally."

"Ugh, but how?" she said, tugging on his twenty dollar tie.

He tipped his head to the empty seat beside her "May I?"

"I think," she said, staring at him as he sat. "What do you want?"

"We have a common interest—"

"We couldn't possibly!"

"In Mr. Beckett."

Olivia fell silent in mid-laugh, scooted the stool closer and whispered, "Are you Johnny's *friend?*"

"Johnny? I'm sorry, I don't—"

"Well, shit. What do you want then?" she said, quickly losing interest.

"I know that you're up to something. You're plotting something, aren't you?"

"Look at the balls on you! What on earth could give you that impression? You know nothing about me," she said, curling her lip at his sickly face. "I'm simply having a few drinks with some new friends. Isn't that right, Brandon," she said and tapped the bartender's hand. "And here you are, accusing me of things," she said to Edward.

He grew impatient with her insults. "Emma's journal, amongst other things, suggested—"

"Oh, you're, you're. Shit, who are you?" She snapped her fingers as she thought. "The Butler!" she said, and then cast a stern look at him. "What the hell are you doing reading her personal property? I should have you arrested!"

"Let's skip the inquisition shall we? I have limited time—"

"Damn right you have limited time, explain yourself, peasant boy," Olivia said, turning her attention back to her drink.

"I have sent Craig anonymous packages, with very interesting contents. The first alone, should it fall into the right hands, could ruin him."

"You're the red packages!"

"How do you know about them? How's that possible?"

"Craig came barging into my house the other day; I thought the slimy prick was going to kill me."

"I presume I am correct that you have started a little, *project* shall we say, of your own?" he said.

"I've collected some very interesting information, yes, but despite Johnny's confidence, I fear it's not enough."

"What's in it for you?"

"Excuse me?" she snapped, cocking her head as she glared.

"What's your motive? I'm sure it's not money," he said, helping himself to the olive in her martini.

"He's an evil bastard, the shit he has done to that poor girl...he deserves every bit of payback I can dish out." Not wanting to show emotions, she smiled and lit another cigarette. "What do you want with him?" she asked.

"To ruin him ...' he said, picking up the martini the bartender set on a napkin for him. "Money, everything important to him," he said, spinning the olive in his drink.

Olivia tapped the sword-shaped toothpick on her glass, and then waved it at him as she said, "What do you have on him? I mean how good is it, really? I find it hard to believe someone like you could, well—"

"I have everything straight from his files. It doesn't get any better, honestly."

Olivia's mouth rose to a brilliant smile. "Well then, I think we might be able to work something out. I have money, and you have information," she said, holding her glass up.

Edward nodded, and they clinked their glasses together in a silent toast.

****

Emma didn't hesitate to slip on another pair of old jeans and her faded, slightly shrunken Coca-Cola t-shirt. After twenty minutes of riffling through shoes, she gave up on her search for sneakers and opted for a pair of casual leather flats. She pulled her wavy locks into a loose ponytail.

Her breath quickened as she pulled up to the building, and her tension worn face relaxed into an easy smile. Emma didn't even have her purse out of the car when she saw James jogging toward her. *He must have been waiting at the window* she thought as he picked her up in mid-stride.

"I was so worried," he said through an exhale.

"Why?" she said, burying her face in his shoulder.

"I've just had this weird feeling that I can't shake. Like watching too many scary movies or something before you go to bed," he said and let out a soft chuckle, set her down and kissed her forehead. "Come on, let's go."

"Where?"

"Somewhere, anywhere, I don't care really."

There wasn't much town to drive through, and even fewer places they could go where James wouldn't be bothered with curious intrusions. After his divorce, he swore women off and slipped into a new role as another bitter man burned by a selfish, cheating wife. If they saw him tromping around town with an attractive woman in tow, there would be an onslaught of questions he wasn't sure if he could even answer. For the sake of seclusion, he took her to his small apartment at the edge of town.

As he opened the door, he quickly bent over to pick up misfit socks and empty take-out containers scattered throughout the room.

"I'm sorry, it's awful in here. I don't really have company much."

"No, no, it's fine," she said and tried to offer a smile.

He hobbled through the room picking up random bits from the floor and tables until he had a heaping pile in his arms. He squeezed the stack, using his neck to stop the overflowing belongings from falling. "If you'll excuse me, I just need to…" he said, trying to nod his head toward the other room.

"Sure," she said.

The apartment was the epitome of a bachelor pad, aside from the odd assortment of antiques throughout the room. He lived in a hodgepodge space filled with hand-me-down tweed sofas, mismatched end tables and outdated ceramic lamps with crooked shades. The collected belongings made it painfully obvious to Emma that his ex-wife left with more than just his heart. She took everything. In the center of the small room sat a large, painted coffee table, riddled with old magazines with worn pages and torn corners.

She bent over and flipped through them. Entertainment Weekly, Sports Illustrated, Forbes. A decent-sized TV stood by the window, atop a beautifully crafted old-English armoire scooted in the corner. Small sprinklings of dust fell from the top of the shabby drapes when she pulled them open.

Above the plaid sofa was a chaotic collage of family photos in cheap, wooden frames. She saw pictures of James as a child; a lanky boy with wiry dark hair standing next to a handsome soldier, his glowing mother stood proudly in front of the two at the curb of a small white duplex. She had been so entranced with the photos that she hadn't noticed him standing there.

He chuckled and pointed to a photograph. "My first truck," he said with a nostalgic grin. "I saved all summer for that thing, $600 the guy wanted. Three-hundred and seventy-two lawns I mowed for that. "

"Is that your mother?" she asked, pointing to a slender woman in a tan dress at Niagara Falls.

"That's Mom on their honeymoon," he said, reaching for the frame and rubbed a layer of dust off with his sleeve. "She got so mad at Dad taking her there, she always hated water. She fell off a boat once as a kid I guess, almost drowned, never went near a beach again," he said, gazing at the photo again before putting it back on the wall. "Well, it ain't much, but it's what I've got," he said, gesturing at the room. "I'd give you the tour, but there's only two other rooms."

"No it's, uh, it's lovely," she said.

"Well no, but thanks, I appreciate the effort," he said with a smile then settled himself on the sofa, grabbed a belt loop on her jeans and pulled her down beside him.

"How come you never bought another house after the divorce?" she asked, lying down to use his thigh as a pillow.

He shrugged. "I always thought of homes for *families*, you know? Moms and Dads, kids running around and all that."

"Is that what you want, or, wanted I mean? A wife and kids?"

He rubbed his chin and half-shrugged his shoulders. "I did before, with Mary. After the divorce...I don't know. I like my life all right now, living here, going on the road looking for things for the shop. It's good, it suits me."

She closed her eyes imagining them driving through hidden country roads, searching old barns and homes on a quest for little treasures.

He traced his finger around her ear to the nape of her neck, sighed and said, "But ever since I met you, I've been wondering what it would be like to try again. Get a little house someplace quiet, like—"

"The cottage," she said.

"The things we could do to fix that place up. I know just the place to get hinges for the windows, and the tile—" he said. A sweet fire lit up his eyes and she could see the ideas swirling around inside his head. "This is crazy talk, isn't it? You and me like that?"

She sat up, resting her elbows on her knees. "I don't know, James, I'm trying. I'm here with you now, aren't I?"

"I don't want just *right now*, and then you run home. I want to do things like get the little cottage, I can tinker with that old boat and you can plant flowers in the garden and—"

"Oh, James, please don't—"

"But you want that too, don't you? Like in the photo of us. Don't you believe that's how it's supposed to be?"

"I need another month, James. I have it all planned out, everything left to do so he can't track me down," she said, leaning over hoping to catch his worried stare. "One month, that's it."

"How can I be sure it won't be one month, and then you're just gone? Like I'm your rebound guy or something? Or after a month, you want another month, what then?"

"You don't really think that, do you?" she said, bending her head to lock her eyes with his.

"I really want to trust you, I do. But—" He ran his hand through his hair as he looked at the ceiling. "I mean you get how I might be worried about this, right?"

"And you get that if I'm sloppy about leaving, he'll send goons to track me down, don't you?"

"What a pair, you and me." He tried to laugh to ease the tension as he shook his head. "Stars must've been drunk trying to get us together." He bent and rubbed his forehead. "God, what am I doing?" he said to himself.

"Maybe the stars just took too long to align or something?" Emma said and tried to smile. "We both need to trust each other, hard as it is," she said, staring at her feet.

"You're crazy for being here," he said, cocking his head toward her. "And I'm crazy for inviting you."

"Birds of a feather flock together?" she said, cringing with a hesitant smile.

"What am I going to do with you?" he laughed, wrapping an arm around her shoulder and kissed her forehead.

Twenty-two

"Mr. Mitchell has signed the proposal. And that younger one, Harry something? He wired the money this morning," Sheila said, racing behind Craig as he returned from a morning in court.

"Beautiful," he said with a sly grin. "See, they can't break me!"

"No of course they—"

"Get a hold of my accountant, tell him to transfer the money back here to the States. I need it and it doesn't matter at this juncture. The paper trail is already there."

"Of course, is there anything else?" she asked as she scribbled notes on her yellow legal pad.

Craig sat on the edge of his desk, groaning as he thought about Emma sitting at home, useless as always.

"Rick Schneider, give him a call and tell him I need a favor. Some information."

She peered at him from her notepad, her pen stopped in midswoop on the paper as an eyebrow rose with excited curiosity. He nodded as his pinched, stressed face relaxed into a smirk.

"Of course, I'll do that right now!" she said, trotting out of the office with a bounce in her step.

****

"No, no, no, that would never work! Albeit disgusting, he is a very intelligent man, he would never fall for something so silly," Olivia said. "Sonya! We need more drinks," she hollered over her shoulder.

"Do you have any suggestions then? Seems I am the only one who has come up with ideas," Edward said.

She took an exasperated breath, flicking a wrist toward him as she bent her head and pinched the bridge of her nose.

Edward tipped his head back to soak up the grandeur of the room. Mammoth coliseum posts made a demanding entry to the two-story high room, with a glorious mural on the coved ceiling. Before he left today, Edward thought the Becketts' home something grand and demanding of awe, but compared to Olivia's home, the Becketts' could be the servant's quarters.

"Do you suppose that we should just be honest with him? Tell him our demands and the repercussions should he not fulfill them?" Olivia asked, turning to face the odd butler across from her. "Honesty isn't my usual approach, but in this case—"

Edward rather enjoyed the idea of finding more suitable ways to drag out the demise of Craig. "I'm sure that we can come up with *something.*"

Olivia focused her scowl out the French doors as she leaned against the doorframe. "I don't see how it's possible, without dragging this out far too long. We mustn't let Emma suffer through that torture."

"Yes, yes of course. While I hoped to put him through as much pain as possible, letting him feel every twist of the dagger…she too would be in so much pain because of it." He strolled across the shiny, bamboo floor and stood beside Olivia.

"I suppose your idea is best. When shall we do it then?" he asked.

"As soon as possible, of course. I need to call Johnny, and then I will let you know the details from there," she said, her gorgeous face lighting up with a smooth smile. "I assume I can call you, no?"

"Yes, of course. Every call goes through me," he said, as if that somehow made him more significant than a mere employee.

The horizon hinted at a beautiful sunset on the dazzling home, and she had had her fill of the weasel-like butler. There was much to be done, calls to make, money to be wired, and she didn't need his company to do it. She turned abruptly, crossing her arms on her chest. "Well then, that will be all." She nodded toward the door behind him. "You can let yourself out," she said, turning her back to him as she walked through the opposite doorway.

****

James took Emma to a Mexican restaurant in the next town; a small place with all the expected décor of traditional American dinning. Plush tan chairs, pale mustard walls, frosted pendant lights above the tables, but the moment James opened the door Emma's senses were filled with the aroma of authentic Mexican cooking. She eyed the tostadas on passing trays as patrons devoured the homemade salsa and chips at their tables.

"Are you sure you don't have to go back yet?" James asked.

"I'm not really sure about anything these days."

"So you're just winging it, is that what you're saying?"

"Craig basically said he wants to work on *us*, but that's dead. We both know it." She scooted salsa around with a spoon, with her static stare on the plump chunks of tomatoes. "Something feels strange there, something in the air, the way he's acting. I don't know, I can't really figure it out," she said and brought her gaze up from the bowl.

"I'm not exactly the guy to promote divorce or nothing, normally I'd have a few choice words for a guy sitting here, doing what I'm doing," he said, rubbed his scrunched up forehead then took a drink of his soda. "But you should just leave the guy. Obviously you guys aren't going to work things out. You're just beating a dead horse, aren't you?"

Emma looked up at his pure, emerald eyes. She hated herself for putting him through this. "I suppose I'm just too scared, like he says I am," she said, blinking to wash tears from her eyes. "I don't care about money, really I don't. But I know my husband, know his ways of dealing with people. He'd rather have me buried in a ditch than let me walk away," Emma said, shuddering as she closed her eyes.

"I mean I'm sure the guy probably cared about you at some point, but come on, look at what he's done to you."

"He probably loved me?"

"You know what I mean, don't get defensive, Emma."

"I don't mean to, but you have to respect the difficult position I'm in here."

162

"Emma, stay with me. We'll work it out together," he said, reaching across the crowded table and lay his hand on her forearm.

"Please don't do this to me. I have to do this right. I can't spend the rest of my life always looking over my shoulder, don't you understand?"

"What about love? That has to count for something, doesn't it—"

"Please, James," she said through a sob, covering her face with the sage-green napkin.

He gently pulled her hands down to uncover her face. "It's not about fear or loose ends, it's about doing the right thing. We're meant to be together. I can't figure it out, but you know I'm right." He rubbed his forehead.

"James, I need a month. I need to walk away and know he can't track me down. Okay?"

"If we're going to be together, I mean that's the plan, right? Then why can't we work it out together, I mean really—" He sighed and leaned back.

Emma was grateful the waiter came with their entrees, and tried to lighten the mood with lighter conversation. She shared stories of the days from her past, on the farm and at the factory. Word by word, her past rumbled to the surface. Slowly they started to relax again, forgetting the strain of their worries and immersed themselves in the moment they shared that night.

With the smallest gesture or faintest smile James flashed, Emma's broken soul started to mend and she felt life churning inside of her. She forgot the lies she told, the people she helped ruin, and the façade she helped Craig paint. She laughed until her sides hurt, joked and flirted.

"So I'm standing in the factory, drenched with sweat because the place didn't have any AC. I'm on my second shift, exhausted," she said, pausing to finish chewing a bite of food. "Then the belt or something on the machine breaks, starts making this weird grinding noise. When all of a sudden, poof!" she said, raising her arms up above her head. "This explosion of brown cotton fluff comes flying out of the machine and sticking to me everywhere." She leaned across the table, helping herself to a bit of his enchilada. "I start thinking about Caddy Shack, the little gopher, you know?"

Emma puffed up her cheeks, wiggling on the seat as she performed her dancing gopher imitation.

James snorted, almost choking on his mouthful of food as he laughed.

"I still don't know how I didn't get fired, man was my boss pissed!" she laughed.

"You make a rather fine gopher," he said and laughed.

"Everyone has to be good at something, right? I'm not nearly as hairy as he is though, so you can't quite get the full effect of the dance."

"God, I hope you're not that hairy," he said with a smirk. "I might have to re-think some things about you if you are, get you some coupons for Nair or something," he said with a playful grin.

She sat back, still chuckling, and rubbed her bloated belly.

"Come on, Hairy, let's get out of here," he said and tossed two, twenty-dollar bills on the table.

"Just let me finish this," she said, and dug her spoon back into the bowl of fried ice-cream. She dragged out dinner as long as possible, even ordering a desert she had no room for to avoid the night coming to an end. *Maybe I could order one more margarita*, she thought, leaning over the table to eat the last bite.

"Crap," she said, watching the chocolate covered ice-cream fall from the spoon and roll down her shirt. *Wonderful*, she thought, *just wonderful.*

The ride back was quiet. Neither wanted the night to end but knew it had to. James helped Emma out of the car, and then waited, fumbling with his keys as they stood in the parking lot of his apartment complex.

"Do you mind if I clean up?" she asked, pointing to the stain on her shirt.

"Of course, come on up," he said with a grin.

Once upstairs, he opened the door for her and flipped on a few lamps.

"Can I get you something to drink?" he asked halfheartedly, knowing she would be leaving.

"I can't believe I dropped the ice-cream like that," Emma said, rubbing the splotch of hot fudge on her shirt.

"You want a wet rag for that maybe?" James asked, walked to the kitchen and started rifling through a drawer.

God what an idiot, I can't believe I did that. Jesus, Emma, she thought. "Um, I think I need to scrub it actually. Do you mind if I uh—"

"Sure, bathroom is through the bedroom there," he motioned with a nod from the kitchen, reached in the fridge and opened a beer.

"Thanks, I'll only be a minute."

Emma took her shirt off in the bathroom, soaked it under hot water and started scrubbing it with a bar of soap. *I can't believe I did that! Why am I so clumsy around him? He looks at me and I turn into rambling, klutzy moron.* As she thought, she scrubbed harder, dragging the bar across the soft fabric so rough it started separating the threads. "Get a hold of yourself, Emma...you're an intelligent, capable woman," she whispered to herself, rinsing out her shirt. "You've hosted parties for Governors, judges. You've had Spielberg over for dinner for God's sake. Pull yourself together," she said firmly to her reflection in the mirror.

"Do you have a t-shirt or something I can borrow till this dries?" she hollered through the bedroom, hanging the soaked, wrinkled shirt on a towel rack.

"Yeah, um, there's probably something in the long dresser there, top drawer," he said from the living room.

She took a quick peek into the bedroom and then flicked on a lamp. She skimmed the first drawer: boxers, socks and rolled-up ties.

"Which drawer?" she said as she pulled open the next drawer.

"The one on the right, it's got some—" he said, halfway through the door and stopped, paralyzed by her exposed skin covered only by a white, lace-trimmed bra.

She instinctively grabbed the first thing she saw to cover her chest. She tried to swallow the lump in her throat as she watched him admiring her.

"I'm sorry, I—" he said, but his eyes never turned from her bare skin. He stopped in front of her, eyeing her smooth chest covered by an issue of Sports Illustrated.

She felt like she was dissolving with him standing so close, her body so exposed and vulnerable. Tingles stood tiny hairs on end, her heart thudded in her chest. She thought she would melt and turn into nothing more than a puddle of water at his feet.

"I should have knocked," he said, sliding the magazine from her grasp and set it back on the dresser.

Utterly boneless when he looked at her, the tidal wave of emotions his gaze brought almost made her collapse into his arms. He glided a hand down her heaving, goose-bump covered chest. Her mouth cracked open, *don't, don't,* she thought as his fingertip traced the waves of her tight stomach muscles. *You'll say something stupid. I should stop him, this isn't right to be doing this...*

"You're so beautiful," he said, with his hands around her back and rubbing below the clasp on her bra.

"James, I—we shouldn't," she said, but found her hands pulling his shirt over his head as he unhooked her bra.

His hands studied her naked torso, then wrapped around her neck and gently pulled her forward and pressed a hard kiss on her lips. She almost crumpled from the pleasure of his tongue. He guided her to the bed, sat down and ran his hands down the curves of her waist as she stood in front of him.

"God, you're sexy..."

"James, I—" she breathed, feeling beautiful in his presence. She wanted to stop, but stepped closer and ran her fingers through his wispy hair.

He pulled her into an embrace and slid her onto the bed. "Say that you'll have me," he whispered, nuzzling his face on her neck and pecked slow kisses on her hot skin.

She wanted to protest, knowing it was wrong. *You're a married woman, what are you doing,* she screamed inside her head.

"I've never felt so wanted before," she said, almost embarrassed by his awe.

"You're the sexiest woman I've ever seen," he whispered, sat up and ran his hand down her stomach and stopped at the button on her jeans.

The air in his tiny bedroom was palpable. Her breath stuttered, she thought her heart might implode from the tenderness of his touch. She reached down and unbuttoned her jeans.

"Are you sure?" he said.

She let her hand rest on his smooth, firm chest and felt the pounding of his heart underneath her fingertips as their eyes locked. "Absolutely," she whispered, and pulled him into her arms.

She never felt awkward or like she had to perform for him, be sexier than she really was or more excited than she felt. She felt his love pour through in every touch, in every sweet word whispered in her ear as they each rolled around and explored the other's body. She felt sexy and desired, safe and loved. She found herself moving in ways she never thought she could.

They lay exhausted and panting in feverish satisfaction. He wrapped an arm around her as she snuggled up beside him, resting her head in the crook of his arm. He caressed her sweaty shoulder and leaned forward to kiss her on the forehead.

"All these years, I never knew what I was missing," he whispered.

"I love you..." she said. Content, she curled up inside his arms, laid her head on his heaving chest and closed her eyes.

The warmth of her delicate skin against his immersed him in a comfort he didn't know he missed. James let himself slip into a daydream of the life they might have together. Of the life they maybe already had together. He was lightly rubbing her hand when his finger caught part of her wedding ring.

Emma felt his muscles tighten. "What's the matter?"

"Nothing I, I just..." he mumbled, rolled over and pulled the covers up. "This isn't right."

Her sagging eyes were now fully awake from the guilt and worry that charged through the momentary pleasure. She rolled over and put a hand on his shoulder, unsure what to say. *He's right*, she thought as her palm lay on his stiff arm, *I can't do this to us, it'll ruin us. I can't be married and be with James and not expect him to be angry.*

"I know," she whispered and kissed his bare arm.

"I don't want to lose you, but I can't be...I don't want to be the other guy, I don't want to sneak around. I hate people like that, and I can't be one."

"I know, I'm just...I don't know what to tell you," she said, pulling on his arm to coax him to look at her. "Please?" she whispered, and finally he rolled to face her. She tried to force a smile as she held her hand to his cheek. "I'll, I'll make this right," she whispered. "I will," she said, leaning forward in hopes of him returning her kiss.

The second her plump lips touched his, he softened, wrapped his arms around her and squeezed the warmth of her body against his chest. He wasn't quite sure what she meant by making it right, but he hoped it meant staying with him. He closed his eyes and pictured them together; her face covered in paint as they worked on the cottage, her swollen belly as they worked in the baby's room, until he drifted to sleep with visions of moments they might never have.

Twenty-three

Craig's car crept down the trash-riddled street. He peered out the window as he read the graffiti covered signs and tried to ignore the menacing onlookers leaning glaring at his car rolling down the street. He found the right building, yet was grateful and utterly terrified to set foot outside of his car in this neighborhood. But he had to do it. She left him no other option at this point.

He stepped into the dimly lit bar, and instantly felt underprivileged eyes boring holes into him from across the room. It smelled of stale beer and cigarettes, and he almost gagged from the overwhelming stench of sweat and filth. Craig paused next to a man at the bar wearing a plaid flannel shirt and grease covered overalls, slouching and chatting with the bartender.

"Um, excuse me?" Craig said.

The man in flannel flicked a peanut shell at Craig's face.

"You lost?" groaned the bartender.

"I'm looking for Derek," Craig said, trying not to look over his shoulder at the man beside him flicking shells at his shoulder. He was old and fat, but the man had huge, bulging arms that twitched almost like they craved to snap Craig in half. He swallowed hard and thought the bartender would never answer him. "Do you know him? I'm supposed to meet him here."

"He's in the booth in the back, sweetheart. Over by the pool tables," the bartender said, nodding his head with a grin.

"Thank you," Craig said.

"Yeah, yeah…" the bartender said waving a hand. "I don't want to hear it, man."

Craig heard the bartender mutter something to the man in flannel as he walked away, and they erupted in laughter at his expense.

"Fuckin' suited pansy!" one of them said, filling the room with their coarse laughter. Craig cringed and tried to keep a calm step.

All he could see was thick smoke swirling around the stained-glass light fixture above the booth. He stopped at the side of the booth and said, "Excuse me, are you, Derek?"

"Hello, Craig. Please, sit down," Derek said, extending his hand to the empty seat across from him.

Derek was a good-looking man, in his late-twenties, Craig would guess, dressed in a fine gray suit, much like something Craig himself would wear. His mousey brown hair was slightly slicked back, and his bright blue eyes felt as if they pierced right through Craig. He looked classy, like he could be charming and easily weasel his way into the likes of Craig's crowd. Craig could see now why Rick recommended him; looking like he did no one up-town would give him a second glance.

Derek slouched, leaning against the dark, wood-paneled wall, one hand cupping a Budweiser bottle as the other held a fat, woodsy smelling cigar.

"So what's your problem, Craig? Rick was a little vague on the details. Little twit is so worried about phone taps, paranoid shit he is," he said, laughing before he sipped his beer.

"Well, it's my wife—"

"It's always the women! God, how them bitches screw us up, huh?"

Craig offered an apprehensive smile and a forced laugh. "Yes I suppose so."

"So what's she done, cheated on you? Take your money? Run off with the pool boy?" he said, sat up and put his forearms on the grimy table.

"No, no, nothing like that."

"Damn, must be a brutal bitch you got. Not many other reasons I can see you needing my employment."

Craig almost chuckled at the word *employment*, as if he were being hired to do something by any means moral or upstanding.

"She, well, she has become quite the problem for me lately. Causing certain people to, let's just say, dig into my past a bit. Which, I'm sure you can understand, that being something I don't want," Craig said.

"And you think I'm the one to handle this problem?"

"I can't see any other option, Derek, if you please," Craig said, sitting back and relaxing a little in the burgundy leather booth, hopeful that the stench of the bar would wash off him when he stepped out into the fresh air.

Derek rubbed his manicured hand on his chin, raising an eyebrow as he eyed Craig. "Well, how would you want it done?"

Craig almost flinched, this side of things he wasn't entirely accustomed to. "I'm not really sure what the options are—"

"Yeah, ain't like I got a menu right!" Derek laughed. "See, it can be nice and neat..." he said, easing back into his slouched position, "She can slip when she's getting in the bathtub let's say, or maybe she has a little car accident, flies off the side of the road..."

Craig tipped his head up a little, picturing Emma crash through a windshield, or found in the bathroom, one foot dangling inside the bathtub, her body on the floor and head cracked open with a pool of blood around her.

"Or we can go the other way, clean shot in the head say. I ain't going to do it with her, smack her around or nothing freaky like that though. That's not my gig, you feel me?" he said, eyes wide with importance. "If you want something like a clean shot to the head it's going to cost extra, cleanup's a bitch."

"Oh no, of course, that won't be necessary," Craig said, somewhat disenchanted. "I suppose it should be something uh...tasteful? I don't need any more suspicion around me."

"Okay, sure thing, man. All I need is her usual schedule, a list of people who'll be around her and all that, beauticians and shit, you know? When you want this done?" he asked, waving his empty beer bottle in the air for another round.

"I'll have to get her schedule from my butler, he knows it best."

Derek raised an eyebrow at him. "You don't even know what she do, who she be with?"

Craig felt a little uneasy in his glare and tried to grin. "Well, she uh, she's such a pain in the ass these days, I just don't want to be around her."

"Bitches can make you so crazy, don't even want to step foot in your own house," Derek said as he shook his head. "So when can you get me the info, man?"

"I'll need to be sure I am somewhere that can be easily verified…" Craig said as he thought out loud. "Give me a couple of days?"

"Say, Thursday?"

Craig drummed his fingers on the table, eyes darting around as he quickly thought about steps that needed to be taken. "Yes, yes, Thursday should be wonderful," he said, as if he were planning a golf outing with a friend.

"You have instructions for payment?"

"That should be taken care of as we speak."

"Great." Derek grinned, then stood and extended his hand. "Pleasure doing business with you, and I'm sorry for your loss," he said and laughed as he shook Craig's hand.

Craig raced back to his office with huge strides through the halls, almost running toward Sheila. She stood up with bright, eager eyes. "Well?"

"Come with me," he said as he walked passed her.

Sheila followed his quick pace into the office and sat in front of his desk. "So what did he say, is he going to do it?" she said and leaned forward.

"I need something solid for Thursday, all day," he said

"Okay, of course. I will be—"

"Not with you. I need something highly visible. I don't want anyone casting any sideways glances at me."

Her excitement faltered. "Oh, I see…"

"I'll be in court all morning, so make sure I'm busy all afternoon and evening, understood?"

"Yes, of course, Craig. Anything you need," Sheila said, scribbling notes.

"Have you taken care of the payment?" he said, blew on his name placard and polished it on his sleeve.

"It was confirmed thirty minutes ago."

"Wonderful…" he whispered as he sank into his chair.

She stood beside him, her hand on his shoulder as a smile slowly crept up and she almost giggled.

Craig gently tapped Sheila's hand, finally relaxing with the weight of his worthless wife soon to be lifted from his shoulders. Then he could handle Olivia, find out who the red packages belonged to, and win the election with the sympathy vote. *It's going to be beautiful*, he thought, closing his eyes as a beaming smile lit up his face.

"Are you going home tonight?" Shelia said with a pouting lip.

He squeezed her hand. "I don't want her to ruin this mood for me."

She perked up, standing with confidence. "She ruins everything."

"Come on, let's go get some dinner. All of this planning has made me hungry," he said with a wide smirk.

****

Emma moaned in bliss as she woke up the next morning still in James' arms. She rolled over and snuggled up against his back. He grumbled and moaned, stretching his arms above his head as he blinked sleep out of his eyes.

"Mmm, I didn't dream it," he whispered, rubbing his cheek against her frizzy locks. "Good morning, Hairy, how did you sleep?" he said with a playful grin.

She rolled over, snickered with a smile and slapped his arm. "I slept fine, thank you. Now stop calling me that," she said through a laugh.

"Do you have to go soon?" he said with squinted eyes, still trying to push the morning fog out of his mind.

"I can stay for breakfast, probably."

"Mmm, breakfast..." he said through a yawn.

He looked like a bear waking from hibernation, groaning and stretching his long limbs like that. "I'll go make us something," she said and climbed out of bed, searching for wherever she threw her clothes last night.

"I'm not sure if I have anything in there," he said as he rolled over, gazing at her while she dressed. The rising sun poured in through the window, almost streaming around her as if she were an angel. He couldn't imagine waking up to anything more beautiful than this.

"I'll whip something up," she said with a smile, plopped down on the bed and leaned over to kiss his forehead. "It's been so long since I've been able to cook something, it'd be a treat really. I'll make something work," she said, her brilliant smile coaxing him into submission. "Just call me Helpful Hairy," she teased from over her shoulder.

"Check the expiration dates, I don't really cook you know," he said with a groggy chuckle.

Emma hummed to herself as she moved around the tiny kitchen, flipping through cabinets and drawers as she made a piecemeal breakfast. It had been years since she had been allowed to set foot near a pan and God forbid, actually use it. There was a time when she could move through a kitchen with fluid-like grace, moving from a stove to cupboard in one smooth motion, chopping and sautéing a mouthwatering meal. Now she leaned against the counter, the pan behind her smoking from the burner being on too high, scrunching her lip as she read the back of a pancake mix box.

She strolled into the bedroom with a cookie sheet, carefully sat down and placed the tray on the bed. James sat up, taking a deep breath as the scent of syrup filled the room.

"What do we have here?" he said with a smile.

"Um, I think breakfast. Possibly. You're okay with food poisoning, right?"

"Well, not really." He chuckled while dipping his finger in the syrup. "But I'm hungry enough to give it a whirl. Can you dial 911?"

"You've been warned, so you can't say anything if this turns you green," she said. "The eggs are, well..." she said, skeptically poking the yellow pile with her finger. "They look a little weird, but I *think* they're okay. You try first," she said, handing him a forkful.

"Oh sure, make me the test dummy," he said and slid the fork in his mouth. "Aren't cooks supposed to taste their food before they serve it?"

"I wanted to make a nice berry crepe, but your flour has somehow turned into one big clump. I didn't know it could do that," she said and cringed. "And then I looked in your fridge and realized, um, yeah, single guys don't have fresh fruit."

"I get pineapple on my pizza sometimes, does that count?"

"Not so much, but good try." She chuckled, leaned over and kissed him on the cheek.

They snuggled up together on the bed, picking at the hodgepodge breakfast as he flipped through the sports pages while she read the local headlines. The paper was packed with stories about high school fund raisers, a barn raising celebration and new computers for the Sheriff's Department. The ease of the lazy, normal morning enveloped her, making her so relaxed she forgot that her world was far outside the realms of this one. She belonged in public solitude of the loveless obligation of marriage.

James folded up the paper and set it next to his empty plate. "You're going soon, aren't you?"

Tension crept up her back and shoulders. "I can't stay all day."

He watched her for a moment; she looked stunning sitting there in his button-down shirt, her hair tangled and pulled up into a sloppy ponytail. "You don't have to go you know...this is nice, isn't it?" he said as he reached for her hand.

She glanced up at him, his hopeful eyes looking right inside of her. "It is but..." The thought of stepping back into that vile house was like erosion, slowly tearing her apart. A stabbing pain twisted in her gut, madness brewed in the suffocating air and she was petrified about going back to it. *I can't just disappear.*

"I'm sorry, James, I have to go back. I can't just walk off and not come back. Reality doesn't work like that," she said, a mournful look shrouding her eyes.

"Why can't you just take off? Your marriage is dead right? You don't even like that life."

She chuckled in astonishment. "What would happen if I just took off like that?" she said, almost rolling her eyes.

"You'd have me. I'd take care of you."

"And I'd have God knows how many of Craig's *people* hunting me down. I have to go, I'm sorry. It just, things don't work so easily like that."

He closed his eyes and nodded his head. "I'm not going to argue with you."

She took James' absolute silence as a sign that he no longer cared to continue the conversation, so she helped herself to his shower, washing away the scent of his cologne on her skin, got dressed and pulled her hair back up. She stared at herself in the mirror, hit by a wretched pang from the nagging voice that begged her to stay.

As she walked into the living room, she saw him fully dressed and waiting for her on the sofa. A lost, empty look blanketed the sweetness of his eyes cast toward a splotch of something on the floor.

She coughed to break him from his daze. "I think I'm ready."

They walked to her car without words. She leaned against the driver's door, spinning the key ring around her finger as the silence wore on.

"I don't want to say goodbye again," he said, raising his look from the ground to her eyes.

It knocked the wind out of her, she wanted to gasp but nothing came out. She didn't want to be alone, without him. Her limbs hung at her sides like a bulky purse resting on a tired shoulder, she stammered trying to think of what to say. "I uh..."

He interlocked his fingers with hers. "This has to be the last goodbye. When I see you again, I don't want there to be anymore goodbyes. I don't want to lose you, Emma," he said, his beautiful eyes sagging in despair. "I don't want to say goodbye again."

She bit her tongue, hating what was about to come out of her mouth. "But what if I can't stay the next time I see you? I need another month, you know that," she whispered.

He let go of her hand and slid his into his pocket. "Then it would be the last goodbye...I can't keep doing this," he murmured.

Her eyes started watering, but she could not bring herself to fight with him. She held her breath, tears on the brink of pouring out as she said, "Okay..." turned and got into her car. To kiss him or say goodbye would be more than she could bear, she would crumble before him and be nothing but a blubbering mess.

He shielded his eyes as the car drove into the distance, reached the top of the hill and disappeared into the valley. He slouched, wilted and beaten, like a wax candle that's been burning too long. He slid his hands into his pockets, gazing in the distance.

"Goodbye, Emma."

Twenty-four

Emma pulled into the empty garage hoping Craig was still out, but fear whirled in her stomach like butterflies with razors strapped to their wings. As she crept into the house, there were no voices or sounds to be heard, the air heavy and suffocating all life inside it. She stepped through the foyer heading for the stairs, almost screaming as Prudence popped out in front of her.

"Where have you been?" Prudence whispered, grabbing Emma's hand and pulled her into the sun room.

Emma scooted close as they sat down. "What's the matter?" she said with bloodshot, fear-filled eyes.

"Something ain't right," Prudence said, stretching out her collar to get more air. "Craig hasn't been home, and Edward is gone. I can't find anyone, it's like everyone just disappeared. It's damn creepy here."

Worry grew heavier on Emma's lungs. She thought of James, of jumping in the car and going back.

Prudence put a hand on Emma's forearm. "But that's not it, it gets weirder."

Emma looked up at Prudence with panic swirling in her ocean eyes.

"I came to see you this morning and I found this on your pillow. Something's crazy wrong, Emma," she said, growing more agitated with her scratchy shirt. "Something's gonna happen," she said, handing Emma a small folded note. "I uh, I already read it. I couldn't help it."

The paper shook in Emma's hand as she unfolded it. "I don't know if I can handle this," she said as she started to read.

> **Dearest Emma,**
> I'm sorry that I wasn't here upon your arrival, but I have many things to tend to of grave importance. I kindly ask that you wait for me, I have much to explain to you.
> **Regards,**
> **Edward**

"Edward?" Emma's heart raced as she loosely clutched the letter between her numb fingers.

"I've been trying to figure out what the hell he's up to, but I just don't know," Prudence said, almost out of breath as she whispered.

Emma turned toward her, her eyes refusing to blink. "I don't know," she muttered. "I never would've expected this."

****

Edward stepped into the huge foyer, the old maid giving him an odd look behind her thick-rimmed glasses. "Right this way, Senor," she said, guiding him through a long hallway. He fidgeted with his beige suit jacket, now knowing nothing he owned was up to their standards. They walked through several rooms, toward a wall of French doors leading out to a deck overlooking a slanted mountainside. She pointed toward the doors. "She wait for you."

His Adam's apple seemed too big and he couldn't swallow the saliva pooling in his cheeks. He tried one last time to choke down the anxiousness boiling inside, taking a deep breath as he turned the knob.

"Edward, right on time," Olivia said, motioning to the empty seat across from her. She looked more casual than he had ever seen her, lounging on her patio in a fluorescent-pink bikini with bulky, gold bracelets on her wrists. Seeing her so unadorned and simple, he imagined that maybe underneath the hard, gold-plated exterior hid a woman soft and caring, secretly craving a life outside of her spotlight.

"Good morning, Ms. Child," he said, pulling out the chair.

"Have you brought all my goodies?" she said, rubbing her hands together.

178

"It's all here. I've gone ahead and made a few sets of copies for you, should you need them," he said, and pulled out a stuffed package from under his arm and placed it on the table.

"Well, wasn't that thoughtful of you," she said, half-mocking the beady-eyed butler. She sat forward, flipped the box open and thumbed through its contents. "How far back does it all go?"

"Since before I started to work for him, and then of course when I did start I was able to attain much more information. You probably have his last six years in your hands."

"You are a vengeful little thing, aren't you?" she said as she laughed, closing the box and leaned back in her chair.

"He's quite deserving of it, don't you agree?"

"What has he done to you, might I ask?" she asked, pulling her sunglasses down over the bridge of her nose.

"No you may not," he said, stiffening in his chair. "Have you arranged payment per my instructions?"

"Yes, yes, exactly as you wanted…" she said, and nibbled an olive.

"So you have the million cash, and the rest was wired to the specified account?"

"I said it was taken care of, so it was." She snickered at him, reached under the table and picked up a handsome, black leather briefcase. "It's all in there." She scooted her package closer, opened it and grabbed a handful of papers. "Are you sure this is good information?"

"The best," he said as he opened the briefcase, desperate to keep a straight face as he marveled at the stacks of one-hundred dollar bills in beautiful bundles.

"It had better be, for the money you wanted," she said. "It's gorgeous, isn't it?" she said, watching him stare in awe at the money.

"Yes, quite. Don't worry, you'll get it back from him. You will make out better in this than I," he said as he closed the briefcase.

"I beg to differ, little mole, I will gain nothing from this—"

"You will have helped a dear friend, will you not?" he said. The end of this being close, his manner softened, letting the human side of him creep back into the open.

"I guess this means I'll be left to wallow and wither in the filth of the upper class alone," she said, and then tried to shake off the sadness. "I am rather excited about my meeting today. It's going to be a glorious day dear Edward, we should celebrate!" she said, grabbing two glasses and a bottle of champagne. "A glorious day indeed!" she said as she popped the cork off the bottle and poured the bubbly beverage.

"Hmm, let's say..." she thought out loud as they held their glasses in the air. "Let's say here is to the...oh screw it, let's crush the bastard!"

Edward nodded his head. "Here here!" he said, smiling as they clinked glasses. "So..." he said, set his glass down and got settled in his seat. "Have you decided how to have it done?"

****

Emma wore a drag pattern across the rug as she paced in her room. Prudence sat at the bay window; wrapping and unwrapping a strap on her apron around her finger. Both women were distraught, and neither knew what to do next.

"Sitting here doing nothing seems stupid," Prudence said, tossing her apron onto the bed.

"What else can we do?" Emma said, pulling on a loose thread in her hemline. "Without Edward here—"

"You think he's really going to help? He seems too, too weaselly or something. I don't trust him."

"Who's to say what his intentions are, that's why we're waiting."

"With that little bit stashed away, you should just take off, don't sit around and wait," Prudence said.

Emma finally stopped pacing and sat on the edge of the bed, *I could do it, just take off. Pack up and not look back, right?*

"So what's it going to be, are we packing or do I have to go back and actually work now?" Prudence said, watching Emma's wandering focus.

"Tonight, I leave tonight—"

"Well hot damn--"

"*After* I speak to Edward," Emma continued, her eyes growing wide with insistence.

Emma could barely focus the remainder of the day, wasting time by showering again and changed into something tasteful as she waited for Craig's arrival and Edwards' surprise. She needed to be presentable, but casual enough for Craig to think she was lounging at home for the day. A flared skirt and chiffon blouse did the trick.

"Do you know if Craig called for me at all while I was gone?" Emma said to Prudence as she fluffed up her hair, agitated with her uncooperative curls. "I hate to think what he would do if he knew I was gone all night."

"It's not my job to answer the phone, and Edward wouldn't tell me anything anyway."

"Oh this is just ridiculous!" Emma said and slammed the brush on the vanity. "I can't sit here and just wait all day!" Emma huffed and crossed her arms. "This is stupid, I can't do this anymore."

****

Craig sat with his feet on the coffee table, papers spread out on his legs and across the cushion beside him on the sofa. He pinched the bridge of his nose. "Sheila!" he said. "You need to have that McGregor guy sign this, and this one, too. You should have known that," he said, glaring at her. "I can't file a petition without his damn signature on it."

"I'm sorry, Craig, I must have been preoccupied at the moment and—"

"I don't pay you to be preoccupied, I pay you to be organized and efficient."

She bent her knee and cocked her hip to the side in a full mopy stance.

He sighed and reached out to her. "Oh, all right, come here."

Her pout perked to a smile, her gray suede skirt sliding up her thighs as she sat down next to him. He slowly rubbed her freckled skin. *Now I remember why I pay her*, he thought as he slid his hand up and down.

"I made all the arrangements for tomorrow," she said, sitting straight with a proud smile.

"Have you now? Do tell, my sweet," he said, raising his eyebrows as he questioned her.

"It's for all day. After the hearing you'll have lunch with the three B's, after that is a meeting at the Drixton Firm for mediation. Then you have drinks with Charles Maco, and then a dinner for the AIDS Foundation," she spouted off and then glanced up from her agenda. "There's no way you'll be home before one in the morning."

"Upon which I will go home, discover Emma's poor broken body—"

"Call the police, just in time to make a morning statement with the press," she said.

"A good start to winning the sympathy vote, and wonderful freedom," he said as he grinned, leaned back and crossed his arms behind his head.

"And then we finally can be together!" Shelia said. Her bright eyes looked up into his, waiting for a grand outpouring of love.

"You know that it would be to my downfall should the moment my lovely wife pass, I pop up in the public eye with a gorgeous young woman on my arm." He brushed her hand off his knee. "It would not set the right image for me, forgetting entirely the suspicion it would arouse. I simply cannot take the risk," he said, patting her on the head as he stood and walked to the desk.

"If you'll excuse me," she managed, and quickly left the room.

He rolled his eyes as the door shut. "Women…" He sauntered to his big leather chair and slid into it. "I'll have to rid myself of her, too," he mumbled to himself, glaring at the door. "She's too clingy, tasty as she is." He quivered, shaking off the burdening thoughts of these women, took a deep breath and smiled; in twelve hours time, he would be a widower.

****

Emma couldn't believe the stillness of the house, and found herself wandering aimlessly through the barren halls. She pushed the ladder in the library and watched it glide across the long track. The clank when it hit the end of the rail seemed incredibly loud in the silent home. She jerked at the bang, half-expecting Craig to jump out of the shadows and scorn her for being so noisy.

She curled up on the chaise by the fireplace. "Why did I have to leave?" she whispered to herself. Her heart ached for James. She turned toward the door ensuring she was alone before she reached for the phone.

"Yeah?" his voice cracked on the other end of the line.

He sounds tired, she thought. "James?"

"Emma, is that you? I can barely hear you."

"It's me. Everything is so quiet here today, I'm afraid to make a sound."

"Is something wrong? Do you need me to come get you?"

"Everything is fine. It's just...something feels off. No one is here, like the house has been abandoned. It's weird."

"Where's your husband?"

"I don't know," her voice shook as she answered. "I just needed to talk to you," she said, clutching the phone with both hands. "I'm sure it's just my imagination," she said and tried to chuckle.

"I'm going to come get you. Something is wrong, I know it," he said, putting his jacket on as he spoke.

"No, I'm fine," she said. "I'm just making something out of nothing, just being silly I'm sure. I just miss you," she said, wishing to be back in his tiny, studio apartment.

"You should've stayed here. I don't know what you thought you were going back for..."

Static filled the line, *why did I even call,* she wondered, *what did I expect him to say?*

"I don't want to argue about it, I get enough arguing here—"

"I love you, and he doesn't. It seems like a no-brainer to me."

"This isn't a cut and dry situation—"

"He hates you," he said softly.

"I, I know."

"Then why don't you just leave—"

"I don't want to go round and round like this—" She cupped her forehead in her palm. "Just know that I love you, okay? I called because I missed you and just wanted to hear your voice, not argue." The silence roared in her ears. She thought for a moment he might have hung up and waited for the sound of the dial tone.

"I love you, too," he finally said.

"I should go; he might be home soon and I shouldn't be caught on the phone—"

"Jesus, Emma—"

"I, I have to go."

"I can't keep doing this, Emma."

"I love you..." she whispered, closed her eyes and hung up.

Twenty-five

"Yes, yes, absolutely. You know how it is. People are always willing to spread rumors about someone against their standings," Craig said with a light-hearted chuckle, reaching out to shake their hand.

"Well, I greatly appreciate you taking the time to clear the air for us. I have to say it was a bit unsettling!" the tall one said as he laughed.

"But it's great to hear that it was all fabricated. People have no morals these days," the wiry man said, shaking Craig's hand as they stepped into the elevator.

"It's been my pleasure to clear that up for you, gentlemen. Do stop by or call any time you have concerns," Craig said with a reassuring smile as the elevator closed.

"Everything go all right?" Sheila said as Craig came back to the office.

"They're back on board," he said as he shuffled by. "It's all coming back together," he said with a grin.

Craig propped his feet up on his desk and took in the beautiful, golden horizon outside the windows, bringing with it the end of his last day as a married man. He pictured himself looming over the cold, metal table in the coroner's office, standing beside her stiff, colorless body underneath the white sheet. He leaned back and smirked.

"Oh Craig, Craig, Craig…it's a truly a breath-taking night, isn't it?" Olivia said, smiling as she surprised him at the doorway.

"I'm sorry, she just barged through!" Sheila said from behind Olivia's arm.

"Oh shoo, we have grown-up things to talk about you twit, and I don't have the time to draw pictures to explain it to you," Olivia said, shutting the door in Sheila's face.

"I should have guessed you would be here again," Craig said, lifting his feet off the desk and turning to face her.

"That's what I always liked about you, Craig. You're such a smart boy."

She looked stunning, her long hair draping over her shoulder, strutting in a curve hugging, v-neck dress. He despised her, but she looked delicious. Her dress hugged her firm backside like a glove as her endless legs took delicate strides across the room.

Olivia made herself comfortable in a chair, crossing her legs in an elegant, exaggerated swoop. She looked up at him, flashing a brilliantly white smile that turned his stomach to knots.

"Let's skip the formalities tonight, shall we?" she said, helping herself to a cigarette. "It's been a daunting day for me, and I simply haven't the energy."

"Yes, lets," he agreed.

"What I am about to propose to you is, well, not so much of a proposition as it is demands," she said as a sly grin peeked out from behind her cigarette. "I have a wealth of information on you. Thanks to my new, thorough partner," she said, letting the words trickle from her lips.

"Partner?" he said.

"He's an odd little man of sorts, rather annoying, honestly. But oh, the information he has collected! Such a useful little thing he is," she said with an excited clap of her hands. "I have enough to not only destroy your beloved election, and your worthless career, but your entire life in our regal hellhole."

Sweat started to bead up on Craig's forehead, and he instinctively loosened his tie. "What do you want?"

"Yes, the demands, of course. I don't want a nasty trail like you have left behind yourself," she snickered as she stood, and tossed a piece of paper on his desk. "So with a little *convincing* from some friends of mine, you might call them my thugs—"

"What did you do?" he snapped, bolting upright in his chair.

"Testy, testy, Craig. Good heavens," she said and patted his shoulder. "I had your accountant take money from these supposed charities and had the funds transferred to my own accounts."

"Is that it, that's all you want? Money?"

"No, darling, it isn't," she said, grinning as she tapped him on the cheek. "You will, quietly, file for divorce. Saying something about how you both have just grown apart or some sweet little sentiment about how you're both still good friends."

Craig burst into laughter. "Why on earth would I do that?"

"Because if you don't, you will force my hand. And you don't want to do that, now do you?" she said, leaning into his face. "This information could fall into the hands of the press...and should that not work, well, then..." she stood straight, examining her nails. "Let's just say I'm sure your funeral will be beautiful."

He fell back in his chair, ripped off his tie and unbuttoned his collar as sweat dripped down his forehead. "Since you already have my money, do I get that information back?" His voice was flat as he spoke.

"Do I look like a fool? It buys temporary silence, darling, and covers the cost I ensued acquiring it," she said, helping herself to his whiskey. "So, Craig, what will it be?" she said, pouring them both a glass and handed him one. "Money and divorce, or sit back and watch all of your hard work fall to pieces?" she said and waited for his reply.

He swallowed the whiskey in one gulp, slammed the glass on the desk and spun around to face his prized wall of plaques. His arms felt so heavy he could barely lift them, but a soft calmness washed over his shaky body, knowing that tomorrow Emma would be dead.

"Money and divorce," he said.

"Smart decision, Craig. You are not to go home tonight. Emma will be informed of your impending divorce and make her own arrangements. You are not to speak to her, you are not to track her down. Do you understand?" she said, whipping his chair around to face her. "Understood?"

He paused for a moment and took a deep, hateful sigh. "Understood," he huffed and spun his chair back around.

"I know where to find you, darling, so please don't be stupid and veer from the course. You'll only make me have to up the stakes should you do that," she said, set her glass on the table and moved toward the door. "Oh and, Craig?" she said, glancing over her shoulder.

"What?"

"Have a lovely evening," she laughed through a gorgeous smile.

He clenched his hands into fists, squeezing so hard his nails pierced his skin. He seethed and kept flicking a lighter. Open close, open close. *Click click click click. Emma will pay for this, she deserved it.* It was tempting to track Derek down and have him finish the job tonight, but he had no alibi. He had a sickening taste in his mouth as her sweet face filled his mind. *She has to pay. Click click click.*

Sheila poked her head into the room. "What happened?"

"Get out…" he said, not breaking from his furious trance.

Sheila's eyes flashed from worry to fear in a blink. She backed out of the door, grabbed her purse and jogged to the elevator. She knew better, this time, than to try and comfort him. Let him take his anger out on *her.*

****

An uneasy feeling lingered in the air as Emma sat at the long dining table alone.

"What am I doing here?" she said to herself. She looked down at her hand, how brilliantly bright her diamond ring looked in the candlelight. It felt so heavy, like a cinder block sat on her hand. She ached to take it off, to pack a bag and go where she was loved. "I can't do this anymore, I can't… I've had enough."

She let out a shaky breath, pushed her chair back, and started to walk out of the room.

A wisp of a moving shadow caught her eye as she walked passed the sunroom in search of Prudence. She cocked her head and peered into the room. "Hello?"

"Good evening, Emma." Edward flipped on the lamp beside him.

"What are you doing here in the dark?" she said, pressing a hand to her startled heart.

"We haven't much time I fear, so I must be brief," he said, reaching for her hand to guide her to the chair across from him.

Emma cocked her body away from him. "Edward, I can't, I have to—"

"Please, ma'am, you know I would not ask if it were not imperative."

"I'm leaving, and I won't be stopped," she said and tried to stand.

"It's about Craig," he said as he grabbed her arm.

"What, what is?" she said, hesitantly sitting back down.

"He has done many evil things, far beyond what you know," he said, placing a hand on her forearm, refusing to let her leave. "I have watched in silence for years, just waiting for the right time."

Her body stiffened. She leaned back trying to create an invisible barrier between them. "What are you talking about, Edward?" she said, an unsettling feeling growing into a full storm.

"He has ruined many people, shattered their lives—"

"Edward, please—"

"And I have done many hurtful things, ignored much that I shouldn't have."

"I don't understand what you're saying, Edward—"

"Its time for him to pay for what he's done."

The words seemed to drop on the floor in front of her. She could almost hear its thud.

"What do you mean, time for him to *pay*?"

"Everything will be taken from him. Everything. His career, his money, every superficial thing he clings to."

"Is that what you've been up to? Sneaking around and plotting like Craig does?" she said, pressing a hand to her lips as she tried to breathe. "What have you done? Do you know what he'll do to you—"

"I have partnered with someone, someone much stronger than me. She'll ensure my safety and that he pays," he said with urgency, cocking his head down to pull her focus back.

"You're doing all this because you want, want revenge? Is that it? I don't understand why you're telling me this."

"He won't tolerate you for much longer, especially now. For your safety, you must leave."

The word *tolerate* echoed in her ears, as if her life had been set to a timer, held in Craig's hands. "Edward, I was leaving, right now—"

"Here—" Edward said, reaching behind him and picked up the black leather briefcase. "Craig will be filing for divorce tomorrow morning. You need to take this and hide somewhere safe. Go, before he ki—" he stopped mid-word. He nudged the case on her lap and nodded.

"I wish you'd listen," she snapped, startled by the anger in her voice. "I was on my way to leave, now—"

"Open it, please," he said, nodding to the briefcase.

"What is this?" she said, eyeing him as she opened the latches. Her mouth dropped open, eyes refusing to blink as she stared at the piles of money inside the case. "Where did you get this? Where did this come from?" she whispered as she slammed it shut and pushed it away.

"It was part of my payment, for the information I provided," he said and scooted the case back toward her. "I want you to have it, to start over. Take it, you must."

"Information? What—No I, I can't take this—"

"It's your only chance, don't be stupid."

"You don't understand, I want to leave—"

"Then take it! Now, come quickly. I don't know how much time we have," he said, grabbing her hand and pulled her out of the room.

He jogged toward the stairs with her reluctantly in tow when the front door slammed. He pushed her behind him and cautiously walked to the foyer and peered into the darkness.

"Oh, God," he said in relief. "It's only you."

"That's not the welcome I was hoping to receive, partner," Olivia said.

"Olivia, what are you doing here?" Emma asked from behind Edward's shoulder.

Edward urged Olivia with impatient eyes. "We don't have a lot of time."

"I've told him not to come home—"

"And you're actually going to trust his word?" Edward said.

"I'll be quick, I promise," Olivia said.

"Just what the hell is going on between you two? Don't talk as if I'm not here," Emma snapped, stepping between the mismatched partners.

Edward sighed, and then headed upstairs to the master suite leaving the two women in the foyer.

Olivia stepped toward Emma, took a shaky breath, and clasped Emma's hand inside hers.

"I didn't listen to you, darling. I started a plan of payback for that bastard husband of yours. It was rather thrilling, really. But along the way I stumbled over Edward here," she said, nodding up the stairs, "And surprisingly, he's helped me gain information far better than I did on my own."

"What are you talking about, Olivia, what plan? Someone better start explaining—"

"I couldn't stand by and watch Craig continue on like this anymore. So I set out to ruin him," Olivia said with an apprehensive smile.

"You're destroying someone's life, for kicks?" Emma said.

"He's no prized pig, darling. We both know that."

"You're behind all this?" Emma said, and then looked down at the case in her hand. "Is this dirty money?" Emma snapped, dangling the briefcase in the air. "How did you people get this?"

"Don't be ridiculous, darling, *dirty money*. I'm not The Godfather for Christ's sake. It's my money."

"You paid Edward, but I thought…" Emma mumbled as she rubbed the back of her head. "And he's giving it—"

"When Edward found me, I saw that it would work much better to partner up, odd as he is. But it seems good help doesn't come cheap these days," Olivia said with a half-hearted chuckle.

"So you two, did this together?"

"No worries, darling, Craig will pay me back ten fold," Olivia said as she laughed, gently pushing the briefcase back toward Emma. "I don't know what you will buy, but I know it'll be better than this," she said, pursing her lips into a solemn yet eager smile. "It's time for you to live, darling. To find yourself again without the worries that he'll find you." She pulled Emma into a tight hug. "You deserve this, darling, never forget that," Olivia whispered through a quiet sob.

Edward jogged down the stairs to the two women wrapped up in a tearful embrace. "She needs to hurry."

Olivia tipped her head to the ceiling as she wiped tears from her face. "God, if anyone saw me like this, it would ruin my reputation as a heartless bitch," she said and tried to laugh.

"I don't know how to thank you, Olivia," Emma said.

"It's about time I did something useful with my money, don't you think? Now go with Edward, darling, do as he says." Olivia stepped back, clasped her hands and took her last look at Emma before she turned to leave.

"You've had your goodbye with her, we've no time to dawdle and watch her leave," Edward said, grabbing Emma's hand and pulled her up the stairs.

Emma's eyes filled with disbelief as she stepped into the room to find Prudence standing there with a fully packed suitcase in her hands.

"What, what are you doing?" Emma said to Prudence.

Prudence's lips curled to a faint, shaky grin. "He told me what's happening, so I packed this for you," she said, lifting up the suitcase to hand it to Emma. "It's not much, but it should last you a while. I think it has a little bit of everything in there," she said through a nervous chuckle.

"Wait, wait!" Emma shouted, pressing her hands on her temples. "This is too fast. Just give me a minute to process this!"

Prudence lowered Emma's hands and wrapped an arm around her shoulder. "It's your chance now," she whispered. "Go to him."

"I just need a second to think," Emma screamed to no one.

"I'm sorry, ma'am, there's no time for that now," Edward said.

Emma looked at Prudence; her sweet face so vivid and hopeful. She glanced back at Edward, his posture now light and his eyes unusually kind.

"What about a new ID and birth certificate? I haven't gotten one yet; I can't use my real name."

"There's no need for that now, ma'am. He won't be tracking you down," Edward said.

Her heart pounded faster still. "This is really happening, isn't it?" Emma said, her bewildered eyes locking on Prudence. "I'm going to be free, aren't I?" she said, shifting her gaze between Prudence and Edward. "Free," she whispered, covering her smile with a hand.

Edward checked his watch and then nodded at Prudence. Prudence's grin stretched to a full smile as she nudged Emma's hands with the suitcase. "It's time to go," she whispered.

Emma looked down at the suitcase and then back up to Prudence. A faint smile dared creep out as she took the suitcase from Prudence's hands. "I'm going to do it, I am. We're finally going to be together," she said, set the suitcase down beside her and wrapped both arms around Prudence.

"My dear friend," Emma whispered as she held Prudence tight. She wiped tears on her sleeve as she stepped backward and took a long look at her soft, wholesome face. "What, what about you two?" Emma's voice trembled as she spoke.

"Don't worry, we'll be fine." Prudence said. "And by the way, I quit," she said with a soft chuckle. "Now get!" she said as she pushed Emma to the door.

"Yes, you have to hurry. I don't know when he's coming and it's best you not be here when he arrives," Edward said, reaching out to shake Emma's hand. His voice softened to almost a whisper, "It's been a pleasure serving you, ma'am."

Emma glanced down at his skinny, shaking hand, and then pulled his frail body into her arms. "Thank you," she whispered as she hugged him.

She tried to freeze the moment, painting every feature about them into her memory, hoping age would never let her forget the people who helped her become free. They stood side by side, young Prudence smiling as she tried not to cry and Edward, once so smug but now so relaxed, as if helping Emma had somehow freed himself. He cocked his head at her, his thin cheeks bending to a slight crooked smile as he nodded at her. Emma took a deep breath, turned, and ran out of the room.

"Who would have thought you could be so nice?" Prudence said to Edward as she winked, bumping against his arm with her shoulder. "You think she'll be all right?"

"Most certainly, dear, she'll find her way."

Emma raced through the halls with the heavy suitcase banging against her leg as she ran toward the garage.

"Where do you think you're going?"

She snapped her head around as a foot pressed against her ankle, stumbled, and came crashing onto her elbows. The luggage flew out in front of her as she tried to brace for the fall, but her elbows slipped on the waxed tiles and her head smacked against the ground. She rolled onto her back, her heart pounding as her look darted around in panic.

"Craig, is that you?" she whispered, trying to scoot her trembling body backward. She felt his hand dig into her scalp and grab a handful of her hair.

"I don't think so!" Craig said, bending down and peered into her eyes as he pulled her. "You're not going anywhere tonight, dear wife," he said, squinting and glaring into her eyes. "You can't leave me," his hot breath whispered in her ear.

She screamed, reached up, and blindly grabbed at his hands tangled in her hair. He threw his foot in her ribs. "Never!" he said as his brown loafer slammed into her ribcage.

Emma yelped and curled into a ball as a sharp pain shot through her side. She clutched her ribs, sobbing as she tried to scoot back.

"You were always nothing but trouble," he said, lifting his leg back and slamming it into her side again. "How many years did I waste on you?" he yelled.

She whimpered and closed her eyes as a stabbing sensation coursed through her kidney. She dug her nails into the grout and pulled herself into a corner, bawling and curled up in pain. "No, Craig, please!" she said, wrapping her arms around her legs.

"Begging won't save you, you—"

She heard a gush of air as Craig's head jerked to the side, his eyes flashing shock as he froze. A small trail of blood rolled down his scrunched forehead. He stumbled and threatened to buckle on the floor. She tried to stand, inching her way up the wall as she held the spasm in her ribcage.

"Go!" Edward screamed at her, stepping out from behind Craig with a fire poker tightly gripped in his hands. "Go!" he said, swinging back the wrought-iron poker threatening to strike Craig again.

She scrambled for the briefcase and tucked it back under her arm, bent over and started dragging the suitcase across the floor. "I'm sorry, Edward," she cried, her wet eyes locked on the surprise hero. "Forgive me for leaving you," she said, biting her lip in worry as she backed into the hallway leading to the garage.

"What the hell?" Craig mumbled in confusion, wobbling as he spun around to see his attacker. "Edward?" he said, his head bobbing as his shaky hand reached up to the throbbing bump on his temple.

"Good evening, Mr. Beckett," Edward said with a grin.

Twenty-six

"You remember her?" Edward said, flicking a photo at Craig's face.

Craig flinched as he sat crouched on the floor holding his diamond patterned tie to his head. Edward stood above him with the fire poker pulled back and ready to swing. Craig picked up the picture, his eyes heavy with fog. "That's Angie, my first assistant?"

"Very good, Craig. That's Angie, your first assistant...my wife."

"What?" Craig said, glancing up at Edward.

"You heard me," Edward said, then landed a full swing of the iron poker down onto Craig's shin.

Craig cried out, grabbed his leg and pulled it up to his chest. "What the hell do you mean? What do you want from me?" he said through winces of pain.

"You know, she begged me to move here, to put her career on the fast track to success she said. And being young and in love, I begrudgingly agreed," Edward said, strutting around Craig, swinging the poker like a baseball player warming up before stepping up to the plate. Craig spun his head as he watched Edward walking around him, the cocked arm, listening to the whoosh as the poker sliced through the air.

"And you hired her...but you had to have her for yourself, didn't you?" Edward said, bent down and glared into Craig's eyes. "She left me, for *you*. I lost everything when she walked out. And then—" He paused as he chuckled, throwing his hands up, "Then you didn't even want her!" he said. "You tossed her to the side, and got yourself a new little toy."

"She was your wife?" Craig whispered, scrunching up into a ball, certain he would never see morning.

"Didn't we already establish that? You need to pay more attention, Craig, or this could take a very long time," Edward said with a grin, swinging his arm back again.

"Please, don't—" Craig cried, ducking his head.

"Don't what? Don't do this?" Edward mocked, whipping the business end of the iron poker forward and stopped it inches from Craig's face.

"Are you, are you going to kill me?" Craig said with a light sob.

"Tempting, but that would be too easy," Edward said. "I'm going to ruin you..." he said, his grin stretching to a full, hateful smile. He leaned his head back and chuckled at the sobbing snake before him.

"What are you going to do?" Craig said, casting quick glances up to the vengeful Butler. "I had no idea she was your wife, I'm sorry, I didn't know," he pleaded.

Edward laughed and poked Craig with the pole as he spoke. "As if that would have mattered to you! I was just another nameless face in the crowd to you. Just another measly stepping stone to becoming the great Craig Beckett," he said as his lips twitched with a sneer. "And my Angie, she was just another conquest."

Craig crouched even smaller, frightened and clueless as to how he could talk himself out of this situation. "I can pay you?" he said, bringing himself to his knees as he pleaded into Edward's eyes. "Get you a, uh, a finer job? Worthy of someone of your stature?"

Edward's malicious laugh thundered through the halls. "Money! Craig, you don't have any money now," he laughed. "Olivia and I have taken it all."

Craig cowered back into a ball, pulled his knees up to his chest and ducked his head into his legs. Edward dragged a chair to the center of the room, right in front of Craig, and sat down with an air of cockiness. "And by morning time, there will not be a favor or string to pull, not one hand willing to stretch out and help you," Edward said with a smirk, lifted up the poker and examined its tip stained with Craig's blood.

"What, what do you mean?" Craig whispered.

"You see, Craig, Olivia and I made some revisions to our plan. Seeing how I figured you would break the rules and come home," he said, lowering the poker and looked at Craig. "As we speak, there are at least ten lovely packages finding their way onto journalist's desks. *The Times, The Daily Sun, The Herald,* they all have it now," he said with a grin of satisfaction. "By the time you might manage to crawl out of here, your face will be plastered on every front page."

Craig's body slumped to utter despair, closing his eyes as horrid headlines ran through his mind. There was no doubt journalists would be feverishly typing up the story of their career to finish in time for morning print.

"So you see, Craig, since you so carelessly took everything from me, now I've taken it all from you," he said with a brilliantly evil smirk. "And while hitting you this way really is unnecessary, seeing how physical pain means nothing to you." He stood and stopped in front of Craig. "It's awfully fun…" he said, cocking his arm back above Craig's head.

Craig grimaced and closed his eyes as he saw the iron poker coming down at his head.

Twenty-seven

Emma barely noticed the meandering hookers she passed getting to her room at a dilapidated motel outside of the city. If she had the ability to think clearly, she would have wrapped the bed in plastic wrap before she climbed in. It hadn't set in that she was gone, free. She expected to wake up in her cold, suffocating room having dreamt it all. But it happened, and she now found herself blanketed with unfamiliarity and surrounded by swirly, bold wallpaper and drab, green shag carpeting.

After a long hot shower, she wiped a towel on the steamy mirror, tapped a bandage to her forehead and inspected her swollen, purple side. She grabbed her bags, took a quick look around the room left to go check-out.

By mid-afternoon the paperwork was finished and she pulled into the city limits. An apprehensive ease flowed over her as she parked the car and walked to his store. The gold bell rang above her as she stepped in.

"I'll be there in a minute, take a look around," he hollered from the back of the store.

Her feet nervously tapped as she waited, and blood pumped through her so fast she could barely breathe.

"Can I help—" James said, looking up from an old pocket watch in his hand and stopped in his tracks. "Emma? What are you doing here?" he said, an instinctive smile covering his unshaven face.

Her eyes sparkled as a sense of solace washed over her. "I have to show you something," she said as she smiled.

"What's going on, show me what?" he said, his eyes scrunching in confusion as he set the watch down.

"Let me show you, it's important," she said, tugging on his sleeve as she walked backwards toward the door.

"Show me what?"

"It's a surprise," she said with a smile. "Trust me, okay?"

He took a deep breath, dug into his pocket and pulled out his keys. "I know I'm chasing trouble for doing this, but now I'm curious," he said with a playful glare.

"Here, put this on," she said with a smirk, handing him a soft cloth. "Put it over your eyes, and no peeking!"

With a teasing glare, he wrapped the cloth around his eyes and she helped him into her car. He fidgeted with the scarf, tugging on it and scooting it as they drove. He had no idea how long it had been, but it felt like hours he sat with the blindfold on his face. "Are we almost there? This thing is starting to itch," he said and wiggled his nose as he pulled on it.

"In a minute," she chuckled.

She rolled down the windows. A cool, soothing breeze blew against his face; a hint of lavender filled the air, and his head bobbed back and forth as the car crept down a bumpy path.

"Jesus, where the hell are we?" he said with a chuckle.

The car slowed to a stop. He heard the crunch of loose gravel underneath Emma's shoes as she came around to his side and helped him out of the car.

"This way..." she said, cupping her hand under his elbow to guide him down a path.

She stepped in front of him and untied the blindfold. Green dots filled his vision, he blinked a few times to adjust his eyes to the sun's glare.

Emma continued walking, and then stopped and looked back at him. "Are you coming?"

"What is this—"

"I bought it. It's ours," she said, almost bouncing as she dangled the keys to the cottage in her hand.

"You what?" he said with a confused smile as the keys swung in front of his face.

"Surprise!" she said, raising her arms in the air.

"You must be crazy, or maybe I'm delusional?" he laughed.

"No." She laughed and stepped toward him. "I bought it, I really bought it!" she said through a squeak.

"Are you drunk?" he teased.

"No I'm not drunk, you idiot," she said as she swatted his chest. "I decided to leave yesterday, and as I was… Olivia and Edward were there and…well…so I bought it. I left."

"You, you left?"

She bit her lip as she smiled and nodded. "I left."

They looked at the worn down cottage. The chipped rocking chairs slowly rocked in the breeze, petals from the trees danced across the overgrown grass, dangling willow branches swayed in the wind tickling the blades of grass. He turned toward the broken boat, the uneven dock and the garden filled with bright red tomatoes. His mouth opened but no words slipped out.

"Come on!" she said, grabbing his hand and pulled him up to the porch. She looked up at him smiling and dropped the keys into his open palm, clasping his fingers shut around them. "Go ahead, open it," she said, looking down at the keys in his clenched fist.

He looked down at the worn brass keys and then up at her beautiful face. He tried to steady his hand, grabbed the knob and forced the key in the lock. The old knob wiggled in his hand as he gave it a gentle yank and swung the door open.

"Well, here we go!" she said with an infectious smile, and clasped her hand in his as they stepped into the living room.

"So, this is really yours?" he said as they stood in the empty room.

"No, it's *ours*." She walked up to him and wrapped her arms around his waist. "This is our home, James. I want to spend the rest of my life with you, like we're meant to."

James kissed her forehead, and then dug a hand into his back pocket. He walked to the mantel, and put the photo of the young newlyweds in the middle. "I bet they would have wanted something like this, don't you?" he said as he looked back at Emma.

Emma came and stood beside him as they gazed at their faces from lives they couldn't recall. "I think they brought us together."

"You know, if anyone else hears that, they'll think we're nuts." He laughed as he wrapped an arm around her shoulder.

She nuzzled her head against his chest. "Maybe we are?"

"Nah, but we'll keep it to ourselves, just in case."

"I think they're happy now," Emma said, touching a fingertip to the photo. "I can feel it."

****

James decided to take vacation time for the first time since the store opened eight years ago. Emma and James bought minimal supplies, cheap sleeping bags, and spent the next few nights curled up together on the dirty, warped hardwood floor in their living room. For the first time in months, Emma wasn't plagued with the same nightmare.

Each day brought something new, and this morning was crisp and peaceful. The scent of old wood and pine surrounded the little house while Emma sat lazily on the rickety rocking chair. It became a part of their routine, sitting together on the porch as they drank their morning coffee. She had her feet propped on the porch railing as James thumbed through the morning paper. She reached for the front section.

"James, did you see this?" she said, leaned over and handed him the front page.

"Well holy—" he said, almost paralyzed as he read.

"It says here," she said and pointed to the middle of the article, "that someone anonymously sent the paper a package with copies of every illegal thing he's done. Fake charities, false tax documents, using election contributions for personal reasons. It just goes on and on," she said, astounded and fell back in the chair as James continued to read.

"I don't see anything in here about you," he said, skimming the article.

"There won't be anything about me," she said as she thought of Edward and Olivia.

"Just something about how 'A beaten and battered Beckett tried to quietly file for divorce, before the local authorities barged through the gates of his hillside mansion and closed the cuffs around his corrupt hands. His publicly beloved wife, Emma Beckett, seems to have mysteriously disappeared.' That's crazy," he said, tipping the paper toward her and showed her the caption below an old photo of them together.

"I should feel bad, shouldn't I?" she said.

"You didn't do this crap, he did."

"So much of that, I contributed to…" she said, her gaze shifting out to the pond. "But really, I just feel—relieved."

"He's getting what he deserves, Babe, don't forget that," he said with a gentle tap on her leg. "He made all those decisions, not you."

She took a shaky breath and tried to forget Craig. "So, what should we do today?" she said and tossed the newspaper aside. "I think I really want to tackle that bedroom, so we have a decent place to sleep. What do you think?"

He rubbed his stiff neck. "I'm a little too old to be sleeping on the floor; working on the bedroom is a great idea."

****

Craig sat on the sofa, hunched over, with elbows resting on his knees as he buried his face in his hands. "I can't do this on my own, Baby," he said, glancing up with bruised, pathetic eyes.

"They're calling me a whore, Craig. A whore!" Sheila screamed as she threw a newspaper in his face. "And I wiped out my savings to bail you out!"

"I know, Baby, I'm sorry I—"

"You know my Mom called me today? She said I was a disgrace to the family—A disgrace!" she said, crossing her arms and turning her back to him.

"I can't do this without you, you know that," he said, walked behind her and put his hands on her shoulders.

"Oh really?" she said, spun around and glared in his eyes. "That's not what your statement says. Says there you denied all of it. Our pictures are all over the damn news, and still you deny being with me," she said and shoved him away from her.

"Baby, please, my lawyer told me to say that. Really I—"

"Out!" she said, arm stretched and pointing to the door.

"Baby, please don't say that," he said, his swollen eyes watering as he started to shake.

"The entire country knows about us, but you still want to shush me and put me in the dark. I won't do it anymore, Craig. I want you to get out," she said, turned her back to him, crossed her arms, and stood in cold silence waiting for him to leave.

His head fell and his shoulders slumped. He had nowhere else to turn for comfort, understanding, or sympathy. He glanced up at her, opened his mouth and hesitated. "I should…" he shuffled his feet and thought about reaching out to her. "I have a statement to…" he muttered, realizing she didn't care. He slid his hands into his pockets and turned for the door.

A mass of journalists, photographers and newscasters swarmed the front of the building as the car pulled up. They rushed the town car before it could come to a full stop. The inside of his car lit up with feverish flashes from cameras; reporters banged on the sides and hollered questions with faces pressed against the windows. Police officers quickly encircled the car, demanding the ambitious journalists to back away or be arrested.

Craig's pulse pounded in his neck. He pumped his hands trying to control his shaking. He pressed a handkerchief to his shiny forehead and took slow breaths to calm the swollen feeling in his throat. It sickened him that the statement he was about to give might be his last moments of freedom.

The evidence kept piling up on the DA's desk. Craig's lawyer had almost begged for deals, but the only thing the DA accepted was his last three days of freedom to 'settle affairs.' Today, he was to give his statement to the press, then be quietly escorted to the county jail to await his upcoming court date.

An officer opened the door, police and secret service surrounded him, pushing off the mob of journalists as he made his way to the stage. The flashing cameras blinded him as he pushed his way through the crowd and finally reached the steps, just out of arms reach from the storms of people. He cursed his trembling legs and strained for a face of innocence. He raised his hands to quiet the screaming crowd, waited for the uproar to settle into eager silence, and placed his hands on the smooth wood podium.

His sweaty hands fiddled with sheets of paper, and then a shaky finger rested on the first line. He cleared his throat and looked out at the dozens of cameras and huge microphones dangling over TV cameras.

"I have done the state of California a great disservice, and let the wonderful people of this state down in countless ways. This morning, when I turned myself in to the authorities…"

******

Emma was cleared of any connection to Craig's fraud, and after Craig's conviction the authorities crammed her belongings from the mansion into a storage facility for her to collect. The house and its contents were auctioned off to pay off some of Craig's debts.

She schlepped back and forth from the storage unit, to James' apartment, to the cottage, sorting through the things she never really loved while she packed James' belongings into moving boxes. While she tried to settle into her new life, the small town spent weeks gossiping about this new woman apparently living with James.

Months passed, and Emma finally finished sorting through her horrid, ten-year life with Craig. She drove to the Salvation Army with an overflowing trailer, and as she heaved the last box out and set it by the pile of things she never wanted to see again, her past became complete. She watched the group of employees pass the boxes into the building, looked back at the empty trailer and saw the beginning of her future.

James came home for lunch, worried she might be upset about letting go of so many belongings. "It looks weird in here without all that stuff," he said, sitting in the barren apartment.

"I'm glad to have it gone, really," Emma said.

"And you look better this way anyway," he said, tugging on his sweatshirt hanging on her little frame.

"I don't know about all that," she said as she laughed. "But it'll do for now. I just so glad I don't have to see that stuff again. I don't want to think about it even." She wrapped his arms around her, closed her eyes and laid her head on his chest. "I just want to focus on us."

"It's funny you should say that, because I want to ask you something." He started to dig into his pocket. "I know the timing isn't the best, but I don't think I can wait anymore." He smiled, pulled out a small velvet box, and crouched to one knee.

******

Life was simple, and Emma almost couldn't remember her days without James. He filled his nights with projects around the house, and she found herself doing things she hadn't done since she was a teenager. She climbed into the cobweb-filled attack to help rewire the electric, swung a sledgehammer to bust down water damaged walls, and burned countless dinners attempting to regain domestic skills she had been forbidden to use for years.

On the weekends they treated themselves to short trips to small farming communities, hunting through barns and farm houses for interesting trinkets and furnishings for the house. She loved watching the excitement in James' eyes as he dug through what seemed like a pile of junk, standing up with a childlike grin as he pulled out the latest find.

As the summer settled into fall, they were ready to fully embark on spending their lives together.

Emma taped up the last box as they surveyed the empty apartment.

"I think that's everything," James said, glancing around his bachelor pad. "Feels kinda weird to be moving."

"I can't believe we actually finished," she said, fidgeting with the keys to the cottage. "Are you sure about this? You and me?" she said with a cringe.

"Without a doubt," he said, pulled her forward and kissed the engagement ring on her hand.

"I don't want you having any regrets."

"My only regret is it took so long to find you."

They walked to the management office and James turned in the key to his apartment.

"Are you really ready to do this?" she asked as they climbed inside the rental truck. "Because I'm kind of hooked on you, Mr. Dover."

James laughed and put the truck into gear. "You're not so bad yourself. Come on, let's go home."

Under the umbrella of red, orange, and yellow leaves that canopied their tucked-away home, they had a small wedding ceremony out by their pond. Emma looked radiant in her simple, satin gown. As she pinned the gold brooch to her gown she felt a rush of emotions surge through her.

A gust of wind blew through the windows and knocked the photograph of the newlyweds off the mantel. The wind carried it across the room, and it came to rest at her feet. Emma bent and picked up the photo. As she looked at the black and white image, a wave of relief overcame her. She let out long exhale and smiled.

Prudence started crying the moment she saw Emma coming down the aisle. Even Olivia managed to drag herself out of the city to attend. James' smile beamed across his tender, peaceful face; he couldn't wait to call Emma his wife. They held hands, reciting their vows by heart.

They had a small reception at a banquet hall, losing the world around them as they shared their first dance as husband and wife.

"At last, my love has come along…" the speakers played as they twirled around. She laid her head in the perfect nook of his shoulder. He pressed his lips against the silky sweetness on her cheek and whispered, "I'm glad you found me again…"

Twenty-eight

"I thought for sure I wouldn't see another paint brush for years," Emma said, turning to face James installing a new light-switch plate cover. Her face was covered with speckles of baby-blue paint.

He shook his head and laughed at her. "How do you always get covered in paint?"

She shot him a playful glare, then let out a tired breath as she sat on a box in the middle of the room and rubbed her big round belly.

"I hope the doctor is right. I hate the thought of having to paint all this pink once the baby comes," she said, leaning back on her palms as she surveyed the pastel-colored nursery. "Prudence sure did an amazing job on the mural, didn't she?" she said, admiring the wall across from the crib. Over the years Prudence had grown to be her best friend, and she was grateful that after a lot of convincing Prudence agreed to move closer to them despite her long treks to her gallery.

James walked over and crouched down on his knees, leaned in and gently kissed her stomach. "It's a boy, don't worry," he said with a confident smile.

"How do you know?" she teased, running her fingers through his tousled hair.

"He's fidgety, like me. If it were a girl, she'd be calm like you." He stretched up and kissed the tip of her nose.

She smiled, pressed a hand to his cheek and gazed into his gold speckled eyes. Four years and he could still make her melt.

He jerked away, looked down at Emma's stomach and watched a little wave of movement roll across her belly. "See, fidgety," he laughed. "Our big problem, is his Aunt Olivia," he said with a sarcastic glare. "Baby isn't even born yet, and the spare room is already filled with toys," he said as he laughed.

"I'm trying to control her," Emma said and chuckled. "But you know Olivia, she does as she wants." She sat back as he covered the window with the morning paper to finish painting the trim, and noticed Craig's face. "Is it horrible that I've forgotten about him until I saw the paper today?" she said softly.

He sneered at Craig's face plastered all over the front page, dipped his brush in the paint can and smeared it all over his picture. "Why should you bother to think about him? He made his bed, let him lie in it."

"You're right," she said, shaking off the guilt for his thirty-six-year sentence. "He's the one who embezzled money, not me." She rubbed her sore back and looked down at her moving belly. "So what do you think about the name Ted?" she asked with a smile.

"Ted?" James said with a scrunch face.

Emma started laughing. "What, you don't like that?"

He scratched his head. "Is it a family name or something?"

"I don't think so, but I like it. It's simple, and strangely comforting." She looked down and rubbed her belly. "What do you think, do you like the name Ted?" she said to her belly. "See, he's calm now, he likes it too," she said with a grin.

"Ted, huh?" he said, looking back at her over his shoulder. "I guess it's okay."

"Good. Ted…" she said, caressing her stomach.

****

Craig managed to shave years off his sentence for good behavior and was finally released from prison. His old, battered body barely resembled the handsome lawyer from his glory days. His parole officer got him a job at a local factory, and the Supervisor not entirely pleased to hire someone old enough to retire without a single days experience in manual labor. Yet Craig quietly made it through his days and met his quota, and spent his nights pouring over drinks at a dingy bar by the halfway house he lived in.

His wobbly head dangled over his glass of whiskey, the day's paper on the grungy counter beside him. His coworkers leaned in hushed huddles, making jokes, and laughing at grand stories about what could have the strange coot so distraught.

"Dude, I swear I saw him crying," the stubby one laughed.

"Bullshit, guys like that don't cry," the lanky one said.

Craig hadn't the mind to notice. His glossy eyes scanned the article again as his wrinkled, weathered hand caressed the warmly worded obituary. It was a fine photo; she looked stunning, even in her old age.

He gulped the rest of his drink, glanced down at her death announcement, and couldn't help but wonder how things would have turned out had he done things differently.

"What's got you so down, old man?" the cocky foreman said with a wide grin leaning on Craig's shoulder.

"You see this? She was my wife," he slurred as he tapped the paper with a wrinkled finger. "We used to be something back in the day."

"Your wife, huh?" he said and glanced at the article. "Hey guys, Craig here says he used to be married. Him and his old lady were something back in the day!" he mocked as the small group broke into laughter.

"It's true you mindless shit," Craig said, jerking his arm back that the cocky young man rested on.

"Oh, getting sensitive, huh?" another man joked. "What, were you some famous movie star?"

"Yeah, man, didn't you see him in The Terminator?" the foreman laughed.

"I was almost the Senator!" Craig said with an evil glare. His drunken head bobbing as he glowered at the man. They laughed so hard they almost choked, faces bright red, keeling over through exaggerated chuckles and snorts.

"You hear that, Eddy? Craig was a Senator! Oh la la!" the stubby one laughed.

"I said *almost*," Craig yelled over the laughing group. "Would've been the youngest Senator ever elected. I saw more money than you could ever hope to see, you little shit…" *Jerks have no idea who they are talking to*, he thought, and bent back over his freshly filled glass.

"Yeah, sure thing, Craig...Senator..." the bartender muttered, tapping the old man on the shoulder as he cleared away the empty shot glasses.

"Senator..." Craig whispered, pressed the glass to his lips for a moment and then gulped the whiskey.

****

It was an odd feeling for Emma, dying. Back when she was married to Craig, she imagined it painful and gruesome: her body being thrown into a ditch in some barren desert. But then James came and filled her life with love, laughter, and three beautiful children.

She lost him a year ago, heart failure like his father, and only six months after she lost Olivia to a car accident. Now, she found the thought that she would soon see them again peaceful. She was content lying in her bed with her kids curled up beside her. Prudence sat beside the bed, caressing Emma's hand in her last few minutes.

The doctors could find nothing wrong with Emma and simply called it old age. But she just wanted to see James again, and her body finally caved under her forceful desire.

The sun drizzled through the French doors across from her bed, the pond almost sparkling in the soft summer sunrise. As she lay propped up with pillows, somehow she could smell James' scent lingering in the air. She felt his soft lips against her cheek, his low voice whispering her name and calling her to him.

"Can you hear him, too?" she whispered to Prudence.

"No, honey, I can't," Prudence said with tear filled eyes. She pressed her lips tight to hold back her tears and patted Emma's hand. "He's calling you home, I think," her shaky voice whispered in Emma's ear.

Emma tried to turn her tired head. A weak, drowsy smile stretched across her sunken cheeks as she strained to see her beautiful babies, now with babies of their own. Ted looked just like James, tall and handsome with his boyish charm. He sat beside his brother, and wrapped his arm around him. *Always the strong one*, she thought, admiring her handsome firstborn baby.

Matthew was a mix of them both, with James' emerald eyes and Emma's freckled nose. He held their sister's hand, she was sitting on the edge of the bed rubbing Emma's hand. *Poor boy hasn't slept in days, he's going to be a mess without me,* Emma thought.

Carol, the youngest, took on the motherly role when Emma took a turn for the worse. She laughed and cried every time she realized she sounded just like her mom.

A tear rolled down Emma's cheek as she looked at their heartbroken faces. She took a labored breath and whispered, "It's time for me to go see Daddy…bunches of whole pumpkins…" Carol broke into sobs, burying her face in Matthew's shoulder. *They would be all right, someday,* she thought, laying her head back on the plush pillow and closed her eyes.

Darkness filled her mind; sounds of crying around her faded to silence; it was like she was falling asleep.

A faint light flickered in her mind. She felt her eyes opening, sloshing sounds slowly trickled into her ears, salty scents filled her nose and she took a huge, gasping breath. The stunning full sun shone down upon her. She wiggled her toes and looked down at them, watching them get covered in the soft white sand and she dug her feet in. The cool, clear waves rolled up on the shore in a big foamy whoosh. She glanced around the vast, beautiful beach wondering where she was. She looked down at her hands with a dreamy gaze. They were no longer wrinkled and worn, but the flesh tight and young again. She pressed a hand to her face, slowly feeling the smooth, flawless skin underneath her fingertips.

In the distance she saw a long, skinny pier reaching out from the shore. A young woman gazed back at her, sitting alone and swirling her feet around in the water. Emma strolled toward the pier, the hot sun beating down on her shoulders, and the cool sand soothing her feet as she walked. She stepped onto the old, wooden planks, walking toward the woman who looked at Emma over her shoulder with welcoming eyes.

Emma stopped beside her, glanced down, and the young bride looked up at her and patted the spot beside her. Emma sat down, rolled up her pant legs and stuck her feet in the soothing, gentle waves.

The young bride sat peacefully, her long train bunched up around her as her feet hung over the edge of the pier. Emma understood that she was looking at herself, not as she is now, but as she once was a lifetime before her. She cocked her head, examining the bride who sat with her.

"What's your name?" Emma said.

"Carol. I've been waiting for you, Emma."

"Is this heaven?" Emma asked, spinning her feet in the water.

"This is my waiting place. I have been waiting a long time for you, Emma," Carol said, her sweet eyes shifting to the woman next to her.

"What were you waiting for?"

"For you to finish it for me," Carol said, turning her head back to the ocean, watching their feet make bubbles in the water.

"Finish what?"

"Finish my life as it was meant to be, finish our love," Carol said, pulling her feet up onto the pier. "I longed for him, so badly, I called for him."

"Did he hear you?" Emma said as Carol stood, fluffing out the wrinkles in her old satin gown.

"I think he did, because you found him for me," Carol said, shifting her look to Emma as she spoke. "We left little clues and hints everywhere trying to find each other, and I thought for so long they would never be found..." she said, turning to face Emma square, "but then he found this," she said, running her fingers across the gold brooch with the delicate swirls she wore on her wedding dress. "My Aunt gave it to me, I wore it on our wedding day," she said with a proud smile. "And when he found it, I had to trust that meant he would find you too."

Emma swished her feet in the waves. "What does all of this mean?"

"I think it means it's finished, fate has completed its course."

"Will I see my husband soon?" Emma said.

Carol nodded to two figures in the distance. "I think we both will," she said, sighing in relief. A loving smile made her face utterly radiant, and Emma was taken aback by her simple beauty. Carol puffed up her skirt, stretched the delicate train out behind her, and started to walk down the pier leaving Emma behind her.

Emma stood up, held a hand over her eyes and peered into the distance to examine the two men. She saw a handsome, young man in a tuxedo, his slicked-back hair gleaming in the bright daylight. A grateful smile stretched across his face as he ran toward the young bride. Emma squinted her eyes to stare at the other man looking in her direction. Her shoulders relaxed and her arms fell to her sides. "James…" she whispered through a brilliant smile, and then started to jog down the pier toward the beach.

A Preview of
Reinventing Claire
By
Darian Wilk

One

You would think Charlie would show me a little sympathy and wait for a day or two to tell me he wanted a divorce. But Charlie never was good at waiting.

I should have known in the morning that my continual misfortune was some sort of omen, a warning from some greater-being that today would get even worse. My breaking point hit me when the heel snapped off my favorite pair of shoes during lunch. I hunched under my desk, trying not to cry as I attempted to super glue them together and praying I could just go home to my husband. Lucky me, my boss called me into her office, promptly fired me, and I could go home just like I wanted. Except now I was unemployed, and I had to change a flat tire on the gravel covered shoulder of the freeway first.

I called Charlie on the way home, and he promised to leave work early and take me to dinner. 'To forget the day with a nice night out,' he said. Little did I know he had his own agenda for the evening.

There we finally sat – Charlie and me, at my favorite Italian restaurant, Linguini's. The plan, or so I thought, was to drown my sorrows over a bottle of wine and a plate of the best manicotti in town.

"I can't believe it. Not living up to my potential! What the hell kind of speech is that to fire someone with? Is it like the 'It's not you, it's me' excuse for employers?"

"You win some, you lose some I suppose," Charlie said, filling my wineglass for me.

"Six years there and nothing but glowing reviews, and she says I'm not living up to my full potential. And I said 'Thank you'. Who the hell says thank you for being fired?"

"You weren't thinking straight. Go easy on yourself, Claire."

"Well, I should be positive and look for that silver lining right?" I said, raising my glass in a halfhearted toast. If I had known what Charlie was about to spring on me, I probably wouldn't have been smiling.

Charlie sat there, slowly spinning his wineglass on the eggplant colored placemat.

"Is your lasagna okay honey? You've hardly touched it. Here, have some of mine instead," I said, already cutting off a portion of my manicotti.

"Claire, I want a divorce."

I froze, the hunk of manicotti on my fork in mid-air over his plate. "What—what did you say?" I barely managed.

He took the forkful from my hand and set it on his plate. "I said I want a divorce," he repeated in that dry, lifeless tone he always used when trying to be serious.

"Divorce?" I said, as if repeating it would somehow make it not real. "But you—we're having dinner and…" I muttered. I tried to fill my glass again, but my shaky hand hit the rim and sloshed wine all over the white tablecloth.

"I met someone else. And she makes me…well, happy. It's like, like I'm alive again!" He smiled, blotting the wine I spilled with a napkin in his calm, tidy way.

"Someone else? Alive again? What is that even supposed to mean?" *This has to be the worst joke ever. When will he give up on trying to be funny on bad days?* "This isn't funny, Charlie. I'm not in the mood for bad jokes."

"I'm not laughing, Claire. I'm trying to come clean—"

"Come clean? I just got fired, Charlie. We're having dinner. What do you mean someone else?"

"We've been together over a year now. I met her at a conference, and we kept running into each other after that. I didn't intend to. You would like her though. But, well, we want to get married. So I want a divorce."

I would like her. Has he gone mad? He can't get married; he's already married. "A divorce…" I whispered to myself, the words dragging across my dry tongue like sandpaper.

"To new beginnings!" He tried to chuckle, but sat staring at me for a moment with an unnerving glean in his gaze. "New beginnings…" He patted my hand as he stood. "Goodbye Claire," he said, pursing his lips into the worst sympathetic grin I had ever seen. He turned and left me there, alone.

I sat there for, I don't even know how long, repeating the words in my head. I kept thinking he would come back and sit down, that he didn't just tell me he wanted a divorce. We would make fun of my former employer and her pear-shaped bubble butt and finish dinner.

I raised the cold manicotti to my lips, trying so hard to believe it didn't happen, that it was another ordinary evening out. But after a while I realized he wasn't coming back. His plate of half-eaten lasagna across from me reminded me I was alone. The big, wet red stain next to my hand where I spilled the wine after his announcement pounded the moment into severe realization.

"You guys want some boxes?" the waiter asked me, shaking me back into reality.

"He wants a divorce," I said looking up at him with tears filling my eyes. The poor guy stood there for a moment, his wide eyes staring at the floor, before he seemed to scoot away. *A divorce? Will he be at home waiting for me, or did he…He probably went to her place.*

I started crying. And not the weepy, sniffle kind either, where you delicately blot a hanky to your eye. No, the snorty, heaving sobbing you only want to do locked in your bathroom with the shower running so no one can hear you. He wanted a divorce. He left, and *oh God, I left my wallet in my other purse! How am I going to pay for dinner? Did he take the car? I can't pay for a taxi.* I envisioned myself getting hauled off by the police, failing at an attempted dine-n-dash, crying as I called out for Charlie. I was never very good at rebellion.

A customer handed me her napkin, rubbed my back a little and said, "Are you okay honey?" I think I said something to her, but I don't really know what. Probably something profound like I said to the poor waiter. "I, my husband—and I—" I filled the napkin she handed me with snot, and then another one. I muttered something else as she excused herself and flagged down a waiter.

After some apologetic mumbling to the waiter about not having my wallet with me, the manager called me a taxi despite my crying that I couldn't pay for it. He slipped the driver a wad of cash. I should have told him I only lived five minutes away and could walk if my feet weren't so sore, but instead I slid into the backseat without so much as a thank you. The driver asked me 'Where to' about three times before I managed to get my brain to cooperate with my mouth. I just wanted to get out of there as fast as possible but couldn't manage 'Just drive.'

"761 West 24th Street, please," I said, clutching the box of leftovers against my chest like a lifejacket.

The taxi stopped in front of my house, a sage-green Victorian with all the gingerbread house trimmings. We spent years working on that house, getting paint colors approved from the historical society, spending Saturdays at English Gardens for peach-colored rose bushes for the side patio. It was our baby. All the lights were off, and his car wasn't in the driveway. The whole house seemed to sag, the color dripping off the wood siding and vanishing into the grass.

"Lady, you gonna get out or what?" the driver said, leaning over the back of the seat.

"Yeah, I'm sorry," I said as I scooted across the dirty vinyl and opened the door. He peeled off and left me standing on the curb. I guess tonight was a good night to ditch me. *How can I go in there*, I thought, staring at my suburban beauty.

I trekked around to the backyard, by the Koi pond Charlie built last summer for my birthday, to get the spare key from under the sapphire looking rock. My keys were in my other purse too. I didn't think I needed them with Charlie driving. I walked back to the front door and let myself in.

The foyer felt cold, broken, and lonely. Just like me. It was like standing in a stranger's house. I crept into the living room, half expecting to see Charlie sitting there in his leather recliner, reading Forbes and waiting for me. But the room was vacant, just like my thoughts.

The house never seemed so empty, not even the day we bought it. We had broken open a bottle of champagne in the barren living room to celebrate our new path in life. I wanted to cry. I wanted to call my sisters. I wanted to go find Charlie. *Maybe if I call him…*I sank into the sofa, still clutching the takeout containers in my arms, and sat in the cold silence of a broken marriage.

The answering machine startled me. *Did the phone even ring?*

"Hi, it's Claire and Charlie. We're not home right now…"

I shot up from the sofa and ran to the phone, hoping it was Charlie, crying and begging to come home.

"Hello?"

"Hey Claire Bear, I got your message. I can't believe that bitch!" my sister said.

"Oh…Sam, I uh—"

"I could storm right down there, poke her in the eye with—"

"Sam, it's really not a good time," I said, my lifeless hand barely holding the phone.

"What's the matter? You sound weird?"

"Nothing I, it's just been a long day."

"Well no shit. You got fired."

"Sam, please," I said, rolling my eyes. *I should have let the machine get it.*

"I can tell something's wrong. What is it? Is Charlie giving you shit about it? Look, just tell him—"

"He's not here Sam."

"Where the hell is he? I thought you guys were going out to dinner?"

What time is it? It feels late. I glanced at the cable box, only seven o'clock.

"He, um, he had to go into the office." I couldn't handle Sam right now. God love her, but she would be like a crazed badger on the rampage if I told her the truth.

"Really?"

She knows me too well. "He forgot some files he needs to go over tonight I guess." *That sounds believable, right?* "Big meeting coming up—"

"He could at least take you with him. Leaving you alone after the day you had, I tell you—"

"Sam, I'm tired," I said, rubbing between my eyes. My head hurt like a jackhammer had been pounding on it all day so I dug through my purse for the Tylenol. I struggled with the damn childproof lid as I pressed the phone between my shoulder and ear. "Can we please do this tomorrow?" I said as the bottle broke open, sending little white pills flying into the air. *Damn it*, I thought as tears filled my eyes again.

"Oh, all right. You sure you're okay, you don't sound—"

"I'm fine. I'll call you tomorrow." I bent over, picking up two pills off the floor.

"Okay, night, Claire Bear."

I could tell her tomorrow, when I was done crying and could handle her berating my soon to be ex-husband. Not caring how early it was, I went upstairs to our bedroom. It was beautiful; I loved our bedroom. I decorated it in this sweet, country, shabby-chic motif. A big, puffy white comforter with a pastel flower print was the perfect touch with the gold headboard I bought. I found this gorgeous wrought-iron dress form at an estate sale. I'd never touched a sewing machine in my life, and would probably blow the stupid thing up if I tried, but the dress form looked great tucked in the corner by the window.

I loved coming in here at the end of a long day, curling up beside Charlie and listening to Jazz drizzle into the room from the bar down the street. It didn't feel right in here, not now. It was one thing to go to bed alone when Charlie was on a business trip or after we had one of our stupid arguments and he slept on the recliner, when I knew it was only a matter of a day or two before he would be back in bed with me.

I couldn't curl up in *that* bed, knowing he'd never sleep with me in it again. I grabbed a sheet from the hall closet and headed for the futon in the office, the one place neither us ever slept. Maybe tomorrow this would make sense. Maybe Charlie would realize his mistake and come home with caramel lattes and a bag of apple muffins from Kate's Kitchen. Some women got flowers when their husband screwed up, I got coffee and muffins. But I would gladly take it, if it meant he was coming home.

I changed into a pair of yoga pants and a blue tank top, pulled the sheet over my head and hoped tomorrow could somehow undo today. My heart jolted when I heard the phone ring, and I tossed the sheet off as I bolted up and fumbled across the desk for the phone. I knew it wasn't Charlie. Charlie wasn't coming home again. I curled up, buried my face in the lumpy spare pillow and let the scrunched up cotton muffle my frantic sobs.

ABOUT THE AUTHOR

Darian was born in Myrtle Beach , South Carolina, the youngest of two children. While still a toddler, her family moved back to their home state of Michigan, where she continues to live today.

Darian married her husband, Steve, in 2005, and is the mother to two wonderful kids. When not writing, she is happiest spending time with her family and friends.

Darian loves to hear comments from readers, and welcomes you to contact her at her website:

www.DarianWilk.weebly.com